You want too much, Lesley, an inner voice said

You want to call your days your own. You want Matt all to yourself and that isn't possible.

They stepped into her room, which had increasingly become their room. She felt him come to stand behind her and slip his arms around her waist. When he kissed her nape, she turned and found the solace she always found in his arms.

Yet, even with his warm mouth grazing her cheek, her troubled mind reeled. She wondered if she was being terribly disloyal to Matt by hoping that someone else would be chosen as president of Hamilton House. She was going to be his wife, and loyal wives wanted the moon for their husbands, didn't they?

Suddenly, she recalled something he had said the night they had first made love: *We live with our choices a very long time . . .*

ABOUT THE AUTHOR

Oklahoma-based author Barbara Kaye is well-known to Superromance readers, who have told us they admire her keen powers of observation and her insight into human nature. The Hamilton House trilogy was years in the making, and readers are sure to find the wait was well worth it! Barbara is married to a USAF colonel and has five grown children.

Books by Barbara Kaye

HARLEQUIN SUPERROMANCE

46–A HEART DIVIDED
124–COME SPRING
161–HOME AT LAST
206– SOUTHERN NIGHTS
219–JUST ONE LOOK
257–A SEASON FOR ROSES
270–BY SPECIAL REQUEST
316–THE RIGHT PLACE TO BE
332–TRADITIONS
379–RAMBLIN' MAN

HARLEQUIN AMERICAN ROMANCE

19–CALL OF EDEN

Don't miss any of our special offers. Write to us at the following address for information on our newest releases.

Harlequin Reader Service
901 Fuhrmann Blvd., P.O. Box 1397, Buffalo, NY 14240
Canadian address: P.O. Box 603,
Fort Erie, Ont. L2A 5X3

Choice of
a Lifetime

BARBARA KAYE

Harlequin Books

TORONTO • NEW YORK • LONDON
AMSTERDAM • PARIS • SYDNEY • HAMBURG
STOCKHOLM • ATHENS • TOKYO • MILAN

Published July 1990

ISBN 0-373-70411-9

Printed in U.S.A.

CHAPTER ONE

THE CORPORATE OFFICES of Hamilton House, Incorporated, Western Division, occupied the fifth, sixth and seventh floors of a downtown San Francisco skyscraper. On the seventh floor was Matthew Logan's inner sanctum—as tastefully elegant as the man who presided over it. The office was very up-to-date San Francisco, with its teal-blue carpet and drapes, stainless steel desk, brushed aluminum blinds, recessed lighting and expensive works of art. Vanessa Hamilton, the company's cofounder and C.E.O., insisted that her executives surround themselves with all the trappings of success, for that reflected favorably on the company as a whole. None of Hamilton House's vice presidents followed that dictum with more relish than Matthew Logan.

He had known when Vanessa had made him a vice president of the company that a certain stylish elegance, a dignified flair was expected of him. Although Hamilton House consisted of fifty-two restaurants located throughout the United States, Vanessa had managed to keep each one exclusive. "Stuart insisted on it," she had once told Matt, referring to her late husband, who had been the guiding hand behind the company's growth. Stuart had liked to play up regional styles and tastes, and so no two decors were precisely the same, no two menus exactly alike. Each restaurant was unique—and exquisite. Vanessa had been subjected to a barrage of contrary advice through the years, but she had never wavered from that policy. She had been smart. Even Matt admitted that dinner at a Hamilton House made for a memorable occasion, and he had been having them for more than twenty years.

He also admitted that it was nice to be associated with such unqualified success. He liked his job. He liked being a vice president, and he thoroughly enjoyed the prestige, privileges and perks associated with the title—and never pretended otherwise.

Matt looked the part of a vice president, if indeed there was such a look. Distinguished and impeccable were adjectives that suited him to a tee. He was tall and trim and had an admirable physique, maintained by constant vigilance in regard to both diet and exercise. His clothes were purchased at places like Bullock & Jones and Saks, and he wore them with the ease of a man accustomed to fine things. He had been blessed with thick, dark hair that had not thinned but was now laced with enough gray to attest to his forty-nine years. He had an angular face with chiseled, definite features that might have looked hard and cold had it not been for the warmth in his gray eyes and his charming, uneven smile. His manners bordered on being courtly. Women seldom forgot him, and even men admitted that Matt Logan possessed a certain finesse. Most assumed—wrongly—that his gentlemanliness was an inherited trait. In fact, it had been studied, practiced and perfected. The only trait Matt had inherited was a hunger for success.

It was Friday afternoon, and Matt was checking off items on his agenda. He would be in Phoenix during the coming week, attending the annual meeting of the Western Division's managers. It would be nice to get away to some sunshine; they had suffered through the dreariest January he could remember, and February so far was more of the same. There also was a lovely woman named Denise Somners in Phoenix, who could be counted on to be a delightful diversion if his schedule permitted. He momentarily thought about calling Denise to tell her he was arriving Monday, then decided against it. Two dozen things could prevent him from seeing her this time.

All day long a steady procession of employees had filed in and out of the office, receiving his instructions. Satisfied that everything had been taken care of, he was mulling over possible weekend activities when his intercom buzzer sounded. Depressing a button, he heard Helen Johns, his secretary, say, "Carol's on her way in, Matt, and she's very upset about something."

No sooner were the words out than the door opened and his obviously distraught eighteen-year-old daughter flew into the room. She was dressed in what Matt thought of as her uniform—faded jeans and a sweatshirt with a risqué message splashed across its front. Matt felt certain that Carol owned a closet full of lovely clothes—her mother would insist on it—but he never saw her in any of them. She was amazingly unconcerned about clothes, makeup, jewelry and all the other things that most women took such great interest in. In fact, there was nothing flashy or flamboyant about her—until she skated. Then she could dazzle, but off the ice she tended to fade into the woodwork. She was a quiet person, even shy with people she did not know well, and she knew very few people really well. When others remembered her at all, they mostly recalled the mane of dark, springy curls that framed her face, and her luminous eyes, gray like his. This afternoon those eyes were flashing distress signals.

Matt was on his feet like a shot. "Carol, honey, what—"

"Oh, Dad!" she wailed plaintively, plopping into one of the chairs facing his desk. "Positively the most terrible thing that could happen has happened!"

"What on earth?" His heart lodged in his throat.

"Sondra's retiring."

Matt's pent-up breath oozed out of him like air from a balloon, and he slowly sank back into his chair. Thank God! At least no one was dying. For a minute all sorts of disasters had occurred to him.

But, of course, to Carol this would be a calamity. Sondra Baines had been her figure skating coach for eleven years and was the woman who was supposed to guide Carol to the Olympics in 1992. "You mean...immediately?" Matt asked in disbelief.

Carol nodded. "Yes, right away. She says she can't give it her all anymore."

"Isn't this something of a surprise?"

"Oh, there have been rumors, but Sondra never said anything to me, and I wasn't about to ask."

"I don't know how her conscience will let her just drop you like that."

"I kept telling myself she wouldn't do it to me, that she knew how much '92 meant. Well, I was wrong, and I should have known it. I should have known that once her precious Eric Zito won his Olympic gold she'd lose interest. He always was the one she cared about most. I'm surprised she stayed with me as long as she did." Bitterness dripped from every word.

Matt tapped his mouth with a forefinger, studying his daughter with interest. He knew that Sondra's retirement was enough to have caused Carol's distress, but he wondered if perhaps that distress had been compounded by Eric's absence from her life. The two young people had trained under the same coach since Carol was seven; for years they had seen each other six hours a day, six days a week unless one of them was off at a competition. And Eric was just enough older—five years—for her to look up to him as a sort of idol.

But now he'd won his gold medal, retired from amateur skating and hired an agent to negotiate all sorts of lucrative offers—ice shows, product endorsements and guest appearances on television. As hard as it was for Matt to believe, the young man had quickly become one of the best known sports figures in the country, a genuine celebrity who hardly had a minute to call his own. Carol flippantly referred to him as "figure skating's resident hunk." She always affected flippancy when talking to or about Eric, but Matt thought she did it to disguise her very real affection for him. Unless he had forgotten all the signs, he was sure his daughter had a king-size crush on the young man.

But Eric had moved on, leaving Carol floundering in his wake, and now Sondra was deserting her, too. Who could blame her for feeling a tremendous sense of loss?

Carol jumped to her feet and walked to the window to gaze out over the skyline, a skyline that, sadly, was becoming increasingly New Yorkish. "I'm so close," she muttered, more to herself than to her father. "What am I supposed to do now?"

Matt frowned. She really sounded low. He didn't like the defeatist tone in her voice. When it came to skating, Carol had always been a positive thinker, upbeat and full of enthusiasm. She was still growing as a skater, making improvements daily. She had placed fifth in the nationals only a few weeks ago and would do better in the next competition, perhaps even place high enough to get to the world championships. Certainly they hoped she would be world champion by the time the Olympics rolled around. Everything had been sailing along so smoothly they might have been marking off items on a checklist. Now, who could predict what would happen?

Damn Sondra! Talk about throwing a monkey wrench into the works!

"Have you told your mother about this?" he asked.

Carol turned to him with incredulous eyes. "Mom? You've got to be kidding! I wish I didn't have to tell her. She'll think Sondra's retirement is the best thing that ever happened to me. Now I'll be able to go to Stanford and concentrate on finding some nice young man and taking my rightful place in society, whatever that is. Believe me, Mom is not going to go into a decline over this. She won't even pretend she's sorry about it."

Too true, Matt thought. It was a pity that his ex-wife had never taken Carol's interest in skating seriously, but she hadn't. He'd always been the one who'd attended the competitions and forked over the money for her training, even though Olivia Logan Bannister and her wealthy husband, Louis, could have paid the cost and hardly realized any money was gone.

But Olivia persisted in treating skating as nothing but a hobby, a pastime that was keeping Carol from more meaningful pursuits. The first time she'd gotten a look at the less than elegant neighborhood where the practice arena was located, she'd almost gone into cardiac arrest. No, Carol wouldn't be able to count on her mother for moral support or a sympathetic shoulder. It was up to him, as usual.

Getting to his feet, he walked to the window and drew his daughter into his arms. She looked so sad, and that tugged at his heart. Carol was something of an introvert, but she'd always been an optimistic one, so certain from the beginning that she could be a champion skater if she applied herself. *She has a lot of me in her,* he thought proudly. *She's ambitious and tenacious, and there are worse things a person can be. An empty-headed, frivolous socialite like her mother, for instance.*

The minute the thought formed, he regretted it. It was petty and unworthy of Olivia. She simply was the product of a pampered upbringing—hardly her fault. Her life might seem frivolous to him, but it was the only way she knew how to live. Olivia was kind-hear .d, though impatient with anything that didn't interest her. And she once had been his wife, albeit not for fifteen years. If their marriage had been disastrous, and it had, at least it had produced Carol, who was his special joy.

His work and his daughter were the two controlling passions of Matthew Logan's life. He had never regretted his divorce, since he honestly believed it had saved two people's sanity, and he had discovered he did not mind living alone. If anything, the solitude sometimes seemed like a reward. His social life usually consisted of attending select productions at the Civic Center or parties hosted by longtime friends. The numerous invitations he received were accepted or regretted according to their relative benefit to himself or to the company. When he reciprocated, he entertained with style and flair, and of course there were the inevitable business lunches and dinners. He wasn't a celibate, but his sexual experiences were superficial and always conducted with women like Denise Somners, who expected them to be nothing more. He had no real hobbies or interests outside Hamilton House, save for Carol's quest for the Olympic gold. He did not know if that was a desirable state of affairs, nor did he ever think about it. It simply was the way things were.

He thought back through the years, back to when Carol had first started badgering him for ice skating lessons. He couldn't remember exactly what had brought it on—maybe she'd gone to see an ice show— and he certainly couldn't remember when skating had changed from a mere diversion into the single-minded pursuit of an Olympic medal. But somewhere along the line the fun and games had turned into something serious, and she had begun talking competition. Once she had her first junior championship under her belt, the die was cast. While Olivia had fumed and begged him to dissuade Carol, Matt had just dug deeper into his pockets.

And he would do something now. He wasn't sure what, but he would do something. After all, he had a lot of money tied up in Carol's career. It cost roughly twenty-five thousand dollars a year to train a world-class skater, and he was too smart a businessman to sit back and watch that kind of money go down the tubes.

"Tell me something, honey," he said. "Is Sondra the only figure skating coach in the country?"

Carol's bent head came up. "Huh?"

"You heard me."

"Well, no, of course not."

"Then the way I see it, we find a new coach."

Carol smiled sadly. "You're sweet, Dad, you really are, but no one's going to want to take me now. It takes time for a coach and skater to... well, to get on the same wavelength. You almost need to know what the other is thinking without having to put it in words."

"But you have eleven years with Sondra behind you. That has to count for something. And I know how small the skating world is. By this time next week, everyone in it is going to have heard about Sondra's retirement. Your phone might start ringing off the wall."

"I doubt it. That small world is also a highly competitive one. I'll just be someone the others don't have to worry about anymore."

Matt gave her shoulders a gentle shake for emphasis. "You can't quit now, not after all you've been through."

She had almost quit once before, when she had begun to feel the burden of being Sondra's "other" student. She'd felt as though she were skating in the shadow of the great Eric Zito, who had been national champion three consecutive years and had just won his first world title. It was Matt who had talked her into continuing—something Olivia didn't know and hopefully would never find out.

Not that there hadn't been times when he'd doubted the wisdom of encouraging Carol's devotion to the crazy sport. At some point it had occurred to him that she was reaching young adulthood without ever having had a boyfriend. He also realized that she knew the girls she met in a steady stream of competitions better than she knew her classmates. In her world there were no parties, proms, corsages or pep rallies. In fact, she had finished high school with a private tutor so she could give a full six hours a day to skating. It was a rather isolated life, dedicated to a dream that so very few ever realized, and it was such an uncertain one. One lousy bobble in a major competition and—poof—all those years of working and training went up in smoke.

Then he would wonder about life after the Olympics. At a time when most young women were graduating from college and beginning their careers, she would be retiring from hers and just starting her higher education. Or perhaps she wouldn't retire but would turn pro and not go to college at all, which Matt thought would be a damned shame. Then he would brood and worry that he actually was doing her a disservice.

The confusion never lasted long, though. He would attend a competition or simply go to the rink and watch Carol practice, would see and feel her dedication, and then he would think, *She's just a chip off the old block.*

"Don't worry," he said gently. "This isn't the end of your career, not by a long shot. Cheer up. Have I ever let you down? How about having dinner with your old man tonight? Anywhere you like."

Carol sighed ruefully. "I wish I could, Dad, but Mom and Louis are giving another party, and I have strict orders to be there. They've invited this 'divine young man.' I think it's really funny that Mom knows so many divine young men when most women go their entire lives without meeting even one. This guy—I can't even remember his name—is supposedly very handsome, very rich and very available, but let's get real. If he's so handsome, rich and available, how come he doesn't have anything better to do on a Friday night than to go to one of Mom's parties? I know one thing—if he's anything like the other ten divine young men Mom's produced, he'll be a crashing bore."

Matt tried to stifle a smile but couldn't. Olivia just didn't understand that an Olympic medal was far more important to Carol than a young man, unless the young man was Eric Zito. "Well, try to be patient with your mother." His thoughts returned to the immediate problem. "Carol, is Joe Hylands still teaching?"

"Uh-huh. Just little kids, though. Why?"

"Oh, his name popped into my head suddenly. Seems to me he always kept up with who was doing what. I think I'll give him a call when I get home. He just might come up with someone for us."

Carol brightened. "I wouldn't have thought of Joe in a month of Sundays, but he's the perfect one to talk to. What would I do without you, Dad?"

"I hope it's a very long time before you have to find out."

FOR ONCE Matt did not linger late at the office. Instead, he left promptly at four-thirty and drove straight to his Nob Hill house. Of all the knolls casting their shadows over San Francisco, perhaps Nob Hill was the most famous. Once the domain of the city's crusty rich, men who'd built a railroad across the continent, it now was home to its finest hotels and strings of lovely town houses bordered by manicured hedges. Matt's own on Sacramento Street was trimmed by wrought-iron grillwork. When he arrived, he went straight to his study and telephoned Joe.

Joe Hylands had been Carol's first coach, the man who'd seen her potential early on and had sent her to Sondra. And his interest in her career had not waned during the ensuing years. He telephoned frequently for updates. He was pleased to hear from Matt but stunned at the news of Sondra's retirement.

"Carol must be taking this pretty hard," he commented.

"She is, Joe, and that's why I'm calling you. We need to find someone else. Damned if I'm going to let the past eleven years go for nothing. I was wondering if you have any suggestions."

There was a lengthy pause. "I can think of a couple of people who would jump at the chance to coach Carol, but she would have to relocate. If you mean here in Northern California...maybe. There's one person. She coached out of a rink near Denver for years and developed a couple of promising skaters. But then she quit—said it was playing hell with her marriage—and once you quit it's hard to get back in it. I don't have to tell you that doing the international circuit requires tunnel vision. She might not be interested."

"Then again, she might be. Carol's hardly a novice. Anyway, I can ask. What's the woman's name?"

"Lesley Salazar."

"Salazar," Matt repeated. "It doesn't ring a bell."

"No, it wouldn't," Joe said, "but if you've been keeping up with skating for twenty years or so you might remember Lesley Ann Kelly."

That name! It was so unexpected that Matt almost choked, and he gripped the phone so tightly his knuckles turned white. "Lesley?" he blurted out.

"Yes. Do you know her?"

"I...met her once, a long time ago." Sixteen years ago, to be precise. "Olivia and I spent a weekend at her parents' house. I...had no idea she was back in the Bay Area."

How could he have known? It wasn't as though they had stayed in touch or even had ever seen each other again. He had seen her for two memorable days, that was it. He'd been a married man then, and by the time his marriage had given up the ghost, Lesley had been a married woman living somewhere else—now that he thought about it, it seemed as if it were Colorado.

They had been little more than ships that passed in the
night, and though he'd thought of her off and on
through the years, chiefly when Carol began asking for
skating lessons, he had not seriously entertained the
notion of ever seeing her again. Furthermore, he
imagined Lesley's memory would have to receive a
severe jolt for her to remember him at all.

"How long have they been back?" he asked Joe.

"They?"

"She and her husband. I never even knew his
name."

"Arturo Salazar, the photographer. Won a couple
of Pulitzer Prizes. Lesley's a widow now. Arturo got
himself killed covering a revolution in some little
country I never heard of."

Lesley! Wasn't it strange that of all the women he
had met in his life, one small redhead had remained so
vividly in his memory? They had spent a grand total
of perhaps three hours together. Yet, he'd never forgotten her.

Matt knew he had to see her again, which bordered
on the ridiculous and was totally out of character for
the sensible man he considered himself to be. Usually
he scoffed at nostalgic nonsense, knowing how disappointing former places and former faces could be.
Lesley would be...forty now, not at all like the twenty-
four-year-old enigma who had captured his imagination sixteen years ago. Then she had been a bewitch-
ing blend of vulnerability and toughness, innocence
and sexuality, and she had briefly, so briefly, touched
his life at a time when he was in turmoil. Now she was
a widow, probably a mother. She wouldn't be at all as
he remembered her.

Yet, he wanted to see her again, and he would. He had a perfect excuse, one that he had momentarily forgotten. He experienced a fleeting second of regret at relegating Carol's need for a new coach to number two on his list of priorities, then forgot it. "Where is she?" he asked.

"She inherited the old homestead. Her folks are both gone now. I think I have the address and phone number."

"Never mind. I know where the house is, and I don't want to call ahead. It's too easy for people to say no over the phone."

"Well, good luck. Who knows? Now that she's widowed she might be looking for something to do."

Whether she would or wouldn't no longer mattered that much. The main purpose of his visit to Lesley had ceased to be Carol. He wanted to satisfy his curiosity. "Thanks a lot, Joe. You've been a big help."

For long minutes after he hung up the phone, Matt sat slumped in the chair in his paneled study, chiding himself for his foolishness. But at no time did he consider not trying to see Lesley Ann Kelly Salazar again. The prospect was too appealing. Perhaps, depending on how their meeting went, he would muster the courage to tell her what their brief encounter sixteen long years ago had meant to him.

Inevitably, his thoughts went back in time, and long-forgotten details came back to him with such amazing clarity that they might have happened only last week....

CHAPTER TWO

IT WAS EARLY SUMMER. The year was 1974, a good year in one way, a not-so-good one in another. Matt was thirty-three years old, rapidly climbing the corporate ladder, but in a rotten mood more and more often. He had found a comfortable niche for himself within the confines of Hamilton House, but he couldn't find one in his own home, literally or figuratively. Olivia was redecorating their Russian Hill residence yet another time, so the place was in a state of upheaval. He didn't know why she bothered, since she would never be happy with the house. Russian Hill was not Pacific Heights, and Pacific Heights was where Olivia longed to be.

Perhaps deserved to be, Matt conceded. She had, after all, been born to money, while he was working for his. From a very early age, Olivia had possessed more of everything that most people yearned for, and, Matt discovered, the very rich really were a different breed. Olivia, who was one of them, found it impossible to understand a man who would not seize any opportunity to join their exalted ranks.

Matt supposed theirs was not an unusual story. He refused to go into Olivia's father's fantastically successful construction business, something that had been "suggested" to him both by Olivia and her father more times than he could remember. But Matt liked what he was doing. He had risen from accounting to become assistant manager of restaurant operations in six short years and felt he was destined for great things, at least within the limited universe known as Hamilton House. Being the boss's son-in-law held no appeal for him, even though his standard of living would have risen immediately and dramatically.

Olivia's father was dumbfounded that the only son-in-law he thought he would ever have didn't want to take advantage of all that was being offered him. Matt didn't dwell much on how his father-in-law felt, but he wished there was some way of making Olivia understand how important it was to him to succeed on his own. That, however, was hopeless. The lines of communication between himself and his wife had been down for some time ... almost from the beginning.

They had been married four years. They had met at a cocktail party, a tedious affair that had been a business obligation for him and a social one for her. Their eyes had met, as in the song, across a crowded room, and Matt, after first quizzing a mutual acquaintance about her marital status, had wrangled an introduction. They later left the party together and spent two hours at an all-night pancake house, talking and drinking coffee. By the time the evening ended, he had known she excited him as few women ever had. Bewitched him might have been more accurate.

In those days Olivia's beauty had been legendary in San Francisco society. The thoroughly spoiled only child of wealthy parents, she was almost a law unto herself, and she ruled her coterie of friends like a czar. However, none of them seemed to mind. She was so beautiful, so witty and so charmingly vivacious that no one noticed how manipulative she could be, particularly when in danger of not getting her way. Everyone longed for her acceptance, which she bestowed on a select few with the air of a monarch conferring knighthood.

And she had been the first truly sensuous woman Matt had ever known. From the beginning, the physical attraction between them was strong and undeniable, and unlike other women he had dated, Olivia was frank about sex. After dating for several months, he had proposed—in the first flush of a sexual afterglow—and for a while he had thought himself deeply in love.

Soon, however, Olivia's campaign to change him had begun. Accustomed to having her way, she'd never considered that Matt might not want to change, that he was happy as he was. Confused by the one man who could resist her pleas, Olivia often resorted to nagging. Eventually, Matt admitted that their union had been one of total opposites, that only the sexual attraction was real, and even that had begun to pall. It sometimes seemed that the only thing holding the marriage together was Carol, which was asking quite a lot of a two-year-old.

The day of their marriage that he remembered most vividly, even after sixteen years, was a Friday, a Friday that had begun with a quarrel. He had not wanted to drive to the peninsula to spend the weekend with Ross and Alicia Kelly at their splendiferous mansion, and Olivia had declared she wouldn't hear of not going. If he wouldn't take her, she would go alone, but she couldn't understand how he could pass it up. The

Kellys were the crème de la crème of society; their home was a showplace, and it was a real mark of distinction to receive an invitation to a weekend soiree there.

In the end he'd relented. And as often happened in life, the weekend he so dreaded became the one he never forgot.

The Kelly estate was on the bay side of the peninsula, nestled in the foothills of the Santa Cruz Mountains. Its opulence was almost indescribable. Floors were inlaid with rich designs, and marble work and murals abounded. Even Olivia, who was familiar with fine things, gaped openly. Guests would spend the weekend either in the main house or in one of the guest cottages located on the estate. Matt and Olivia were staying in the big mansion itself. They were shown to an upstairs bedroom that Matt guessed had once been a young girl's domain. It was quaint and done entirely in blue and white. After getting settled in, they were invited to make themselves at home.

The Kellys did not hover over their weekend guests, but a gaggle of servants saw to it that no one wanted for a thing. There was a surfeit of food and drink at all hours, a swimming pool, tennis courts and plenty of grounds for strolling. Matt had to admit he was impressed. He thought in many ways it was like being on a cruise ship.

Olivia was in her rightful element and fairly bubbled with excitement. Watching her, Matt marveled at how alive she became at such affairs. Sometimes he envied her the energy that never flagged. In fact, she seemed to gain strength as the festivities progressed. Naturally, she was anxious to see and be seen, so Matt assured her he didn't in the least mind being left on his own. She changed clothes quickly and was off, while he took advantage of the relative privacy to wander through the rooms of the grand house, inspecting, admiring.

He had just stepped into what he guessed was the library when an engaging figure uncurled herself from a high-backed leather chair and stood. Matt stopped dead in his tracks, partly from surprise, but mostly because he was stunned by the sight of the young woman. She was small, not more than five feet four inches, delicate looking and incredibly beautiful. With hair the color of burnished copper, sparkling green eyes and a smooth, creamy complexion, she was the quintessential colleen. Her spectacular hair was pulled back into a single neat braid laced with a ribbon, showing off her excellent bone structure. Matt did not think he had been so instantly impressed with another human being in his entire life, not even that night at the cocktail party when he'd first seen Olivia.

"Are you lost?" she asked in a melodious voice, her mouth curving into a sweet smile.

"I don't think so. The kitchen's that way, and the front door is that way."

"Then you aren't lost. You're probably just bored. I wouldn't blame you if you were. Mom and Dad's bashes bore me, too."

So she was the Kellys' daughter. He offered his hand. "I'm Matt Logan."

"Hello, Matt. It's nice to meet you. I'm Lesley." Her hand was smooth and soft, her grip firm. "I don't think I've ever seen you here before."

"No, this was my first invitation. Or rather, my wife's first invitation, and I was unsuccessful in my attempts at begging off."

Lesley laughed delightedly. "At least you tried. Not many do. Everyone seems to swoon with happiness over being invited to these things."

Chagrined, Matt feared he was coming across as a snobbish boor. "I'm sorry if I sounded high-and-mighty. And the house alone is worth the trip. It's very impressive."

Lesley leaned against the back of the chair and crossed one ankle over the other. She was wearing a full-skirted, pale yellow sundress that complimented her smooth, fair skin, and she had the tiniest waist he'd ever seen. "Where do you live?" she asked.

"San Francisco."

"Are you staying the entire weekend?"

"Yes."

She smiled, and when he smiled back at her, he thought he saw her cheeks color slightly. Perhaps his smile had been too bold. He felt strangely daring, for she was having the most curious effect on him. He forgot he hadn't wanted to come, and he almost forgot his wife was with him.

"Would you like me to show you the house?" Lesley asked.

"I'd love it."

"Then we'll start downstairs with the game room. That seems to be everyone's favorite."

Matt could see why. It was a cavernous retreat on the lower level with a stunning view. One certainly never could complain about a lack of things to do when visiting the Kellys. He noted a pool table, a pinball machine, game tables and an old-fashioned juke-box. And along one wall was a curved bar that was at least as large as many hotel bars Matt had seen.

Then his gaze fell on the most impressive sight in the entire room—a large framed photograph of a beautiful young figure skater in flight. The skater happened to be his tour guide. He stared at it a minute, then turned to Lesley, quizzing her with his eyes.

"That was taken the year I won the nationals," she said nonchalantly.

"Did you go to the Olympics?"

"Yes."

He waited, but she said nothing. "Well?" he finally asked.

"Well what?"

"Aren't you going to tell me how you did?"

"It wasn't my year, I guess. I fell during my long program and had to settle for the bronze."

"But an Olympic medal is an Olympic medal."

She smiled. "Not really. Who remembers who won the bronze? It's like trying to remember who was second runner-up in the Miss Universe Pageant."

"Can't you try again? You're very young."

"I'm twenty-four," she said, which surprised him. She didn't look it. "That's over-the-hill for most amateur skaters—including me, I'm afraid. That's something I've just begun to realize. And there are so many great young skaters coming along all the time. Don't you watch the Games on television?"

"No, I hardly ever watch television."

"Or read the sports page?"

"Only during football season."

Lesley laughed her delightful laugh again. "There's more to the sports world than football. So tell me, what do you do?"

"I'm in the restaurant business."

"Do you own one?"

"No, I work for a corporation that owns many. Have you ever heard of Hamilton House?"

"Yes. Nice places." She then took him by the arm. "Come on. I'll show you the rest of the house. Some of it is quite spectacular. My mom has made a career out of keeping it that way."

The touch of her hand in the crook of his elbow was light, gentle. He found it difficult to believe that such a dainty woman could be an athlete. She reminded him of a filly—lean, limber and spirited. Her fresh gaiety and spontaneity charmed him. She was at that delightful age when life had yet to destroy illusions— and how long had it been since he'd spent time with a woman who didn't have at least a nodding acquaintance with disillusionment?

Yet, there was a touching vulnerability to her, too. She seemed the kind of woman a man instinctively felt protective of. Together they strolled in and out of rooms. Matt tried his best to make appropriate comments as she told him the history of the house—originally built by a man who'd made his fortune in mining and lumbering—but his interest in the house had become negligible. Lesley was the delight. As long as he was with her, he found it impossible to wipe the foolish grin from his face.

The afternoon fairly flew by. Matt almost resented it when the other guests began drifting toward the house to begin getting dressed for dinner. He had liked it better when Lesley was his only companion.

WHILE THEY WERE DRESSING for dinner, Olivia kept up a running chatter about all the important people she had met that afternoon. "Where were you?" she asked. "I kept thinking you would show up any minute and at least make an effort to be sociable."

"The Kellys' daughter was kind enough to give me the grand tour of the house."

Olivia uttered an impatient sound. "Honestly, Matt, the way you lurk in corners distresses me—really it does. Now I want you to mix and mingle tonight. The Hunters from San Jose have asked us to sit with them at dinner, and I insist that you do. He's in electronics."

Matt resisted the urge to say, "So?"

"Try to be charming," Olivia pleaded.

"Isn't that asking a great deal of me?" he asked, making an attempt at teasing, but Olivia never took his teasing the way it was intended. She merely shot him one of her I-don't-understand-you looks as they left the room to join the other guests downstairs.

Dinner was delicious, a culinary masterpiece, but not even excellent food could alleviate Matt's boredom. The dinner partners Olivia had been so anxious for him to meet were two decidedly uninteresting individuals. Jonathan Hunter could not stop talking about himself, and his wife, Sylvia, never said a word. Since Matt couldn't think of anything to add to the fascinating account of Jonathan's life story, conversation was pretty well dominated by Jonathan and Olivia.

The only minute of relieved tedium came when Lesley walked out onto the terrace where everyone was dining. Matt allowed himself that minute to feast his eyes on her. She was dressed in red, and he thought anyone who said redheads couldn't wear red had never seen Lesley in the color. She was a vision. Her face was angelic, radiating innocence, but when she threaded her way through the tables, her supple body exuded potent sensuality. While she scanned the crowd, their eyes met for a fleeting heartbeat of time. She smiled at him, then moved on. For the remainder of the meal, he plotted how to find time to be alone with her again.

Actually, it was easy. Once the guests began standing and milling around, waiters appeared from inside the house to clear the tables, and from somewhere music began. Matt simply ambled away from Olivia and the Hunters and went to look for Lesley. He found her standing alone at one end of the long terrace.

"You were sitting with the Hunters," she commented when he came to stand in front of her. "Was the woman in white your wife?"

"Yes."

"She's beautiful."

"She would be delighted to hear you say that."

"Do you have children?"

"Yes, a daughter." The last thing he wanted to discuss with this fascinating woman was his marital status. "How about a short walk to work off dinner?"

Lesley hesitated, but only for a minute. "All right."

They stepped off the terrace and strolled across the lawn, heading nowhere in particular. They didn't even speak for several long minutes. Finally Matt asked,

"What will you do now, if you're over the hill as far as amateur skating goes?"

"Oh, I don't know," Lesley said with a little laugh. "Everyone thinks I should teach skating, perhaps take some promising seven- or eight-year-old and lead him or her to the Olympics. Some days the idea appeals, others it doesn't."

"What about turning pro and joining an ice show?"

Lesley wrinkled her nose. "I've considered that. There are those who like it and those who don't. I don't think I would. On the road nine months of the year, doing the same performance night after night, never meeting anyone but other skaters. Someone once told me it was like joining a circus. That makes it almost as impossible to have any kind of personal life as training for the Olympics does. Besides, I never was very good at the show biz side of figure skating. No, I think I'll do something else altogether. I just haven't figured out what yet." She sighed. "I think I might like trying to live a normal life for a change, if that's possible at this late date. I sacrificed a lot for skating."

"For instance?"

"Sugar." Another little laugh. "I didn't knowingly eat sugar for years. My coach believed it made me sluggish. And I've never had a boyfriend. Or a girlfriend, for that matter. I never could relate to people my own age because they didn't understand the drive."

"What about your parents? Did they encourage you?"

"If you mean did they willingly dole out the money, yes, but they didn't really understand. I was sort of this strange child of theirs who didn't like to do the same things their friends' children did. That bothered Mom, especially. I guess I was rather solitary. That's the trouble with pursuing a dream. You focus solely on that to the exclusion of all else, and then one day it's all over, and you're at loose ends.''

She sounded so wistful. Matt badly wanted to touch her in some way, give her a sympathetic pat or something, but he wouldn't have dared. "Dreams die hard,'' he said softly.

"But when something is over, no matter how important it was to you, it's over. You have to accept that, put it behind you and start all over again. Clinging to an old dream doesn't make any sense. Life's too short to waste on longing for things that are over.''

Her words jolted Matt, reminding him as they did of his marriage. He had no idea what had happened to it, but something had, and he knew Olivia couldn't be any happier than he was. But she never wanted to talk about it, and whenever he tried he only ended up feeling helpless. He'd analyzed his marriage until he'd reached the only conclusion that could be drawn— they just liked different ways of life. There was nothing wrong with either of them; they simply were incompatible.

He looked at Lesley. "Thank you,'' he said.

She cocked her head. "I don't understand.''

"For pointing out something that I've been refusing to admit.''

She uttered a little laugh. "I still don't understand.''

"I know. It's not necessary that you do.'' He took both her hands in his, lifted them, turned them over, then bent and lightly kissed both palms. It was a completely impulsive gesture. When he lifted his head, he looked into her startled, puzzled green eyes.

"N-now, I . . . I really don't understand," she stammered.

"I can imagine."

They both smiled, but though each seemed to relax in the other's presence, nothing could have been further from the truth. Something was happening; the air around them suddenly seemed charged with a splendid energy force, and both of them felt it, knew it and knew the other felt it, too. She was looking directly into his eyes, her lips parted in surprise, and he had the almost overwhelming urge to cover them with his own.

Lesley recovered first and backed up a step, looking embarrassed. One hand went to her breast, as though to steady her heartbeat. Matt saw her embarrassment and suffered some of his own. Good God, he was thirty-three, a married man with a daughter, and here he was, drooling over a nubile nymph almost a decade younger than himself, his head swamped with thoughts he had no business thinking.

And he was making her nervous, the last thing he wanted. Giving the one hand he was still holding a gentle squeeze, he released it and stuffed his own hands into his pocket. "Perhaps we should rejoin the party."

"Y-yes." Abruptly she turned and walked toward the house, her head held high, and Matt was left to rejoin Olivia and the Hunters and endure the remainder of the evening.

At some point during the night, while his wife lay sleeping peacefully beside him, Matt had an erotic dream, and it was a beauty. There was nothing unusual about that; he knew most men had such dreams from time to time. But in the past, the women in his dreams had been fantasy creatures, none of them remotely like anyone he actually knew. This time, however, he dreamed of a woman whose name he knew—Lesley—and the feelings she elicited in him left him limp and utterly content. He wanted to be ashamed of himself, but he couldn't. The dream was too magnificent. He hated for it to end.

The following day, Matt caught only brief glimpses of Lesley, and it occurred to him that she was avoiding him. At the poolside party on Saturday night, he didn't see her at all. When his curiosity threatened to eat him alive, he casually asked his hostess where her daughter was.

"Some of the younger people were going into the city for some dancing, and for once I was able to convince Lesley to go," Alicia Kelly told him. "She really doesn't have many friends her own age. Isn't that a shame? The skating, you know. I'm so glad that's behind us."

It was the longest evening of Matt's life, and not all the self-chastisement in the world could change that. The next morning all of the guests prepared to depart after a lavish breakfast. Again, Lesley did not join them. Matt ruefully realized he would not see her again. While Olivia was offering her drawn-out goodbyes to the Kellys and anyone else she could corner, he headed for their car, suitcases in hand.

Suddenly he was aware that someone was walking beside him. Turning, he saw Lesley, dressed in jeans and a plaid shirt, her hair in a ponytail. She looked all of seventeen, which made Friday night's dream seem unconscionable.

"I wanted to say goodbye," she said in a low voice.

"I'm glad you did. Good luck with...whatever you decide to do."

She glanced hesitantly toward the house, and her gaze seemed to rest on Olivia. "You, too," she said. "I hope... I hope you'll be happier in the future."

For one breathless moment they stood staring at each other. "What makes you think I'm unhappy?" he finally asked.

"I know you are," she said. "Goodbye, Matt. I really enjoyed meeting you." Then she turned and walked away.

THAT WAS IT, only a brief encounter, and Matt didn't understand how he could remember the details of it so clearly after all this time. Less than a year after driving away from the Kellys' mansion, to the astonishment of family and friends, he and Olivia had finally ended their sham of a marriage. The Russian Hill residence had been sold, Olivia and Carol had moved in with Olivia's wealthy parents, and Matt had rented a bachelor pad. If he had felt anything, it was a sense of relief that neither of them needed to put up a front any longer. His initial worries about Carol had been quickly dispelled. He had been given unlimited visitation rights, and father and daughter had quickly established a closeness that many dads in nuclear families would have envied.

A few months afterward, on an impulse, he had telephoned the Kellys' house and asked for Lesley. The housekeeper who answered the phone paused, then informed him that she had married that past spring and now lived in Denver. Matt still remembered his acute disappointment.

He had thought of her only a few times since then, usually in association with Carol's skating, and had vaguely wondered what interests she had pursued, if any. Perhaps she had found contentment in being a wife and mother. He hoped so.

Now, as the evening shadows deepened, Matt shook himself out of his reverie. He hadn't even changed clothes after work, and if the aroma wafting into his study from the kitchen was any indication, dinner would soon be ready. The bachelor pad was gone, replaced by the small but elegant Nob Hill town house he'd inherited from his father. He got to his feet and went into the kitchen to ask Horace, the manservant also inherited from his father, to put dinner on hold while he treated himself to a shower and a cocktail. Then he went upstairs, shedding his clothes along the way.

A curious excitement was building in him, impossible to stifle. Tomorrow he was going to see Lesley again. At least, he hoped so. She could be away. She could be busy. She could have company or a dozen reasons not to see him. He told himself it was unreasonable to think she still would interest him or be interested in him. He would feel like a king-size fool if he had to spend the first five minutes explaining just who the hell he was. He kept reminding himself that he was going there to speak for Carol.

Yet, if Lesley was half as enchanting as she had been sixteen years ago, he just might speak for himself, too.

CHAPTER THREE

LESLEY SIGHED in mock exasperation as she looked at the earnest, spectacled man seated at the bar in the game room. He was Garson Morman, an agent for a prestigious San Francisco gallery and Arturo's friend and confidant for years. He came to see her occasionally, usually on the weekends, and they talked. Or rather, he talked and she listened to whatever new scheme he had in mind for her. Garson desperately wanted Arturo Salazar's widow to "do something important," meaning something very artistic and creative, since artists were the only people he could relate to. Lesley always said no. She was saying no this time, too. "Garson, what is it with you? Haven't I said no often enough? Am I not speaking English? What?"

Garson continued studying the collection of photographs that had been spread out on the bar. "You refuse to believe I'm serious, for whatever reason I can't imagine, but I am deadly serious, Lesley. They're good, very good. Let me mount a show for you. It might be the start of something wonderful for you, a whole new career."

Lesley smiled and shook her head. "Why do you find it so difficult to believe that this is nothing but a hobby for me?"

"You studied under the master himself."

"I didn't study anything. What I know about photography I absorbed by osmosis from living with Arturo for almost fourteen years. I don't have his eye, I don't have his talent. And I'm not in the least interested in beginning a new career, certainly not in photography. Everything I did would be compared to Arturo's work, and he was incomparable."

Garson shifted on the bar stool and looked at her. "Lesley, you're only forty. You need an interest in life, something to do."

"Is that what this is all about? Are you afraid I'm going to sit around and go to seed?"

"It's happened to many a childless widow."

"It won't happen to me. I have many interests. I'm just not interested in letting any of them become my life's work."

Lesley didn't tell her friend the entire truth, that all the various hobbies she had sampled comprised a constant search for something she could really sink her teeth into, something that would make her want to get out of bed in the morning. So far she hadn't found that, but, she reflected wryly, she certainly had become a jack-of-all-trades. Painting, gardening, photography, every imaginable kind of craft—name it, and she probably had tried it. Nothing lasted long, and she still felt purposeless.

But she was an optimist by nature. Something would come along; she just knew it.

Garson sighed, then began carefully gathering up the photographs and putting them back in their portfolio. While he was doing so, the front doorbell rang.

A minute passed, then Clarice, the housekeeper, came into the room.

"Ma'am, there's a gentleman at the door who wishes to speak with you."

"Who is he?" Lesley asked.

"He says you might not remember him, but he was a guest here some years back. His name is Matt Logan."

Lesley's head came up. Matt Logan! She felt her heartbeat accelerate. How odd that after all these years—all the places she had been and all the famous people she had met because of Arturo—she still vividly remembered the handsome gentleman at that long-ago party. "For goodness' sake! Show him in, Clarice." Even as she said it she quickly scrutinized herself in the mirror over the bar.

Garson slid off the stool. "You have company, so I'll be going now, Lesley. Are you sure there's nothing I can do for you?"

"I'm sure. Thanks for coming by. Give Sally my love."

"I'll do that. She was just saying that we should have you over for dinner some night soon."

"I'd enjoy it anytime." She lifted her face to accept the light brush of his lips on her cheek.

Garson walked toward the stairs but stood back to make way for the man entering the room. He nodded to Matt, then continued on. Lesley did not watch him depart since her eyes were riveted on her unexpected guest. Even though sixteen years had passed since she'd last seen him, she would have known him anywhere. As with so many men, time had only enhanced his incredible good looks. She had fantasized about him for a long time after her parents' weekend party, conveniently forgetting that he was a married man with a beautiful wife and a daughter. She had been so young in those days, younger even than her years, and she had needed dreams. At the time, Matt Logan had been the only exciting man she had ever met.

Now she hurried across the room to take both his hands in hers. "Matt! How good to see you again!"

A wave of relief swept through Matt as he smiled down at her. "I wondered if you would remember me. It's been a long time."

"Of course I remember you, and it has been a long time, hasn't it? Please, come over here and have a seat. Can I get you something to drink?"

"No, thanks." Since she sat down on one of the bar stools, he took the one next to her. Mature beauty had replaced the ingenuous good looks he recalled, but the years had been very good to her. She still had a small waist, and her coppery hair was still thick and lustrous. She had become a beautiful woman. Once again, in the space of a few minutes, she had succeeded in beguiling him.

"I suppose it's only natural to ask what on earth brought you here this afternoon," Lesley said, full of curiosity and more than a little excitement.

"Joe Hylands mentioned you and told me you were back here."

Lesley's brow furrowed. "Joe? How do you know Joe?"

"He was my daughter's first skating coach. We've stayed in close touch for years."

"Your daughter is a skater?"

"Yes, a very good one. If you still keep up with that world, you might have heard of her. Carol Logan."

Lesley brightened. "Yes, the nationals. What did she place ... fourth?"

"Fifth. Carol's what brought me here."

"I don't understand."

"Her coach is retiring. Have you heard of Sondra Baines?"

"Seems like I have."

"She was Eric Zito's coach."

"Ah. Now that young man I know about. He can do things on the ice I wouldn't have thought a mere mortal could."

"Carol's good, too, as you know. She promises to do better in the next nationals, but Sondra's retirement has left her in the lurch. I called Joe to ask if he knew someone who might be willing to take her on, and he mentioned you. I must say, your name came as something of a surprise to me." An understatement if he'd ever uttered one.

Lesley struggled to hide her disappointment. He had come because of his daughter? She hadn't had time to speculate on what might have prompted the visit. Being honest, she supposed she had half hoped he would say something like, "I just heard you were back and wanted to see you again." But that was nonsense, and she knew it. "Matt, I haven't coached in several years."

"So I understand, but Joe says you're quite good. And you're here. I really would prefer that Carol not have to relocate."

"I...don't know. I'm not sure I want to get started again. I know I don't have to tell you that coaching a

world-class skater requires as much time and dedication of the coach as it does the skater.''

"I know, but she needs someone, Lesley. She's
worked so hard, and she's good, damned good." Matt
hadn't prepared himself for a refusal. Perhaps he
should have, but he hadn't. "Listen, I have an idea.
Just watch her skate. Watch her, that's all. Then decide. Even if the answer is no, you might offer her
some words of encouragement, give her a lift. That
would mean a lot coming from a former Olympian.
She's awfully down right now, and she doesn't have
anyone but me to look to for moral support. You
know what her youth's been like—total dedication, no
close friends, no one to really talk to woman-to-
woman.''

"What about her mother?''

"I'm afraid Olivia doesn't take skating seriously.''

Lesley's eyes widened slightly. "Do you mean that
you encourage your daughter's career but your wife
doesn't?''

"She's not my wife anymore.''

"Oh, I…" An image of the woman in white on that
long-ago night sprang to Lesley's mind. She also recalled sensing that the Matt Logan of sixteen years ago
had not been a happy man. She wondered which of the
Logans, if either, was to blame for the split. Had his
beautiful wife broken his heart? Had he remarried?
Did he know she was a widow? Would he care one way
or another? Why was she still so curious after all this
time?

She didn't know, but the fact was she had never
forgotten Matt and the excitement he had generated in
her that weekend. She had almost always thought of

him—his suave manners and his nice smile—when Arturo was being difficult, which had been far too frequently. "I'm sorry," she finally said.

"It was a long time ago," Matt went on. "Less than a year after we attended that weekend party here. I...telephoned you after my divorce."

"You did? No one told me."

"I didn't leave my name. You were married by then."

Lesley's eyelashes dipped, then lifted, and she looked at him. "I wish I had known."

"Why?"

She shrugged and uttered a small laugh. "I don't know. I just do."

The air between them thickened. Again, just like that night in the garden sixteen years ago, something was happening between them. A powerful magnetization. Lesley knew she wasn't imagining it. Her imagination wasn't that vivid.

"Will you watch Carol skate?" Matt asked again. "I know Joe will set up some rink time tomorrow afternoon."

Lesley knew she was going to, and the reason she was had nothing to do with Carol Logan's skating ability. "You took the time and trouble to come here to ask me, so it must mean a lot to you. Yes, I'll be happy to watch her skate. But that doesn't put me under obligation, right?"

"Right. Two o'clock?"

"That's fine."

"Do you know the rink where Joe teaches?"

"Yes, I'll meet you there."

Matt covered her hand with his. "Thanks. This is going to mean a lot to Carol."

Lesley smiled. "I've never known a rink dad before. Moms, yes. A bunch of them. But never a rink dad."

"I'm far too busy to be a rink dad."

"Are you still with Hamilton House?"

It pleased him enormously that she remembered. "Yes. Vice president, Western Division."

"I'm impressed."

Matt's eyes swept the big room. "It's hard to believe it's been sixteen years since I was last here." Then his gaze fell on the wall behind the bar. "It's gone," he said.

"What's gone?"

"The picture of you."

"Oh." Lesley laughed. "I took that down ages ago. What woman my age wants her baby pictures scattered about?"

"Why? You haven't changed all that much."

"Sorry, you'll never make me believe that."

A moment of silence followed. Matt shifted his weight on the stool, knowing he should make some kind of move to leave. His business here was finished. He was trying to think of a plausible way to prolong the visit when Lesley took the initiative.

"Matt, will you . . . stay awhile?"

He seized the overture. "I'd love to. May I make a couple of quick phone calls?"

"Of course." Sliding off the stool, she touched his arm lightly. "There's a phone behind the bar. I'll get it. And I have a chilled bottle of Soave just waiting for a special occasion. This seems to qualify. I'll open it, then you can fill me in on what you've been doing these past sixteen years.''

After calling both Joe and Carol, Matt accepted the long-stemmed glass of wine from Lesley, and from that moment on, time stopped. They talked...and talked...and talked. It was something of a shock for both of them to realize they didn't know each other at all, yet each had thought of the other for so many years.

Lesley learned that Matt had never remarried. He learned that her marriage to a Pulitzer Prize-winning photographer had not produced children, and Matt was very curious about the man who had been her husband.

It was difficult for her to talk about Arturo, who had been a complex individual. "He was brilliant in his field," she said, choosing to discuss only the professional side of the man. "There were those who said Arturo could smell news an ocean or continent away. Others thought he simply had a knack for being in the right place at the right time. I belong to the latter group. For instance, he just happened to be in Buenos Aires on another assignment the day Argentina invaded the Falklands. His dispatches and photographs were the first out of the country. You can't tell me blind luck didn't play a part in that." She didn't add that he had spent a month in Argentina without so much as phoning or relaying a message informing her that he was safe. Lesley often had suspected that when Arturo had been on a story, he forgot he had a wife.

As she spoke, Matt realized that her marriage had introduced her to a way of life far different from the one she had grown up with. Yet she had retained a lot of her captivating freshness. He looked for the vitality he remembered and found it in her eyes when she was speaking enthusiastically about something. Several times while she was talking, he found himself so mesmerized by her face, her eyes, her voice, her scent, that he had to look away, amazed that she could have such an effect on him.

While Matt tried very hard not to study her too intently, Lesley began to memorize everything about him, tucking her impressions away for easy recall later. She noticed the way the skin around his eyes crinkled when he smiled and how white his teeth were. She stared at his slender fingers, with their perfect, square nails, as they curled around the wineglass, and she wished he would touch her. It was a crazy, intoxicating moment.

After a while, Clarice stuck her head in to say that dinner was ready, and Lesley insisted he stay. Matt was having too good a time to consider refusing. As it turned out, it was almost nine o'clock when he finally tore himself away, and then reluctantly. The knowledge that he would see her again the following afternoon mitigated the reluctance somewhat.

At the door, Matt placed both his hands on her shoulders and looked down into her smiling, upturned face. "This has been the most enjoyable day I've spent in a long time, Lesley. Would you think it terribly forward of me to act on an urge I had sixteen years ago?"

She knew what was coming and welcomed it. "No. Please...."

The kiss was quick, soft and sweet. To Lesley it seemed as endless as eternity. She stood watching him walk down the flagstone pathway, and she did not go inside until the wrought-iron gate had clanged shut behind him.

She couldn't stop thinking about him, not that she particularly wanted to. Nor could she stop silently thanking Carol Logan's coach for retiring and Joe Hylands for telling Matt that Lesley Ann Kelly was back in the Bay Area. Long after she had climbed into bed, she lay awake, reliving their first meeting.

There wasn't that much to remember. Lesley didn't think either of them had said or done anything unusual or noteworthy. She had shown him the house, and the first night they had taken a stroll across the grounds. That actually had been the only time they spent together. Yet, once she had set eyes on him, she hadn't wanted to look away. By doing absolutely nothing, Matt had made her heart pound.

Her reaction to him had been so peculiar that it frightened her, so she'd avoided him for the remainder of the weekend, until just as he and his wife were leaving. Totally inexperienced with men, she had feared making a complete fool of herself, but at the last minute she hadn't been able to let him leave without saying goodbye.

Still, she'd never forgotten him. Even now, lying alone in her dark bedroom, Lesley shook her head in wonder at the incredulity of that. And off and on through the years, the most unexpected things had triggered her memory of Matt—a remark, a face in a crowd, her mother's reminiscing about "those great weekend parties we used to give." Once it had been a writer who, at Arturo's insistence, had stayed with them in Denver for two weeks. The man had borne such an amazing resemblance to Matt that she'd been distinctly uncomfortable. She had spent the entire time playing the charming hostess while trying very hard not to stare at her guest. For weeks after the man left, she had thought of Matt to the point of preoccupation.

Odd, she mused, *the memories that just stay and stay and stay.*

CHAPTER FOUR

SUNDAY DAWNED overcast and misty. Matt had told
Carol he would pick her up around one o'clock that
afternoon, and good manners dictated that he go inside the twin-turreted mansion on the palatial ridge
known as Pacific Heights and exchange the obliga-
tory pleasantries with Olivia and Louis. Normally he
didn't mind that since he and Louis Bannister had
what was known as a civilized relationship, and there
were no lingering traces of bitterness or resentment
between himself and his ex-wife. In fact, they liked
each other more now and got along better than they
ever had when they were married. But if Olivia knew
of the trouble he was going through to get Carol a new
coach, he had a feeling their exchange would be anything but pleasant.

He was right. He called at the Bannister house
promptly at one and was ushered into the parlor. Almost immediately, Olivia swished into the room, her
eyes snapping. She was wearing a vivid blue
garment—Matt thought it was called a hostess gown—
and the effect was electric. She was still a stunningly
attractive woman, he observed, and she had all the
time and money necessary to keep herself that way. He
suspected that a plastic surgeon had had a hand in
preserving her good looks, not that it was any of his

business, and if that was true, she was a hell of an advertisement for cosmetic surgery.

"Hello, Olivia. How nice you look." A true statement if one could ignore those stormy eyes.

"Honestly, Matt, I'm very unhappy with you," she said, not bothering with pleasantries. "This would have been the perfect time to put an end to this skating nonsense. Carol has spent most of her life on ice, slouching around in leotards, hanging out at those dreadful rinks, and I ask you, what kind of life is that for a girl with her background?"

Matt always strove for patience with Olivia, chiefly because impatience was a waste of time. "It's what she wants, Olivia, and I'd hate to see the past eleven years count for nothing. Besides, I know you—you'll be the proudest person alive when she wins that gold medal."

"But it all seems so pointless. Then what will she do? The child should be in college. It's not as though she's learning anything useful."

"Well, now, I disagree. Training for the Olympics is teaching her to focus on a goal. That has got to serve her in good stead for the rest of her life."

A pained expression crossed Olivia's face, and her shoulders slumped. "I had such great plans for Carol when she was younger. A girl with her advantages could be anything. She's really attractive—or could be if she would take the time to do something with herself. She could be something outstanding."

"I believe there are those who would say that winning an Olympic medal falls under the heading of 'outstanding.'"

Olivia often suspected Matt of deliberately provoking her for the sport of it. She set her mouth in a tight line. "I wish you were an ally, Matt, but I never could get you to see my side of any issue."

Matt truly regretted that she felt that way. When they were married he honestly had tried to see her viewpoint...at least part of the time. "That's not true. I know what you want for Carol, and there's nothing wrong with it. It just doesn't happen to be what she wants."

"Why are you even getting so involved? I thought Hamilton House was the most important thing in your life."

Matt took a deep breath. "I'm involved because Carol needs moral support. I wish you would try to muster a little of it yourself."

Olivia fastened him with an icy look. "I find it difficult to believe that you and I were ever married."

"I know, dear. So do I."

Thankfully, Louis strolled into the parlor at that moment. Matt seized on the man's presence and engaged him in a discussion about the 49ers' prospects for next season until Carol showed up. He hated it when he and Olivia were at odds over something, usually Carol's skating. It was a relief to drive away from the stately mansion.

"What did you and Mom talk about?" Carol asked.

"You. You're the only thing we have in common."

"I don't think you're one of her favorite people today. She almost had a cow when I told her Sondra's retirement wouldn't make any difference, that you were going to find me another coach."

"I can imagine. How was Friday night's 'divine young man'?"

Carol rolled her eyes. "Impressed with himself. They always are. Frankly, I thought the party would never end, but Mom gave it an eight and a half. That's top drawer. Did you know she keeps a file?"

"File?" Matt asked, perplexed.

"She has one of those little recipe boxes and all these little cards. Every time she gives a party, she takes a card and writes down what she wore, what she served and who was there. Then she gives it a rating from one to ten. If you think the way the judges score figure skating is complicated, you should get a load of Mom's rating system. She says skating's pointless, but please tell me what is more pointless than that?"

"Be tolerant, honey. That sort of thing is probably very important to people in your mother's social position. Give her an A plus for organization."

"I guess you're right. Oh, Dad, I couldn't sleep last night. I was too excited. Tell me who this woman is."

"She's a former Olympian. She won the bronze in '72."

"How did you find her?"

"I met her once years ago. Joe told me she was back in the Bay Area, so I went to see her. But please don't get your hopes up. She only agreed to watch you. She isn't sure she wants to coach again, so we might very well strike out. Did you bring your music?"

Carol nodded. "Oh, God, I feel so hyper. I hope I don't bobble a jump or, worse, fall."

"She's seen plenty of bobbles and falls. Just relax and do your best."

The streets outside the ice arena were far from the loveliest in the Bay Area, but inside the building the walls had been painted to look like a winter wonderland, a nice effect. Lesley had arrived ahead of them and was seated in the stands, talking to Joe Hylands. Matt spied her before she saw them, and he took advantage of that to study her. She was turned toward Joe, smiling and nodding, which gave him a perfect view of her sculpted profile. She was wearing a red jumpsuit, and he recalled the red dress she had worn that night in the garden. Strange that he did, because he wasn't the sort of man who paid close attention to what women wore, just the overall effect. But he'd never entirely forgotten Lesley in red.

"Hello," he called, his voice reverberating through the empty arena. "I hope you haven't been waiting long." He and Carol stepped up into the stands.

"Not long," Lesley called back. "Joe and I haven't seen each other in a while, so we had plenty to talk about."

Introductions were made, and Carol greeted Joe like a favorite uncle. Then, while she put on her skates and Joe took care of the music, Matt sat down beside Lesley.

"Carol's lovely, Matt," Lesley said, "and that's important. It shouldn't be, but it is. Nothing should matter but the program and the performance, but judges look at the whole package. Attractiveness helps—it just does. And Carol doesn't have any worries on that score. If she ever wins a gold medal, her face will be everywhere, simply everywhere."

Matt's stomach was in knots. He was usually nervous when Carol skated in competition, which was normal, but he didn't understand the butterflies this afternoon. It suddenly seemed of paramount importance that Lesley think Carol was wonderful, and he had to remember that Lesley had seen plenty of wonderful skaters in her time. Too, he was worried that the business with Sondra might have Carol not up to par.

He needn't have given it a thought. She skated to the kind of jazzy, vibrant music that usually brought out the best in her, and when she nailed two triples in the opening minutes of the program, he knew she was on. She seemed completely relaxed and spontaneous, so he tried to simply enjoy the performance. He, who couldn't even stand on skates, had never ceased being a little in awe of his daughter when she took to the ice.

He could see that she had improved since the nationals. Matt knew this program, her favorite, by heart, and he felt himself tense again as she moved toward her final jump, the most technically difficult one in her repertoire. As she approached the takeoff point, she pivoted backward, coasting, legs flexed. Then she set her toe pick in the ice and exploded! Launching herself skyward, she became a gyrating blur, impossible to follow. Then her blade hit the ice; there was a final flourish, the music stopped, and the program was over.

For a minute silence reigned in the cavernous arena. Then Matt and Joe applauded enthusiastically. When there was no sound from Lesley, Matt glanced sideways at her.

She was transfixed, hypnotized, spellbound, whatever one wished to call it. Carol really had gotten to her. Lesley had given two-thirds of her life to skating, and she had never ceased loving the sport or being excited by an outstanding skater. "My God," she breathed at last. "I'm having hot flashes! When I was coaching I often dreamed of getting my hands on a champion, and one's been handed to me on a silver platter. She's superb!''

Matt's heart started pounding like mad. "Does that mean that you—"

"Technically, she's brilliant," Lesley told him. "I'd like to see her open up a little more emotionally, but that might come with maturity. How old is she?"

"Eighteen."

"In school?"

"No, that's been put on hold until '92."

"Perfect."

Out on the ice, Carol was making some perfunctory moves. Then she coasted past them, her hands on her hips, catching her breath. Matt shot her a thumbs-up gesture, and she pivoted, skating toward them. He could tell from her expression that she knew she had skated beautifully.

"How often do you nail four triples in a program, Carol?" Lesley asked, all business.

"Almost always . . . at least in practice. I turned the final two into doubles at the nationals, and that probably cost me. I don't think I chickened out. I think I just got tired and figured it was better to stay on my feet than to risk a fall."

"You skate out on the edge, which is exciting to watch when it works. I'd like to see you employ a little flair or moxie or showmanship, whatever you want to call it. I'd hate for you to be known as simply a skating technician. Judges like to be moved. They like panache. And panache attracts sponsorship money."

Carol's eyes clouded. "That's hard for me to do— 'work a room.' I'm not much of a ham by nature."

"Have you ever considered using a choreographer?"

"Not seriously. I know there are a lot of skaters who surround themselves with all sorts of people—choreographers, sports psychologists, nutritionists, I don't know what all—but I always figured my coach and I could do whatever needed to be done. Besides, Dad's shelled out enough money as it is."

Matt listened to the exchange between the two experts with interest. He wondered if a choreographer would help Carol. He imagined good ones did not come cheap. He was an affluent man—he commanded a six-figure salary and had made some good investments through the years—but he didn't have a fortune and never would have. However, if a choreographer was deemed necessary, he'd see to it that Carol had one.

Lesley and Carol continued talking, almost oblivious to Matt and Joe, to anything but each other. Lesley suggested an adjustment in the middle of the program, and Carol skated out onto the ice to try it, the blades of her skates making little snicking noises.

"There. How did that feel?" Lesley asked.

"Better," Carol said. "Much better. I'm thinking I might have been a tad too forward, though."

"Want to try it again?"

"Sure."

Lesley turned and caught Matt grinning at her. She grinned back. "She's irresistible. How could I refuse?"

And Matt's grin broadened.

They stayed at the arena much longer than they had intended. Finally, they made ready to leave. Matt thanked Joe profusely, blessing whatever fates had prompted him to call the man, and while Carol was taking off her skates, he managed to have a word with Lesley.

"A simple thank you doesn't seem adequate."

"You're welcome," she said with a sheepish smile. "I don't know why I'm doing this, but I seem to be, nevertheless. Maybe it gets in your blood or something. I wouldn't have thought so, but apparently it does."

"Lesley, if I promise to be witty and charming, will you have dinner with me tonight?"

She fastened him with her engaging smile. "I'll have dinner with you even if you aren't witty and charming."

"I'll take Carol home, shower and change and come to your place. Be thinking about where you want to go."

"Sounds wonderful. Seven?"

"Seven's fine."

"See you then."

Lesley watched Matt take his daughter's arm and walk out of the building. She felt so strangely exhilarated that she wanted to yell. She had come to the arena convinced she didn't want to go back to coaching. She hadn't been sure she could summon up the dedication again. But Carol hadn't been skating more than thirty seconds before she'd known that was what she wanted to do. During the past several years she had felt so aimless, taking up and discarding all those hobbies. Now she had a focus, and that felt good.

Getting to her feet, she turned to Joe and discussed a schedule for Carol. Then she glanced around the arena one more time before leaving the building. This was where she belonged. In fact, she hadn't wanted to quit the ice in the first place. She had done it only because Arturo insisted, complaining bitterly about the time she spent on the road with first one skater, then another. Never mind that he was off at the drop of a news story. It had been an odd existence. When Arturo was gone, which was much of the time, she led quite an independent life—coaching, making decisions, having her students look to her for advice. That was what Arturo had encouraged her to do in the early days of their marriage. "Live life as you want to live it," he would say, "not as everybody else wants you to." She truly had thought she had found her knight in shining armor, the man who would allow her to be herself.

Then quite suddenly everything changed. Arturo had begun to resent the youth and vitality that had attracted him to her in the first place. He'd become jealous of anything that diverted her attention away from him. He'd wanted her there waiting whenever he returned, and that hadn't always been possible when she had a skater in competition. So she had quit. Lesley had always moved heaven and earth to make the difficult marriage a success, but she had not done it completely free of resentment.

It was strange the twists and turns life could take, she mused a few minutes later as she was driving home. The only reason she had agreed to watch Carol skate was to see Matt again. She wanted to try to keep him in her life this time. Sixteen years ago she had been instantly attracted to him, and it was happening all over again. Not being able to sleep last night for

thinking about him was absurd. It was one thing for a
twenty-four-year-old woman who had never had a
boyfriend to fantasize about an attractive older man,
quite another for a middle-aged widow to still be
thinking about him sixteen years later. A starry-eyed
dreamer was not the image she wanted to project.

More than anything, Lesley wanted to age grace-
fully. She did not want to fight the calendar. She did
not want to live in mind-numbing fear of bags, bulges,
wrinkles, age spots, menopause, living alone or any
number of other mid-life calamities. She did not want
to become a slave to expensive spas, hormone treat-
ments and plastic surgery. Above all, she didn't want
to succumb to the kind of foolish man-woman behavior she had seen in so many older women, and a
woman her age with stars in her eyes was just about
the most foolish thing she could imagine.

Still, she was percolating with excitement. She
would go home, pick out something fabulous to wear,
then give herself a full beauty treatment. It had been
a very long time since she'd felt the urge for such self-
indulgence. With luck she might even dazzle Matt tonight. She hoped she remembered how to.

THAT NIGHT Carol paced her room on the second
floor of the Pacific Heights house, excited and restless, impatient for her first day of practice with Lesley and wishing she had someone to share her news
with. The house was too quiet. Her mother and Louis
had gone to a party and wouldn't be home until long
after she was in bed. Occasionally she could hear
muted voices coming from the kitchen below, where
the servants were enjoying their most relaxed night of

the week. For as long as she could remember she had hated Sundays because she hated being away from the ice. "Quit for a few days and relax," Sondra had once suggested, but Carol didn't know how to relax, and she would never quit.

Throwing herself across her bed, she propped her chin in her hands and stared ahead. Her closet was open, giving her a splendid view of the poster tacked to the back of the door. She had seen it in a sporting goods shop last week and had bought it, then sneaked it home as stealthily as if it were an illegal substance. She would have died of embarrassment if anyone knew it was there, but on the back of the door it was safe. Her mother rarely came into her room and never went in her closet. The maid did, of course, but she wouldn't have had the first clue who Eric Zito was. If she even noticed the poster she would think it was of an actor or rock star.

He looked it. No skates, no snappy costume. Just a brooding, dark-haired, dark-eyed hunk in jeans and a leather jacket. She'd seen that look on his face a thousand times, and it always did odd things to her stomach. That photograph had, no doubt, been taken with an eye toward the little teenage girls who were figure skating's biggest audience. They would go into a collective swoon over it. *Ass,* Carol thought miserably. After so many years, a person might think that a certain other person would call just to find out if she was still alive.

She had been crazy about Eric for almost as long as she had been skating, from the time she was seven and he was twelve. Since then she had seen him six days a week except when one of them was away competing.

They practiced every day but Sundays, and she wondered if that had something to do with her dislike of Sundays. For years she had regarded him as Zeus—unflawed, perfect. Then, as time passed and she grew up, she had flirted with him, made awkward adolescent advances toward him and worshiped the ground he walked on, all to no avail. To him she simply had been Sondra's "other" student, someone to tease unmercifully. Fearful of frightening him off altogether, she had adopted another manner toward him, one of friendly indifference, sassy flippancy. The more she yearned for him, the more flippant she became.

On those terms, they had become good friends. All the skaters on the circuit remarked about their "special" relationship, but none suspected how much more special she had wished it was. She had never stopped wanting his approval when she skated. The simplest compliment from him, and she walked on air for days. Now Carol could see that her hero worship of him had pushed her to a level she might not have attained otherwise.

She had cried copious tears of happiness the night he'd won his gold medal. She, too, had been scheduled to skate in the Games, not with any realistic hope of finishing much higher than perhaps tenth or eleventh, but to give her a taste of the white-hot pressure of Olympic competition. However, the flu had felled her, and she had been forced to withdraw, but nothing could have kept her away. She'd blubbered all over Eric while he'd laughed and kissed the top of her head. Those might not have been such happy tears if she'd known what was coming. Eric had vanished from her life. The only news she'd had of him since then had come from Sondra or *Sports Illustrated*. Now, if half of what she had heard was true, she would have to read about him in *People* and *TV Guide*. There were even rumors that he'd taken up with the gorgeous Swede who'd won the women's silver medal. *Ass!*

Carol rolled over and stood, then crossed the room to close the closet door. Whenever she was in this kind of mood she experienced the desire to eat something forbidden, like a piece of the chocolate cake her parents had enjoyed last night. Sondra hated sugar as if it were poison. Carol wondered if Lesley did, too. What the heck? She was between coaches now, if only till tomorrow. If one little sliver of chocolate cake threw her diet completely out of kilter, so be it.

She had reached the bottom of the stairs when the doorbell rang. "I'll get it," she yelled, and no one came out of the kitchen. Crossing the foyer, she opened the door.

The poster hunk stood in the soft glow of the porch light, his hands shoved into his pockets. Tiny explosions went off inside Carol, but from years of practice she was able to disguise her reaction to the sight of him. One corner of her mouth lifted. "Well, well, look who's here. Hans Brinker, in the flesh."

"It's nice to know that some things never change. You're as sassy as ever," Eric said with a half smile. Then he sobered. "I heard about Sondra. I'm sorry."

"That's life, I guess. At least she was able to stick it out until you got your medal."

For a split second he looked stung, but he recovered quickly. Reaching out, he tweaked her nose. "You'd better be nice to me or I won't ask you to be president of my fan club." Then he brushed past her and entered the house.

Carol was appalled to discover that the hand covering the doorknob trembled.

CHAPTER FIVE

CAROL CLOSED THE DOOR and turned to face Eric. She hated it that merely seeing him could have such an unsettling effect on her, but it had been so long—months and months. During that time she often had been tempted to call his mother and simply ask, "What's everyone been up to?" That would have opened the floodgates. Rosie Zito would have told her every single thing her children, their spouses and their children had done for the past six months, and somewhere in the lengthy account Carol would have gleaned some information about Eric.

She had never done it, though, chiefly because she suspected that Rosie knew exactly how she felt about Eric and might have guessed the real reason for the call. Besides, Eric had his own apartment, so Rosie might not even know everything Eric had been up to.

Now he was here, and her insides were churning. "I was on my way to assault a chocolate cake," she said. "Want some?"

"Chocolate?" he asked in mock horror. "Cake? You really have gone off the deep end. Next you'll be telling me you're hitting the sauce. You shouldn't let Sondra's retirement lead you to a life of decadence."

"Just a sliver?"

"You have a sliver. I'll have a nice thick piece with lots of icing."

"Sondra would pass out. When did you take up sugar?"

"About twenty minutes after I got that medal."

"Well, it's your weight . . . and your teeth. Wait in the den. It's down at the end of the hall."

"Yeah, I remember."

When Carol came into the den a few minutes later carrying a tray that held two plates and two glasses of milk, Eric was studying the photographs, plaques and commendations that filled one wall of the room, all of them testifying to her wealthy stepfather's lifetime of community service. She took advantage of Eric's preoccupation to study him.

Until she had fallen for him, Carol wouldn't have believed that a heart could actually flutter, but hers did with alarming frequency whenever he was around. He had shed his jacket and was wearing a velour shirt the color of Burgundy wine. He was almost six feet tall and had a very muscular build, more like that of a hockey player than a figure skater. His dark brown hair just skimmed his shirt collar, and he had soulful dark eyes and a sensuous mouth. At that moment he shoved his hands into the pockets of his jeans, which pulled the denim tautly across his rump. He also had the best-looking set of buns she'd ever seen.

Besides having a crush on him, she envied Eric. Of course she envied him his Olympic gold—that was natural—but there was more to it than that. To Carol, he seemed to have the perfect life. He was the youngest member of a large Italian family, a brood that had grown to include in-laws, nieces and nephews. They did a great deal of laughing and crying, singing and arguing, hugging and shouting. They made her family seem so quiet and dull. Olivia Bannister would have been appalled at the absolute chaos that ruled supreme in the Zito household, but Carol loved being with the family. For years Eric's mother had thought to include Carol and Sondra in the family's gatherings, but Carol couldn't remember that Olivia had ever invited Eric to their house. She supposed her mother considered him too closely associated with the part of her daughter's life she would have liked to forget. Carol doubted Eric had been inside the house more than a dozen times in the eleven years she'd known him.

She gave herself a shake and approached him. "Here you go," she said. Eric turned, smiling, and took the tray from her.

They sat side by side on the sofa, eating the cake and indulging in idle gossip about mutual acquaintances. Carol was curious about the reason for the unexpected visit. She would have liked to think it was prompted by an overwhelming desire to see her, but she knew better. Long ago she had accepted that they were destined to be nothing but friends. She didn't like it, but she was resigned to it.

"What's it like on the pro circuit?" she asked.

"Different. The pressure's gone, and you make some money."

"Do you like it?"

Eric shrugged, which didn't tell her much. She guessed that after a gold medal, everything was anticlimactic.

"Are you sore?" Eric suddenly asked.

"What?"

"At Sondra."

"Oh. Well...a little. Sure I am. I think it was a crummy thing for her to do." Carol knew she probably shouldn't have said that. Eric thought the world of Sondra, believing that he owed her everything. But if he had eyes, he had to realize that there had been an enormous difference between the way he had been treated and the way she had.

If Eric took umbrage at her remark, he didn't say anything. He settled back on the sofa and looked at her seriously. "So, what are you going to do now?"

"Do? Do about what?"

"About getting a coach, of course."

"Accomplished. Dad found someone for me."

"Oh." Eric looked disappointed. "Well, that's good. I thought you might need someone."

Carol's breath caught in her throat. "Don't tell me you were going to offer your services."

"The thought crossed my mind."

"But... you're so busy."

"I've got some irons in the fire, sure. Some television people are mulling over the idea of an ice extravaganza for the Christmas season. The money they're talking about is almost unbelievable. I might do that since it's a one-time thing, but the urge to take the big bucks and run has passed. My agent's advised me to be selective." He grinned sheepishly when he said that.

"Your agent, yet! I really have been remiss, haven't I? You've been here almost twenty minutes and I haven't even asked for your autograph."

His grin broadened. "Well, I'm glad you found someone. I couldn't have taken that sassy mouth day in and day out for long. Who's the coach?"

"Her name's Lesley Salazar. She was Lesley Ann Kelly. Ever hear of her?"

"Seems like I have. From way back."

"Won the bronze in '72."

Carol's mind was racing. He actually had come to offer her his help! Day in and day out, he'd said. Lord, she almost was sorry her father had found Lesley. To think of working with Eric, just the two of them, made her heart do a dance. No Sondra around to hover over him. Their coach had been so protective and possessive of Eric that Carol hadn't been able to get as close to him as she'd wanted, but Eric meant nothing to Lesley. Carol couldn't believe she was going to have to let an opportunity like this pass her by.

Then she was struck by an inspired thought. At least she hoped it was inspired. Years before, when Eric had burst onto the scene, he had given figure skating something it had never had before—a technically brilliant skater who could hypnotize an audience with his showmanship. And he was media sophisticated, having had microphones shoved in his face and cameras trained on him since winning his first junior championship many years ago. The media adored him. After winning the gold he had been asked to do color commentary for all the important skating events, and he was wonderful on television. Besides being knowledgeable about skating and all the participants, he exuded an irresistible charm. Was that something instinctive, or could it be learned? She wondered . . .

"Lesley thinks I need . . . a choreographer," she began hesitantly.

Eric pursed his lips. "Yeah, it's probably time."

"I . . . ah, wondered if . . . you'd be interested in the job." She prayed he wouldn't think that presumptuous. "I mean, we already know how to work together, and . . . it's not as though you would be stuck with it for long stretches of time. You'd be able to do other things."

For a minute she was sure he was going to turn her down, and she couldn't say she would blame him. For Pete's sake, the man was a celebrity now, a star! Stars did their own choreography, not someone else's. She'd best come up with a snappy retort when he said no, or the atmosphere could become strained.

But he surprised her. "Sure. I can help you, if you think it'll do you some good," he said modestly.

It was all Carol could do to keep from throwing her arms around him. Of course, that wasn't the first time she'd experienced that urge, not by a long shot. To preclude the possibility that she might give in to it this time, she jumped to her feet and gathered up their plates and glasses. "That new miniseries they've been touting all week starts tonight. Want to watch it?"

"I guess so. What channel?"

"I'm not sure. There's the *TV Guide*. I'll be right back."

Carol's heart tripped wildly. She had to forcibly wipe the silly grin off her face as she carried the dishes to the kitchen. With luck, Eric was now firmly in her life until 1992. By then, if she had any smarts at all, she might have thought of a way to keep him there.

THE RESTAURANT Lesley had suggested was rustic, western in decor, and its saloon featured live music—very loud live music—that attracted a young crowd like a magnet. Lesley and Matt, however, were more interested in food and conversation, and the dining room was reasonably uncrowded. They settled into an oak booth, ordered sautéed scallops and white wine and became absorbed in each other.

Matt hated staring at his dinner partner, but he couldn't help himself. She was so lovely she took his breath away. Her femininity was blatant, and he couldn't figure out why. She didn't employ the usual womanly embellishments. She wore no jewelry save for tiny gold studs in her earlobes. She smelled more like soap than perfume. Her makeup was so skillfully applied that she seemed to wear nothing but a touch of lipstick. She didn't engage in the harmless flirting that most women did when in the company of a new man. She was too real to be real, which caused him to wonder if he was seeing in her just what he wanted to see.

She wasn't the twenty-four-year-old beauty who had enticed him sixteen years ago, but in many ways she was more beautiful now than she had been then. Of course, as he had matured, his ideas about what constituted beauty had changed. What he now noticed first and liked most in a woman was a certain—for want of a better word—radiance. It had nothing to do with age; Vanessa Hamilton had it, and she was nearing eighty. Lesley had it in abundance—she seemed to glow from within. But what he found most charming about her was that she appeared to be totally unaware of the impact she had on him.

That, however, wasn't true. Lesley was old enough and had seen enough admiring masculine glances to recognize admiration in Matt's eyes. The knowledge that he found her attractive was unbelievably exciting. Once again she thought about her personal list of behavior no middle-aged woman should ever engage in but at the moment she couldn't think of any items on the list. The reason, she supposed, was that tonight she didn't feel middle-aged. She felt young and free and unfettered, like a girl who finally had been asked for a date by the best-looking boy on campus. She felt like laughing when nothing was funny. She felt like singing, and she had trouble getting through "Happy Birthday to You" on key. It was wild . . . and wonderful.

The scallops were divine, but Lesley suspected anything would have been on a magic night like this. Their conversation seemed to sparkle, but in fact they talked about nothing in particular. Mainly she asked about Matt's youth.

"Average," he said. "Not lavish, but easy and comfortable. Dad was a banker and Mom stayed home, the way moms did in those days. I had a sister, but she died in infancy. Then my mother had a miscarriage before I came along, so they spoiled me shamelessly. I had to go away to school to get some of the cockiness literally knocked out of me."

A cocky Matt Logan was something Lesley had a hard time envisioning. Confident, maybe; cocky, no. There was no need for her to tell him much about her childhood. He already knew what it was like. She had spent it much the way Carol had spent hers—practicing and entering competitions. Matt was, however, curious about what had turned her on to skating in the first place.

Lesley smiled. "I was crazy about roller skating, and I got this older kid to teach me how to do all sorts of stunts—leaps and spins. Now it scares me to think of a seven-year-old doing those crazy things on a concrete sidewalk, but I was fearless in those days. Then one day my dad came home early and caught me." She laughed. "Oh, he had such a fit and told me if he ever caught me doing those things again... You get the picture. I cried and carried on and said I loved to skate. He decided that ice skating might teach me some discipline. I'm sure he regretted that decision many times. No one ever dreamed it would go so far."

"What about you? Did you have any regrets about giving your entire youth to skating?"

Lesley thought about it. "There was one thing. I always regretted never having a girlfriend, a best friend to share a thousand secrets with. I missed feminine confidences. But I honestly think that was the only thing."

And that reminded her of the one important thing she had on her mind. Over coffee she talked to Matt about it. "Would you entertain the notion of letting Carol move in with me until after she's competed in the Olympics?"

Matt looked surprised. "That's two years away."

"I know, but I lived with my coach and his family for a few years prior to my inauspicious attempt at the gold, and it worked out beautifully. I know you think Carol's training has been intense up until now, but as the man said, you ain't seen nuthin' yet. The closer she gets to '92, the more demanding her training will become. Does she take ballet?"

"No."

"She's going to start. I have an acquaintance who teaches it. We won't be turning her into a prima ballerina or anything like that, but it's marvelous for a skater. And weight lifting to increase her stamina."

"Good Lord, Lesley," Matt said with a little laugh, "the girl hardly has a minute to herself as it is."

"I know, so maybe you understand why I want her living with me. She's going to be busy almost from waking to sleeping, and I want to keep a strict eye on her diet. All outside influences will be distractions, and Carol can't afford distractions at this point. It's not easy for 'normal' people to live with someone on that kind of regimen."

"Particularly someone like Olivia?"

"Well...yes. If Carol's mother isn't enthusiastic about her skating now, she will find what I have in mind for her impossible to take. Carol needs someone around her who's as committed to that medal as she is."

Matt thought about it. The idea appealed to him, and he knew it would appeal to Carol. He was beginning to realize that she'd needed someone like Lesley for a long time. The lion's share of Sondra's attention had been reserved for Eric. And as interested in her skating as he himself had always been, he had Hamilton House and his own interests. She would have Lesley's undivided attention.

But there was Olivia to consider. Matt didn't think for a minute that she would docilely go along with the idea. "If it were up to me, Carol would move in with you immediately, but it's not up to me. Tell you what—my plane leaves for Phoenix at one tomorrow. That'll give me time to try to talk Olivia into this. At

least I can get her to start thinking about it. Between
Carol and myself, I think we can put enough pressure
on her.''

Lesley smiled. ''That's great. Oh, Matt, I'm so excited about Carol's prospects!''

Matt reached across the table and covered one of
her hands with his. ''I wish she'd had you all along.''

The husky timbre of his voice, the warmth of his
hand, the gentleness in his eyes were intoxicating. For
a moment Lesley felt disoriented. She hoped her decision to ask Carol to move in with her had been
prompted by all the right reasons, that Matt had
nothing to do with it. She reminded herself that they
really didn't know each other very well. Why, then,
did it seem they did?

''Are you looking forward to this week?'' she asked.

''The conference? Oh...I suppose so. They're
hectic, though. Something's planned for every minute. And there's a lot of socializing involved. Dinners, cocktail parties, that sort of thing. You know
how those affairs go.''

Lesley laughed lightly. ''No, I don't. I don't have
any idea how the world of business operates.''

''That's right, you don't.'' Matt frowned, thinking
of how tightly scheduled the next two weeks were. He
would return from Phoenix on Friday, then he was to
attend a dinner meeting with some prominent local
citizens and a group of city planners Saturday night.
Sunday he was scheduled to play golf in Marin
County, weather permitting, and then it was on to another dinner. These were both civic and business
obligations, for Vanessa insisted that the division
V.P.'s be community leaders. Matt had always wel-

comed a full schedule, but that was before Lesley. He made a mental note to keep his weekends as free as possible from now on.

They lingered over liqueurs, commenting on the other patrons and the raucous music coming from the bar. Neither was anxious to leave, but the restaurant was filling up with late diners. When Matt noticed people waiting for tables, he signaled for the check. During the drive back to Lesley's house they were mostly silent, but it was a comfortable, compatible silence. Matt thought how nice it was to be in the company of someone who didn't require constant conversation, and he truly regretted not being able to see her all week. He hadn't left town yet, and already he could hardly wait to return. Never before had he regarded his Hamilton House duties as intrusive, but this business trip certainly was.

At her door he kissed her, tenderly at first, then with more insistence, touching her teeth with his tongue. Lesley's arms went around him, and his embrace became her sole support. Her knees had suddenly gone weak. She momentarily wondered if she should ask him in, then decided against it. Too forward. Too fast. The trouble with middle-aged dating was that the rules had all changed since she'd last had a date, and she hadn't been too well versed in the old rules. She supposed she would let Matt take the initiative, just follow his lead.

He lifted his head. "Where can I reach you tomorrow after I talk to Olivia?"

"Call the house and leave a message with Clarice."

"Right." He kissed her again, sweetly this time, though he pressed her tightly to him. "I'll call the minute I get back in town Friday."

"All right." Lesley backed off, composing herself. "Have a safe trip. I had a lovely time, Matt."

"I'm glad. So did I."

"Good night."

"Good night, Lesley."

When Lesley closed the door behind her, she leaned against it for a minute, her eyes closed, a smile on her lips. Matt had injected a much needed dose of spice into her life. He couldn't help knowing she was good and interested in him. She had no patience with man-woman games, so she'd made no attempt to disguise her fascination with him. Coyness simply wasn't in her, and playing hard to get was for youngsters whose futures stretched seemingly into infinity. If Matt didn't become part of her life this time, she wouldn't get another chance.

Lesley thought of the poem about "time's winged chariot." A woman of forty didn't have all the time in the world. She would risk rejection rather than waste a minute. She had wasted far too much of her life as it was.

THE NEXT MORNING, Matt faced his implacable ex-wife. "Olivia, please be reasonable about this," he pleaded. "If you'll stop and give it some thought, you'll see that it's a sensible suggestion."

It was unfortunate that he had awakened her, but it was ten in the morning, for heaven's sake. The maid who had answered the door had been aghast over his demand that the mistress be summoned anyway. He had explained that he had a plane to catch and something urgent to discuss with Mrs. Bannister. Could he help it if the alarmed woman had gotten the impression that an emergency was in progress? Still, he'd had to cool his heels a full twenty minutes before an out-of-sorts Olivia had put in an appearance.

"This had better be something that requires notifying the police or fire department" was her opening statement, and their conversation had gone steadily downhill after that. She had listened to him in stony silence, then issued a firm no.

"Matt, I want you to listen to me for once in your life. I seem to have a very hard time getting across to you that I do not consider figure skating and the Olympics to be life's pounding core, and nothing is going to change that. I am trying, God knows against all odds, to introduce Carol to a broad range of interests and to teach her the social graces, things that will be of value to her later in life. The child is completely one-dimensional."

"It's too late," Matt said. "She's already too committed to an Olympic medal, and for the next two years she is going to live, eat, breathe and sleep skating. You simply must accept that. She's adding ballet and weight lifting to her training schedule, and she's going to have to adhere to a special diet, all aimed at increasing her stamina." He was trying to remember everything Lesley had told him and hoped he hadn't forgotten anything. "Things like that can disrupt a household. She won't even be here except to sleep. Her coach lives close to the practice arena. It will be so much easier for Carol if she lives there, too. It's not as though she'll be moving halfway across the country.

For our daughter's sake, please let her go live with Lesley. Make it easier on everyone, especially yourself.''

He saw Olivia's chin tremble, and for some reason, he felt an unexpected rush of tenderness. She meant well. There was no question in his mind that she loved Carol. But she wanted something for her that Carol herself didn't. Olivia had to learn to accept the inevitable.

"Does Carol want to do this?" Olivia asked more quietly.

"I'm sure she will, but I didn't want to discuss it with her without talking to you first."

Olivia lapsed into silence for a minute. Then she walked to a window and peered out, seemingly deep in thought. When she turned, there was a look of resignation on her face. "I'm sure she will, too. I know what you think, Matt—that I want to turn Carol into a spoiled society brat."

"No, I—"

"I don't. But I've never, not for one minute, approved of the life she's chosen for herself. It's sheltered, insular, unnatural. I don't worry so much about the next two years. There'll be people looking after her every need, her every whim—people who will choose her music and costumes, people who will see to her accommodations, people who'll fuss over her health, pamper her moods and all but carry her around on a satin pillow. It's the years after the Olympics that concern me. I've never heard her express an interest in anything but skating, and I hate to think she'll be an adult who's an intellectual invalid."

"My God, Olivia, the travel alone is broadening. She's been more places in eighteen years than most people go in a lifetime. She has friends who are German, Russian, Swedish, French. How can you possibly think she's receiving no intellectual stimulation?"

Olivia made an impatient sound, then sighed. "Who is this woman, this Lesley who's her new coach?"

"Lesley Salazar. She was Lesley Kelly, Ross and Alicia's daughter—you remember."

That got a slight reaction from Olivia. The Kellys had been high society, and that always impressed Olivia. "Why would she want a stranger living under her roof?"

Matt could see her relenting. "It's the pressure of their schedule. And I'm sure you remember the Kellys' house, how enormous it is. Lesley is a widow now, and I think Carol's company will be welcome. And she needs to be in complete charge of . . . well, of practically every move Carol makes for the next two years."

There was a pause, then Olivia shrugged. "All right. From now on, I butt out. You and Carol do as you wish. I lost my influence with her years ago. Now, if you'll excuse me . . ." She swept out of the room.

Matt wished he could feel better about his victory. He let himself out, glancing at his watch as he did so. He had time to stop at the office, call Lesley's house and leave a message with Clarice. He would have liked to tell Lesley and Carol themselves, but they had been at practice since seven-thirty. He could envision the look of delight on Carol's face when she heard the news, and he wondered if she would move immediately. What a time for him to have to leave town. He would spend the entire week in Phoenix wondering what was going on back home.

CAROL WAS RESTING while the ice was being resurfaced. She had practiced figures for three hours and had three hours of free-style skating ahead of her, but she didn't dream of complaining. She hadn't ever begrudged the sacrifices skating called for. Not that she hadn't occasionally wished she could take some time off to think about nothing but new ways to wear her hair, giggle over boys and borrow her best friend's nail polish. That had never lasted long, though, and once she was sixteen or so she never thought about such things at all. She recalled the other students who had begun with Joe Hylands at the same time she did. Not one of them was still skating except recreationally, and some of them had been good. She guessed ability without tenacity didn't count for a whole lot.

Eric and Lesley were engaged in a mild argument. He wanted Carol's music changed. "The finger-snapping stuff is okay for the short program, but I'd like something more dramatic for the long."

"But she's so good at the jazzy numbers," Lesley protested. "It will mean a whole new program."

"That's why I'm here."

Lesley shrugged. "You're the choreographer. I'll give you a free hand with the artistic side."

"And another thing. No more beads on the costumes. Simplicity, simplicity. The judges ought to watch Carol, not the lights dancing off her dress."

Carol listened and smiled. She'd never particularly doted on compliments, and she didn't think she had an outsize ego, but she had to admit that all the attention was nice. She'd spent so many years feeling like Sondra's also-ran.

And it pleased her enormously that Eric thought she could be dramatic on the ice, that she didn't need flashy costumes or snappy music to wow the judges. She guessed she'd had his undivided attention longer today than she ever had before. It was a heady sensation.

Carol grinned rakishly as she watched him. When he practiced, he wore Lycra pants—navy blue with a gray stripe up each leg—and since he had very muscular legs, the pants looked as though they had been painted on. He also wore a short-sleeved T-shirt that exposed his strong arms, with their fine covering of dark hair. She almost sighed audibly. Any female who could look at that bod and not feel something stir inside had a heart made out of steel.

When Eric was ready to leave the rink, he stopped for a word with her. Resting one hand lightly on her hipbone, he said, "Remember, keep that chin up. You want to look in control out there. You want to show 'em your soul. I'll be thinking about the new music tonight. You looked pretty sharp today, kiddo."

Carol wondered if it was possible to die from happiness.

As their first day together ended, Lesley suggested they stop by her house to see if there was a message from Matt. The news that Olivia had consented to let Carol move in with Lesley had the girl chortling with glee. Could life get any better than this? She had a former Olympian for a coach, Eric was firmly entrenched in her life for the time being, and she was going to be spared her mother's endless parade of parties and divine young men. "When can I move in?" she asked.

Lesley smiled. "Why not begin right now? Do you need some help?"

"No, I'll just pick up a few things and be right back. Oh, Lesley, I don't know how to thank you and Dad for this. Everything is going to be...well, just great." Then she pursed her lips. "I can't imagine how Dad arranged everything. I'll bet it wasn't easy."

Later that evening, when Carol had returned with some clothes and a few personal items, Lesley showed her to an upstairs guest room. "Do anything you want to the room, Carol. I imagine you'll be living here for some time."

"This is so neat. I didn't bring much stuff, just what I absolutely had to have." Carol picked up something and shot Lesley an impish look. "Like this. You're the first person I've ever shown this to, but I have to know if it's okay to hang it on the back of the closet door." She unrolled Eric's poster.

Lesley laughed. "Hang it over your bed for all I care."

"Oh, God, no! What if he came in here sometime? I can't imagine why he would, but what if he did? I'd die of humiliation!"

"He might be flattered. Did you ever think of that?"

"No. I've spent years making sure Eric doesn't know how I feel about him. Now it's a way of life with me."

Lesley lounged on the bed while her new boarder put her things away. "Was it difficult...with your mom, I mean?" she asked.

"Oh, not really. I think Mom's getting resigned to my strange ways." Carol shot Lesley a little smile. "I've given a lot of thought to her feelings about me and skating, and I've come to the conclusion that Mom doesn't think competing is ladylike. It's too aggressive, and that's something a lady should never be. More than anything, Mom wants me to be a lady and to marry well...especially marry well. Lord, the guys she's invited to dinner! Like we're really going to fall in love over the lobster bisque."

"It was the generation," Lesley said with a sigh. "Legions of us were taught that we needed a husband like we needed straight teeth, clear complexions and a good black dress. Any husband was better than no husband at all."

"Weird. Maybe that explains Mom and Dad. I wasn't much more than a baby when they split up, but for the life of me I can't picture the two of them ever being married to each other. They're so different."

Lesley's ears perked up at the mention of Matt. "Opposites do seem to attract," she said nonchalantly, hoping Carol would continue talking. She was eager for any conversational tidbit about him.

"They're opposites, all right. Mom's a goer, a real party animal. I guess she'd go out every night if she could. Either that or give a party herself. She loves to entertain. Of course, Dad's pretty good at that, too, but with him it's different. Mom gives parties because she enjoys them. When Dad gives a party, you can bet your life it has something to do with work. Do or die for dear old Hamilton House, that kind of thing. I guess just about everything he does is somehow tied to the business...except for my skating. By the way, what did you think of Eric?''

"Hmm? Oh...he's very nice, very knowledgeable."

"He's the best skater there ever was. A natural, Sondra said. Apparently when he was eight years old he could jump like a deer. He doesn't even have to work on the height of his jumps. Isn't that something?''

Carol then proceeded to hold forth for fifteen minutes about Eric. It wasn't hard to see that, after skating, her two favorite subjects were her father and Eric. One was her hero, the other her idol. Lesley smiled and made appropriate remarks, but she actually heard very little of what Carol had to say about the young man she was so crazy about. She was thinking of what the girl had said about Matt.

The quintessential company man, a workaholic. She couldn't have been more disappointed. Arturo had been married to his work, and he had not been an easy man to live with. He'd often been thoughtless, not because he didn't care but because he was so preoccupied with what he was doing that he forgot she existed. Half the time Lesley had felt like an afterthought, someone to come home to when all the important things had been taken care of. A man like that never allowed a woman to occupy center stage in his life. She had vowed that if she ever again became deeply involved with a man, he would be someone who knew how to leave work where it belonged and enjoy life a little.

Matt had seemed too good to be true, and apparently he was.

CHAPTER SIX

MATT PUSHED his way through the crowd gathered in the hotel's hospitality suite, shaking hands with people he knew, smiling at the ones he didn't, disarming everyone with his urbane good looks and the force of his personality. Within moments of entering the room, he'd effortlessly lassoed the spotlight and placed it directly over his head.

Most of the men present were slightly intimidated and overly obsequious. The women fell into two groups: employees and spouses of employees. They were not difficult to tell apart. The employees conversed more animatedly, dressed more flamboyantly. Loyal company wives invariably wore something simple and black, and they rarely spoke except to each other, for they never called attention to themselves and away from their husbands. They worked very hard at having a good time, but he'd often wondered if they really liked these things. He imagined most of them came because their husbands told them it was mandatory, not because they wanted to.

This cocktail reception was the final social event of the annual managers' conference. Matt had been restless for days. Normally he relished the gathering since he was always the star attraction. This time, however, he had quickly grown bored with the busi-

ness meetings, all the shoptalk and the endless socializing. This time he hadn't even called Denise Somners,
which was something he always did when he was in
Phoenix. He and Denise had shared a lot of laughs
and uninhibited sex through the years, but Denise was
a part of yesterday. Now all Matt wanted to do was get
home.

There had been no opportunity to call Lesley. The
few brief lulls in his hectic schedule had occurred
during the day, when she and Carol would have been
at the rink, and he always returned to his room much
too late to consider calling. He was curious about how
she and Carol were doing, of course, but mostly he
just needed a good dose of Lesley.

He thought about her at the oddest times and actually had found himself daydreaming through the
breakfast session that morning. The man conducting
the program had been forced to ask him the same
question twice, which was damned embarrassing when
one was supposed to be in charge. Worse, later in the
program when he stepped onto the dais to speak, he
had looked out over the sea of faces, and Lesley's face
had intervened. Common sense told him that she
couldn't have invaded his mind so thoroughly after
one date, but perhaps the invasion actually had occurred sixteen years ago. Only now was she digging in,
establishing possession, getting under his skin.

A cacophony of voices swirled around him. Matt
accepted a drink someone handed him, murmured his
thanks, then dipped a chip into something green that
looked like guacamole but had no taste. They would
have been fed better at the Phoenix Hamilton House,
he knew, but it simply wasn't large enough to accom-

modate this crowd, not unless they'd wanted to close their doors for the evening. At that moment Matt felt someone tap him on the shoulder, and he turned to face Jerome Levine, his Seattle manager.

"Another one wrapped up, Matt. How many of these things do you think we've attended together?"

"A dozen or more, Jerry," Matt said with a smile.

"Do you know who I miss?" Jerry asked. "Vanessa."

"Me, too. Five years ago she would have been all over the place. You just got back from Dallas. Did you see her?"

"No. She was recovering from bronchitis and wasn't in the day I was there."

Matt frowned. "Lord, it seems like she's had a lot of that in the past few years."

"I know. As hard as it is to believe, she's fast approaching eighty. She won't be around forever, and I can't imagine Hamilton House without Vanessa."

Matt agreed it was a sobering thought. "I guess Dolph Wade will steer the ship when she's gone."

Jerry stepped a bit closer and lowered his voice. "I heard some company gossip while I was in Dallas. Seems Dolph really ripped his knickers with Vanessa over that conglomerate's buy-out offer."

"Oh? I haven't even talked to the home office in a couple of weeks. Do you mean Dolph was for it?"

Jerry nodded. "That's what I heard."

Matt let out a little whistle. "Vanessa would sell her firstborn, if she had one, before she'd sell Hamilton House. What in hell got into Dolph?"

"Who knows? It's occurred to me that you just might wind up the C.E.O. If you do, try to remember what a superlative job I've done for you all these years.''

Then the two men were approached by others, so the gossip was terminated and forgotten until much later, when Matt was in his room getting ready for bed. He couldn't imagine Dolph doing such a dumb-ass thing. The man had been with Stuart and Vanessa Hamilton since Hamilton House had begun. His official title was executive vice president, but everyone in the company knew that was a euphemism for heir apparent.

And he had been Stuart Hamilton's best friend. Stuart wouldn't have sold out while he was alive, and his widow was even more possessive of the business empire they'd built. Surely Dolph was aware of that. Obviously, he wasn't nearly as smart as Matt had always thought. The question now was, if Dolph didn't succeed Vanessa, who would?

The question had no more than formed in his mind when he recalled Jerry's words: *You just might wind up the C.E.O.* Matt's pulse quickened. In the corporate chain of command, the six division vice presidents were immediately under Dolph. Unless Vanessa brought in someone entirely new, her successor would be one of the six. Matt sank onto the edge of the bed and stared into space. Mental images of his colleagues came into view.

Roger Burroughs in Hartford. The oldest of the six, Roger had been a vice president the longest and was the logical choice. But Roger was a dyed-in-the-wool New Englander. His wife came from a prominent family that could trace its ancestors back to the *Mayflower*. Roger wouldn't leave New England for Dallas if he was offered the ownership of every establishment flanking the L.B.J. Freeway, and Vanessa knew it.

Sharon Carpenter in Kansas City. A real comer, but she'd been a vice president only two years. Who could predict how she would perform over the long haul? No chance.

Hugh Reeves in Houston had announced his retirement next year, and his successor would be in Sharon's shoes—unproven.

Grady O'Connor in Mississippi, in charge of production and development. Vanessa thought the world of Grady, but Matt dismissed him as more of a farmer than anything.

That left Paula Steele in Nashville . . . and himself. Matt smiled. Paula was sharp and probably the best manager in the entire organization. Like himself, she was fiercely loyal to Vanessa. Paula could very well be the one. *And so could I,* he thought. He realized he was indulging in a flight of fancy, but it did no harm. He'd never coveted the top spot in the company, feeling it out of his reach and not really wanting to leave either Carol or the Bay Area. But what would he do now if the presidency was offered to him? He grinned as he slipped between the sheets. He'd accept. As fast as he could pack his bags.

LESLEY AND CAROL had spent a busy, productive week together. Their personalities meshed, so they got along famously. That they hit it off immediately wasn't surprising since they were two of a kind, their lives amazingly similar. Both had grown up in affluence, and both had chosen lives far different from the ones their mothers had led. After a few days of working together, they discovered they often could communicate without benefit of words.

Eric was the icing on the cake—dynamic, energetic and completely devoted to skating. Plus, Carol considered him infallible. *We make an invincible trio,* Lesley thought. It had been a long time since she'd felt so useful, so confident of her own abilities, so sure she was doing exactly what she should have been doing.

But by Friday, her feelings had turned petulant because Matt hadn't called all week, and that was absurd. Hadn't he said that every minute of the week was tightly scheduled? He'd also said he would call as soon as he got back in town, and she had been poised for the telephone's ring ever since she and Carol had gotten home from practice. Perhaps he had stayed another day. From Carol she had learned that, with Matt, Hamilton House always came first. "Dad would take a flying leap off the Golden Gate if Vanessa Hamilton asked him to" was the way Carol had so succinctly put it.

And every time Lesley caught herself daydreaming about Matt, she tried to remember those very words. She might not know anything about business, but she knew businessmen like her father, and she knew men like Arturo, whose work had been a jealous mistress. As a young girl she had pitied her mother all the broken dates, all the vacations that had never materialized because "something important" had come up. Then she had grown up, married and experienced them herself. Never again. No thanks.

Lesley sat cross-legged on the sofa in the game room with a bowl of popcorn on her lap, thoroughly engrossed in one of the vintage movies she was addicted to. She was so absorbed in the film she didn't hear the doorbell, so she was taken by surprise when Matt sauntered into the room. Promptly forgetting all her qualms and misgivings, she started to rise. Her face broke into a radiant smile of welcome.

"No, don't get up," he said, quickly crossing the room to sit beside her. "Am I interrupting one of your favorite movies?"

"Anything made before 1955 is my favorite movie. When did you get back?"

"My plane landed at four, but I made the mistake of stopping by the office. Shouldn't do that when you've been gone a week. I thought I'd never get away. I suppose I should have called first."

"That's not necessary. Your daughter lives here now. I hope you'll feel free to stop by whenever you want."

Matt glanced toward the television set. A commercial came on. "Did the movie just start?"

"No, it's about over."

"Where's Carol?"

"She and Eric went out for a frozen yogurt."

"Eric?"

"Uh-huh. He's her new choreographer."

"Well, I'll be damned! When did all this happen?"

"When Eric heard about Sondra, he went to see Carol to offer his help. She asked him to do her choreography, and he agreed."

"A superstar doing choreography? I guess Carol's in seventh heaven."

Lesley smiled. "I take it you've noticed she isn't exactly indifferent to him."

"She hasn't been indifferent to Eric since she was seven."

"It's really touching to see the way she reacts to him. Can't say I blame her. I think if I were eighteen, he might cause my heart to flutter a little. He's a charming young man. May I get you something?"

"No. I stopped by the house to change. I had a bite while I was there. I thought I'd ask you and Carol out to dinner tonight, but it got too late too quickly. The movie's back on. Watch it by all means. I hate it when I have to miss the end of a film."

But Lesley reached for the remote control and switched off the set. "I don't have to watch it. I've seen this one about fifteen times. The heroine and hero make a date to meet at the Top of the Mark on New Year's Eve. But she'd dying of a brain tumor, something the hero doesn't know. That woman with her who's supposed to be her secretary is really a nurse. Besides, the hero's on his way to the electric chair for killing his business partner. That man with him is a detective. Neither the heroine nor the hero will be alive on New Year's Eve. The nurse and the detective meet, instead."

Matt looked at her in disbelief. "Why in the hell would anyone watch something that depressing more than once?"

"Oh, it isn't depressing. Well . . . maybe a little. But it's so beautifully done, very romantic, and Merle Oberon was too beautiful to be real. I always cry copiously while the credits roll, and I love a movie that makes me cry. Popcorn?"

"No, thanks," he said, suppressing a smile. She was absolutely enchanting.

Lesley removed the bowl from her lap and set it on a nearby table. "So, how was the conference?"

He shrugged. "The usual. I don't know how much anyone likes these things, but I guess the meetings are worthwhile. I always hear a few new ideas and a lot of old gripes. And, of course, catch up on the company gossip. So, how was your week? Are you finding it hard to have a roommate?"

"Not at all. Carol's a very happy, contented young lady these days, and happy, contented people are easy to live with. She's scrupulous about calling her mother every night, by the way, and she's going to spend at least part of Sunday with her." Lesley looked at him with shining eyes. "Eric is going to be wonderful for Carol, Matt. For one thing, she considers him the greatest skater who ever lived, so she'll do anything he tells her to. For another, he knows what he's talking about. He's completely changed the music for her long program. I was skeptical at first, but now I admit he was right. I can hardly wait for you to see it. She's going to be superb!"

"That's good. I take it you have no regrets about going back to coaching."

"Not one. I've needed something for a long time. This is the busiest, best week I've had in . . . I can't remember when. Guess I owe you for that."

"If you're thanking me, you're welcome."

"Sure I can't get you something? I'll have a glass of wine with you."

"Okay, you're on."

Lesley agilely leaped up and walked across the room to the bar. For a minute Matt simply watched her admiringly. She was wearing jeans, athletic shoes and a big shirt tied at the waist. Her spectacular hair was pulled into a single braid, just as it had been the first time he'd ever seen her. In fact, she hadn't changed much in sixteen years. Skaters almost always had great bodies, and Lesley had managed to keep hers. He'd bet she could still put on one of those costumes that wouldn't cover a poker chip and look fabulous. How many forty-year-old women could? Pushing himself off the sofa, he crossed the room to sit on one of the bar stools.

Lesley rounded the bar, sat down on the stool beside him and set a glass of wine in front of him. "How was the weather in Phoenix?" she asked.

"Beautiful."

"It's been so dreary here. I don't remember February as being so...yuk. The paper says we might get some sunshine day after tomorrow. What a welcome change that will be."

Matt took a sip of wine, set down the glass and said "Lesley, I don't want to talk about the weather. I don't particularly want to talk about Carol's skating, either."

"You don't?" His eyes caught hers and seemed to hold them captive. "Well, then, what...do you want to talk about?"

"For openers, I want to talk about the first time we met."

"All right. It was here, at one of those weekend affairs my folks used to give. You walked into the library, looking for all the world like you would have preferred being anywhere else."

"You had me pegged, all right. But you changed that."

"I did? How?"

"Oh . . . by being gracious and charming and making me laugh." Matt took another sip of wine. Earlier, while he was driving to Lesley's, he'd decided to tell her what that long-ago night had meant to him, how he'd never entirely forgotten it or her. Perhaps then she wouldn't think he was moving too fast. For the first time in years he thought of a woman when he wasn't with her, and he knew himself well enough to know that that made her special. If they were younger, he probably would take it slow and easy, court her a little, savor the gradual progression toward lovemaking.

But they weren't younger. At least, he wasn't. He was staring fifty in the face, and he figured he had fifteen years, tops, before the parts went.

Lesley offered him a little smile. "I don't recall that you did much laughing. I thought you were an unhappy man."

"For twenty-four, you were a very perceptive young woman. I was unhappy in those days. And so was my wife, only it took her longer to admit it."

Lesley fell silent, sensing a confidence coming up. She also sensed that whatever was forthcoming was something he wanted to talk about.

"My marriage was not a satisfying one, and I didn't know why. That was the worst part. When Olivia and I got married, I had every reason to believe we'd have two or three kids and grow old together. But before long I found myself wondering what we had ever seen in each other. But we did try, especially after Carol was born. We became masters at the art of dissembling, making sure that none of our family and acquaintances suspected that the marriage was anything but perfect. As a result, most were shocked when we finally threw in the towel."

"What was the catalyst?" Lesley asked.

"Well...it wasn't immediate, but I guess you were."

Lesley's eyes widened. "Me?"

"You said something that weekend, something to the effect that when something was over it was over, that it didn't make sense to cling to something that was gone."

"My goodness, I certainly was a young dispenser of philosophical wisdom, wasn't I?"

Matt smiled. "You don't remember saying that?"

"No, fortunately."

"I thought about it a lot afterward. Olivia and I stuck it out for almost another year, but finally I thought, it's over. It was a relief for both of us. And I never forgot you."

"Never?"

"Never."

Lesley felt her face grow warm. "I . . . can't believe I could have made an impression on anyone in those days. I was at such loose ends, wanting to do something and not knowing what it was." She ran her forefinger around the rim of her glass, frowning down at the amber liquid. "Coming off the Olympics is a difficult time for an athlete. Years and years of training, a moment of glory or defeat, then it's over. All of a sudden you don't have this entourage hovering over you, tending to your every need. I hope I can help Carol anticipate that day and make the transition easier for her."

Matt looked at her and smiled. "I'm sure you will. You did all right."

He had said that as a compliment, but the expression on her face changed dramatically. She looked as though he had kicked her. The reaction was so unexpected that Matt was at a loss to understand it. He waited, thinking she might offer him some explanation since the mood between them had seemed to be so companionable and confidential. Lesley, however, only looked away.

"Did I say something?" he asked.

Lesley was embarrassed at having overreacted. "No, I—"

"I must have. Tell me."

"It's silly, but I always feel terrible when people tell me how well I've done. At twenty-four, life holds limitless possibilities, but I chose to take the easy way, a safe course, rather than to explore and grow and learn. But, please, I don't want to talk about it."

Matt knew he had inadvertently hit a nerve, but if she didn't want to talk about it, he wouldn't pressure her. He also knew he'd better say something quick or the mood would be totally spoiled. Reaching out, he covered one of her hands with his.

"Lesley, on my way over here tonight I vowed I was going to say something to you, and now's the time. I've already admitted that I never forgot you. I was terribly disappointed when I discovered you had married. And when Joe told me you were back here, widowed, I knew I had to see you. True, I wanted to ask you to coach Carol, but even if I'd known there was no chance of that, I would have tried to see you anyway."

He had gotten her attention. She was looking at him, her eyes quizzical, her lips slightly parted, but she said nothing, so he pressed on. "And if you'd given me a flat no about Carol, I still would have asked you out to dinner, and I still would have come over here tonight. I was very attracted to you sixteen years ago, far more than I should have been, given the circumstances, so I'm looking on this as a second chance. The point of all this is, I intend on seeing you as much as possible. If you don't want that, this would be a good time to tell me."

For a minute Lesley was speechless. That his thoughts could have coincided perfectly with her own was incredible. It was even more astonishing that he could so easily give voice to them. She really was touched. Her hand turned under his, and their fingers interlaced. She had been hoping something like this would happen soon, but now that it had, she inexplicably felt shy. "Oh, Matt...."

Her voice came out sounding all fluttery, as though she were on the verge of tears, but she wasn't feeling very teary at all. She wanted to laugh. She slid off the stool, and her arms went up to lock behind his neck, all in one easy motion. She pressed her cheek against his. "Oh, Matt, I'm so glad you're not one for hemming and hawing. I'm also glad you aren't the patient type."

"I don't have time for patience," he said huskily, nuzzling her and pressing his lips into her hair.

"Neither do I. Time passes so quickly."

Lesley felt his fingertips on her shoulders, then his arms went around her, and he, too, slid off the stool to bring her into a tight embrace. As on Sunday, she immediately felt weak. He felt so good, and it had been a very long time since she had known another man's embrace. Matt seemed to sense that and made no move to do anything but hold her for a minute. Desire surfaced slowly and was answered by a long, drugging kiss—the first really passionate kiss they had shared. All her bones seemed to have melted; the kiss went on and on and was broken only when they gasped for air.

Lesley had dreamed of this moment, had lived it over in her mind a dozen times since Sunday night. She had imagined it in any number of places, in all sorts of ways. She hadn't expected it to come quite so soon, but because of all those smoldering looks over the sautéed scallops, she had expected it eventually. Still, there was a dreamlike quality to the entire scenario. She was somewhere off on cloud nine and had no desire to return to earth.

Reality came in the form of the opening and closing of the front door, footsteps and laughter. Lesley and Matt sprang apart like two teenagers caught necking in the back seat of Daddy's car. By the time Carol and Eric entered the game room, they were seated on the stools, pretending to be absorbed in conversation. Actually, Lesley's heart was about to jump out of her chest, and she could feel the flush on her face. She searched Matt's face for signs of lipstick, but there were none. Thank God she hadn't put on fresh makeup since noon.

"Dad!" Carol squealed when she saw Matt, and she bounded across the room to give him a hug.

"Hi, honey. How are you?"

"Great!"

Matt had to admit that she looked happier and more alive than she had in a long time. Whether that was Lesley's doing or Eric's, he didn't know. Probably a combination of both. Carol was a delight when she was happy, her fresh, youthful beauty like a ray of sunshine. At eighteen she was just beginning to blossom. It came to Matt with a bit of a start that he didn't have a little girl anymore. Where had the baby years gone? Although he had always thought of himself as a doting father who gave his daughter more attention than most, he felt a fleeting twinge of regret for all the missed milestones.

Eric came up to stand behind her, so Matt got to his feet and extended his hand. "Hello, Eric, it's good to see you. It's been some time."

"Yes, sir, it has."

Carol turned to Lesley. "There's a sports special Eric wants to watch. It lasts an hour. Is that all right?"

Lesley glanced at her watch. "I trust you know what time it is. We still hit the rink at seven-thirty. Saturday's just another day for us."

"I know, but Eric's leaving for L.A. tomorrow, and—"

"I'll be out the door at ten," Eric promised.

"Then I guess it's all right," Lesley said, and looked at Matt with resignation.

Matt didn't stay long after that. Even if they stole off into another room, he doubted Lesley would be in the mood for passionate romance with Carol in the house. "I'm going to say good night now," he said, "seeing as you're going to have to rise and shine so early."

She nodded and followed him to the front door after he'd said good night to Carol and Eric. When Matt opened the door, she slipped outside with him and found herself gathered into his arms once more. Lesley fully expected him to make a date for the following evening. After a string of kisses, he held her away from him slightly and sighed.

"Damn, I have an engagement tomorrow night that was made weeks ago. I really shouldn't break it since it involves some of our fair city's most distinguished citizens."

"Of course you shouldn't, Matt," she said, swallowing her disappointment. "I understand. I know you're busy."

"Unfortunately, Sunday's the same story. Golf and a dinner that night." He brightened slightly. "I can't miss the dinner, but I could cancel the golf game. Maybe we could do something."

She shot him a rueful smile. "Sunday afternoon is Carol's first ballet lesson. It was the only time that could be arranged. Any other Sunday would be fine, but I really should be there the first time. She'll be going to her mother's afterward, but that won't be until much later, and—"

"And I have that dinner date. Well, so there we have it." Matt bent and placed a kiss on the tip of her nose. "Put me down for next Friday night, no excuses. I'm hosting a party for my employees at my house, and I'd love it if you'd come."

Friday? Would she have to wait until Friday to see him again? And a party for his employees, of all things. Another business obligation. Lesley despised social affairs where she knew none of the guests.

But she knew if she wanted to get to really know Matt, to learn if there was something between them other than the incredible physical attraction, she would have to be with him on his own turf occasionally. "I'd love to come," she said.

"And, Lesley, this is positively the last weekend I'll allow myself to be tied up." He kissed her again, then made his way down the flagstone walk.

Lesley wondered. She couldn't imagine his turning down anything that was important to the company, and she was pretty well tied up, too. A romance, if indeed one was forthcoming, couldn't very well be conducted at her house, not with Carol living there, and she would never go off and leave her charge alone for long. Lesley's sense of responsibility was enormous. Two people had entrusted their daughter to her care, and that was a serious commitment. Lesley had begun to feel like a single parent.

Chief among her concerns was the relationship between Carol and Eric. They were becoming closer every day. In some ways it was a delight to see; in other ways it was a worry. It had occurred to her that she shouldn't allow them to be alone for long periods of time. Eric was as trustworthy a young man as could be found—Lesley would bet on it—but he was a man. And Carol adored him. Eric couldn't remain ignorant of that for much longer. Nor could he miss noticing that she was turning into a beauty. Their biological clocks were ticking away, and their hormones would be working overtime. If their relationship proceeded at the current speed, the inevitable was ... inevitable. All it would take was a little time alone, a place, a look, a touch, a kiss.

Never having been a parent, she had not anticipated a worry that had haunted parents since the dawn of mankind. She thought perhaps she should instigate a woman-to-woman talk. All Lesley wanted to know was how much Carol knew about life and love and men. She hoped it was a hell of a lot more than she had known at eighteen.

Later, when Eric had gone, Carol poked her head inside Lesley's bedroom door to say good night. Lesley asked her to come in for a minute. She wasn't sure how to steer the conversation in the direction she wanted, but Carol made it easy for her.

"Do you know that tonight was the first time Eric and I have been out together, just the two of us?" the young woman said, her eyes bright and alive. "Always before there was someone around—usually Sondra. But tonight there was no one else, so he had to talk to me, just me."

"What did you talk about?" Lesley asked.

"Mostly about what it's been like for him since the Olympics. Sort of a fairy tale, really. Yet, he hasn't changed much. Eric's not arrogant at all, and he's not temperamental. Actually, considering everything that's happened to him, he's pretty modest. You don't have the feeling you're talking to a superstar or anything like that."

"It's easy to see why you're so taken with him," Lesley said. "How does he feel about you?"

Carol pursed her lips thoughtfully. "Oh, he's always thought of me as this bratty little kid, but I think that's changing. I hope it is."

"Carol, I...I don't want to come across as a stuffy old buttinsky, but I'd like to ask you how much you know about men...and love...and sex."

Lesley's charge looked momentarily startled. She recovered quickly, thought, and shrugged. "I guess as much as anyone can know without firsthand experience. How can anyone stay ignorant in this day and age? I mean, starting in the sixth grade, you're bombarded with movies and pamphlets and stuff. And you can hardly pick up a magazine without reading about sex. My friends on the circuit talk about men all the time. It's just that none of us has time to do anything about it. Where are we going to meet men? The male skaters are as busy with their careers as we are with ours."

"I know, but your situation is different. The man you have your sights on is going to be spending a lot of time with you, and..."

Carol smiled. "You're worried about me and Eric getting it on, huh?"

"You could say that, yes. Your parents have placed you in my charge."

Carol looked absolutely delighted. "I sure wish you had something to worry about. Unfortunately, you don't. Eric's never made a pass at me or even acted like he thought of me as female, and he's the only man I care anything about. Oh, I know I'm asking for trouble. There's always a chance he'll find someone he wants to marry, especially now that he meets all these gorgeous women. Then I'd have to rethink just about everything. But as long as nothing like that happens, as far as I'm concerned, other men don't exist."

If Carol thought that would put Lesley's mind at ease, she was dead wrong. *Oh, Lord,* Lesley thought, *how do I feel about that? They are together so much. And Eric is far more sophisticated than Carol is. Maybe it's Eric I should have the talk with.*

But, of course, that wasn't her place, and she wouldn't do it if it was. That would be the same as telling Eric that Carol was crazy about him. If he didn't already know that, Carol should be the one to do the telling.

Though they were young, they were old enough to make their own decisions. Lesley decided she would just have to trust them. And do what legions of other parents did—worry.

CHAPTER SEVEN

ERIC SPENT MOST OF THE WEEK in Los Angeles, popping in for one day before heading to the East Coast for a professional competition. It was only Lesley's second week of working with Carol, and already she could see the difference in her student's skating. She could only take partial credit for that, though. It was Eric Carol was really trying to impress and she was working twice as hard to do it. When those '92 Olympic Games rolled around, Lesley decided, Eric was going to be in France with them if she had to take him there on a stretcher or in handcuffs.

They had seen precious little of Matt, too. One afternoon he managed to catch them at the rink before they called it a day, then had gone on to Lesley's house for dinner with them. But it had meant leaving work early, something Matt never did, so Lesley knew she couldn't expect him to do it often. And they had managed maybe twenty minutes alone that night, making small talk and casting longing looks in each other's direction. Not very satisfying and hardly worth Matt's efforts. So by the time Friday night rolled around, though Lesley was not particularly looking forward to the party, she was looking forward to being with Matt.

He had asked her to come early so they could spend a few quiet minutes together before the party began. Lesley knocked half an hour off Carol's practice time in order to pamper herself a little. The dress she chose to wear was a slightly shaped royal-blue chemise with a dotted silk scarf at the neckline. As usual she wore very little jewelry, only a pair of spectacular antique earrings. Carol said she looked "yummy."

"Are you getting all gussied up for my dad?"

"Not especially. I'll be the lone strange face there. I need to put my best foot forward."

Carol snickered. "Come on. You want to impress Dad. He's handsome, isn't he?"

"Yes, he is."

"Maybe I ought to ask you how much you know about men and love and sex." Laughing, Carol got up to leave the room. "I'm going down to see what Clarice is rustling up for dinner. Have a good time and don't stay out too late. Saturday's just another day for us, remember."

Lesley laughed, too, then gathered up her handbag and keys and left the house. Armed with Carol's directions, she had no trouble finding Matt's place and arrived promptly at six-thirty.

The man who answered her ring might have come straight out of an old British drawing room comedy. "Good evening, ma'am," he said graciously. "I'm Horace. Mr. Logan is waiting for you in his study. Right this way."

Lesley's head swiveled from right to left as she followed Horace across the small foyer and down a hall. Matt's house was a study in good taste and fine workmanship, from the gleaming hardwood floors to the carved moldings. Horace paused at a closed door, tapped lightly, then pushed it open and stood back to allow Lesley to enter the room. The servant soundlessly closed the door behind her.

Matt was standing at one of the arched windows that flanked the study's marble fireplace. He turned, smiling, and walked to her. "Lesley, you look absolutely beautiful. I promise not to smudge your makeup, but I can't resist one little kiss."

Taking her in his arms, he gave her just that—one very light kiss, just a brush of lips. Still, Lesley's nerve ends tingled. He looked wonderful, every inch the distinguished host. He wore a white silk shirt, a vest and dark trousers—no tie, no coat. Just looking at him turned her insides to gelatin. She stroked the back of his neck and pressed her cheek to his before taking a backward step to put some distance between them.

"Let me get you a glass of wine," Matt said. "That is what you want, isn't it? I've never seen you drink anything else."

"Yes, that's fine."

While he got the wine from the wet bar, Lesley strolled around the grand room, admiring its furnishings. The den was a completely masculine retreat, done in cherry wood and subdued patterns. She rubbed her hand over his desk and noticed a framed photograph of an older couple—his parents, she guessed. Yes, it had to be. Matt favored the man in the picture a great deal. The room reminded her of an exclusive men's club... or at least her notion of what an exclusive men's club would look like. And it definitely suited Matt, who was the most refined man she had ever met.

Matt looked at her out of the corner of his eye as he poured her wine and mixed himself a drink. Lesley had no way of knowing that this room had always been his most private place, sort of a hermitage where no one else was welcome. The desk drawers housed his personal papers, the floor-to-ceiling shelves held his favorite books and the stereo cabinet his records and tapes. He never entertained guests in this room; when he gave a party, it was usually locked. Yet, he enjoyed having Lesley browse around.

"This is a wonderful house, Matt," she remarked. "Didn't you say it was your father's?"

"Uh huh." He walked up to her and handed her the wine. "Dad was into restoring long before it became fashionable. He got this place for a comparative pittance, then spent five years getting it exactly the way he wanted. I suppose it will go to Carol someday. She can live in it, if she wants, or sell it. No doubt it will be the bulk of her inheritance from me. I'm too fond of living well to ever amass a fortune."

Lesley smiled. "No one who's paying for a skater's training can amass much of anything but a lot of bills."

"How is my daughter?"

"Tonight she's lonesome. Eric's out of town." Lesley frowned slightly. "Matt, do you mind it that they see so much of each other?"

"I don't think so. Should I?"

She laughed lightly. "I don't know. I'm new at this guardian business."

"Carol's adored Eric for years, but he's always treated her like a little sister... and a pesty one, at that."

"That can't last long. Carol's turning into a beautiful woman, and Eric's a handsome man. When he's in town, they spend a lot of time together."

Matt thought about that a minute. "Well, Lesley, I guess we have to give the kids credit for having some sense. Carol's so focused on that medal. I can't see her letting herself become distracted by anything, not even Eric. And Eric's been there. He knows the kind of single-minded determination it takes to make it to the Olympics. I can't see him trying to distract her. Let's just trust them, okay?" He planted a kiss on the top of her head. "But thanks for worrying. I can see that my daughter is in good hands."

"Was there ever any doubt in your mind about that?"

"Not one." He glanced at his watch. "The guests should start arriving any minute. Funny, I wish you and I were the whole party."

"Funny. So do I."

He touched the side of her face. "Tomorrow night? And Sunday?"

"Your weekend is free?"

"I told you I would try to keep them free from now on."

The doorbell rang. Lesley set down her wineglass and tucked her hand into the crook of his elbow. "We might not get another chance to talk tonight since I have to leave at a reasonable hour. Call me tomorrow after practice."

"Ah, I forgot. Saturday's just another working day for you. All right. I'll phone no later than five." The sound of voices in the foyer reached their ears. Matt opened the door. "Now let's go meet and greet everyone."

THE PARTY TURNED OUT to be exactly what Lesley expected—the kind of thing she normally avoided like the plague. But she enjoyed seeing Matt's beautiful home and getting a glimpse of his life-style. It was enlightening to watch him work the crowd, oozing effortless charm, while his employees and their spouses did their best to ingratiate themselves with him. Lesley was introduced to scores of people—she learned more names than she could possibly remember—but she had heard Matt mention Helen Johns, his secretary, often enough for that name to ring a bell. Helen and her husband, Steve, were a pleasant couple in their forties. They were wildly curious about Lesley, of course, but much too well-mannered to bombard her with questions. But once during the evening Lesley and Helen found themselves alone, circling the buffet table.

"I never saw so much food!" Lesley exclaimed.

"Horace is a wonder," Helen agreed. "Steve and I borrowed him for our anniversary party last year. The man's a genius in the kitchen. Try these little things." She placed a tidbit on a cocktail napkin and handed it to Lesley. It looked like some sort of pastry pinwheel filled with a spicy meat mixture. Lesley agreed it was delicious.

"Don't ask me what it is," Helen said. "I tried to get the recipe out of Horace once, but he just gave me this icy stare. I guess one shouldn't ask a genius to part with his secrets. And speaking of genius..." she cocked her head in Matt's direction. "He does this very well, doesn't he?"

"Yes, he does."

"Watch him work. He'll speak personally to everyone here tonight, and he'll remember positions, spouses' names, children's names and hobbies. It's the same way at the office. He speaks personally to every single employee at least once a week, and that's everyone from his executives down to the newest employee in the mail room. Now, that's genius. I don't know how he does it. It's like he has a computer for a brain. He just punches a key, and all this incredible information is there." Helen shook her head in admiration, then turned to Lesley. "Have you known Matt long?"

"Actually, we first met sixteen years ago but only recently renewed the acquaintance. I'm Carol's new skating coach."

"Ah! Then I'm sure I'll see you and hear about you many times during the next couple of years. Carol and that Olympic medal are the only things I know of that interest Matt outside Hamilton House. He is so committed to the company, but I think you have to be in order to climb to the heights he's reached. Vanessa Hamilton acquired a devoted slave the day she hired Matt, and Matt found his true element."

At that moment Helen was accosted by a woman she apparently hadn't seen in some time. After introductions, Lesley excused herself and wandered off to an unobtrusive corner where she could watch the crowd, especially Matt.

Tonight, for the first time, she began to sort and analyze all the differences between them, and there seemed to be a lot of them. Maybe too many. Matt's social life was active and filled with obligations, which he seemed to enjoy. She, on the other hand, found it ridiculous to attend a function solely out of a sense of duty. He was a master at saying the appropriate thing at all times; she tended to say what she thought. Matt charged into a crowd, immediately feeling he belonged. For most of Lesley's life—with her parents, her schoolmates, Arturo's friends, even Arturo himself at times—she had felt she was on the outside looking in. She was sure Matt had known countless women—one only had to watch him with a few to surmise that—while she had known only one man intimately. He was gregarious; she had a reclusive streak.

Lesley came to the conclusion that she and Matt were total opposites, which might have explained her fascination with him, but experience had taught her that opposites often had a tough time of it over the long haul. Still, the fascination and the incredible physical attraction were there, real and insistent. She couldn't deny them, though she honestly felt there was no more of a place for her in Matt's corporate world than there had been in Arturo's artsy one.

Lesley and Matt exchanged fewer than a dozen words all evening. Finally it was time for her to go. She threaded her way through the crowd to go back to the study in search of her handbag. Out of the corner of his eye, Matt saw her departure. Murmuring an "excuse me" to the people clustered around him, he followed her. When he reached the study, he closed the door and locked it, then pulled her into his arms.

"Don't tell me you have to leave already," he protested.

"I really must. I'm worthless without at least seven hours of sleep. It was a nice party, Matt."

"Every man here asked me who the charmer in blue is." His hands roamed restlessly over her back, and settled on the small of her waist. He pulled her to him and pressed against her insistently. "Be thinking about tomorrow night," he said huskily.

"Yes."

He cupped her face and kissed her—on her forehead, then the tip of her nose, her chin and finally her mouth. Her lips parted. When his tongue slipped between her teeth, she opened her mouth wider. He held her so tightly she thought he was going to crush her ribs. At last he loosened his hold. They stood looking at each other while their chests heaved. "Good grief, Matt," Lesley managed to say. "You've got a house full of guests out there."

"Yeah, I know."

"You need to go back to them, and I need to go home."

"I know that, too." Still he did not release her.

"Tomorrow," she said.

"Tomorrow. And Sunday. Maybe we can drive down the coast and . . . stop somewhere . . . or something."

Lesley sucked in her breath. He was thinking about the lack of privacy at her house. Stop somewhere? That could be exciting and delightfully romantic. "Yes, yes. Sunday. Now, I've really got to go, Matt. I dread running the gauntlet out there."

"There's a side door." He kissed her again. "I'll show it to you. No one will see you leave."

Matt stood in the doorway, watching while she drove away. He folded his arms across his chest and stared at the disappearing taillights. This was one relationship, he thought, that seemed to be having some difficulty finding a place and enough time to develop.

SATURDAY WAS THE PRETTIEST DAY weatherwise that they had enjoyed in some time, so perhaps that explained Carol's lackluster practice session. Lesley wondered if she was suffering a bout of premature spring fever. While the morning session had gone well, the afternoon's freestyle hadn't. She had never seen her student skate so listlessly.

"No, no, no, Carol!" Lesley shouted from the sidelines. "You're doing it again. What's wrong with you this afternoon?" She skated out toward the dejected figure in the center of the ice. "Now, what's the matter?"

"I don't know. I just feel blah."

"Do you mean sick?"

"No, but nothing feels right. I just feel... blah."

"You can't afford to feel blah. Skaters who feel blah don't win Olympic medals. I'm telling you one thing that's wrong. You're not concentrating. You're starting a beat behind the music. It might be only a split second, but it keeps you off during the entire program. No wonder you're missing your jumps and spins. Concentrate, concentrate. Listen to the music and move with it. Ice, music, program. That's what you should be thinking about. And keep that chin up.

Eric wants you to exude self-confidence during this number. You look about as self-confident as an oyster.'' Lesley took a deep breath. "Okay, let's start all over.''

"Aw, Lesley, I'm dead tired,'' Carol complained.

"Then give me something resembling a decent performance, and we'll quit. You're skating like a wimp.''

"Didn't you ever hear of the Emancipation Proclamation? The slaves were set free.''

Lesley turned toward the stands, hiding her smile. "Do it again, and this time listen to the music.''

So went the entire afternoon. Carol's skating never really got on track, and Lesley had a throbbing headache by the time they left the rink. It was Eric, she thought glumly. Carol had let him become a distraction, and she was growing much too dependent on him. Of course, he was wonderful with her, and she always skated like a champ when he was watching, but she had to skate that way when he was on the other side of the country or the world, too.

Lesley chided herself for looking for problems where none might exist. Maybe Carol simply was having an off day; everyone did occasionally. Maybe it was PMS. Monday she might be in top form again.

But she made a mental note to watch her student carefully from now on, to notice what affected her skating. If it turned out to be solely Eric...well, she'd deal with that when the time came. She might be forced to tell Carol what her own coach had once told her.

Lesley had been bemoaning the lack of fun in her life, that she was sixteen and had never even had a casual boyfriend. "You can't have both, Lesley," he'd said.

"Why not? Why can't I be a champion skater and have a boyfriend, too?"

"Because one would have to be more important than the other. You want the boyfriend, the skating suffers. You want the skating, the boyfriend disappears. Someday, yes. Now, no."

She'd chosen skating without many qualms, but now that she thought about it, she hadn't had anyone in her life who was as important to her as Eric was to Carol. Lesley sighed. She just might have herself a real problem.

MEANWHILE, IN DALLAS that same afternoon, Vanessa Hamilton grappled with her own problem. She sat at the mahogany desk in the den of her country estate, going over the legal documents her attorney had delivered to her that morning. After some twenty minutes of intense concentration, she smiled with satisfaction, closed the portfolio and got to her feet. Crossing the room to a sideboard, she poured herself a sherry. *One more detail,* she thought, *and my financial affairs will at last be in perfect order. About time. Waiting so long was risky. Unlike me.*

Vanessa would soon celebrate her eightieth birthday. She was a stunning woman for her age, tall and straight with a regal bearing. In old age she had retained much of the startling beauty that had blessed her youth. Her eyes, though heavily lidded, were as keen and incisive as ever, and the auburn hair that had been her crowning glory now was a blaze of silver around her handsome face. Her figure had softened but stayed trim. Even those who considered her demanding and imperious conceded that she was a remarkably attractive septuagenarian. She looked every inch what she was—a woman of means and power.

But money and influence could not keep her from the grave, and seventy-nine was seventy-nine, after all. Her recent bout with bronchitis had been the impetus needed to goad her into action. Now her financial affairs were almost in order; once she had tended to the last detail, she could rest. And she intended on throwing an eightieth birthday party for herself that people would talk about for years after she was gone.

Vanessa had not anticipated her current problem, which made it even more intolerable to her. Her life was so well-ordered that unexpected surprises annoyed her. Certain recent goings-on within the upper echelons of Hamilton House—most notably a buy-out offer from an international conglomerate—had brought out the worst in some of her once trusted associates, most notably Dolph Wade. How he had disappointed her. Discovering his clandestine agreement with the negotiators representing the conglomerate—in which Dolph would obtain a small fortune in return for his convincing Vanessa to sell—had so enraged her that their longtime friendship was in the deep freeze. Now she was convinced that unless she took steps to protect the future of her business empire before her death, infighting and power plays would occur after it. She couldn't allow that.

It was time—no, past time—to select her successor, and with Dolph no longer an acceptable choice, the selection would have to come from among her six division vice presidents. Pivoting, she returned to the desk and withdrew a folder from the center drawer. In it were the personnel files of those six people. Three of them, for various reasons, were not being considered. Vanessa shoved their folders aside and concentrated on the remaining three.

Matthew Logan in San Francisco. Handsome, urbane, ambitious. Ambition could manifest itself in many ways, but in Matt it was an asset.

Paula Steele in Nashville. Attractive, sharp as a tack, a real southern lady. She was what people referred to as a class act.

Finally, Grady O'Connor in Mississippi. Earthy, unpretentious, innovative. Vanessa had a soft spot in her heart for Grady.

She knew all three of them to be bright, capable, dedicated and, above all, loyal. But the files contained only the dry, impersonal data that such files invariably contained. There had to be a deciding factor, something that would set one of them apart, and it was up to her to find that factor. She had decided to spend some time alone with each of them, to try to get to know them personally instead of just professionally. And there was no time like the present to begin. Suddenly she was impatient. When Vanessa decided something needed to be done, she wanted it done yesterday.

Her eyes flew to the antique clock on her desk. Five o'clock on Saturday afternoon. It would be three in San Francisco. She flicked through her Rolodex, then picked up the phone.

MATT'S FINELY TUNED INSTINCTS were humming when he hung up the phone. Vanessa wanted to see him in

Dallas Monday morning. That meant Sunday travel. He had a lot to do. First he made reservations for the following afternoon. Afterward, he phoned Helen. By the time he had given her instructions, conferred with Horace and chosen the clothes he wanted to take with him, it was five o'clock. He returned to the study, picked up the phone and dialed Lesley's number.

She sounded irritable, which was a surprise. "What's wrong?" he demanded.

"Oh, Carol and I had a miserable day at practice. Just one of those things."

"Would you like to go somewhere tonight? It might cheer you up."

There was a hesitation. "Matt, why don't you just come over for dinner? Carol feels rotten. She is in such a mood. Maybe you can cheer her up. And I've got a granddaddy of a headache that I can't seem to get rid of."

It wasn't exactly what he'd had in mind, but he supposed it would have to do. Maybe they could get away by themselves after dinner. "Take something and lie down. I'll be there in an hour or so."

Matt showered and changed, then left his house. True to his word, he arrived at Lesley's in an hour and fifteen minutes. It was Carol who answered his ring. She threw herself into his arms. "I'm so glad to see you! I've had a miserable day."

"So Lesley said."

"I was flat all during practice. I don't know what was wrong with me."

"Nobody can be up all the time."

He slid an arm around her waist, and together they went down to the game room to join Lesley. "How's the headache?" Matt asked as he placed a light kiss on her cheek.

"Much better, thanks. May I get you a drink?"

"Thanks."

Matt watched her as she crossed the room to the bar. Outwardly, she showed no signs of having had a bad day. She looked fresh and energetic, dressed in a bright print skirt and coordinating sweater. Damn, it was Saturday night, and though many years had passed since Saturday was the most important night of the week for him, it seemed as though they should be going somewhere, doing something. He glanced at Carol, who had hoisted herself up onto one of the bar stools to grab a handful of salted nuts from a dish. At least he and Lesley should have been alone together, but apparently Carol wanted some company. She looked very down and showed all signs of having settled in until dinner was served.

His thoughts mirrored Lesley's perfectly. She longed to be drawn into his arms again, just like last night, only this time he wouldn't release her. Neither of them had to dash off early. They could have a quiet dinner, sip wine, gaze soulfully into each other's eyes, and...who knew? But they'd never be able to do that in this house, not with Carol there. Lesley decided too late that when he'd telephoned earlier, she should have suggested doing something in the city. Then he might have asked her to his place afterward, and...

Carol got up to play the jukebox. Lesley's eyes met Matt's, and he smiled a slow, easy smile. Her heart did an erratic little dance. At least there was tomorrow.

After dinner, Carol received a phone call from Eric. The doom and gloom look on her face vanished instantly. The call was like a badly needed injection of a wonder drug. She bounded upstairs to her room to take it in private. Lesley took advantage of that to maneuver Matt into the library and close the door behind them. "This is the best I can do for privacy," she told him.

"It'll do for now."

Lesley hurtled herself toward him, and Matt reached out to catch her. He held her and caressed her, his hands gentle and restrained but with underlying strength. She could feel herself growing soft and pliant against his hardness. She burrowed her head into his shoulder and rained a shower of kisses on the underside of his chin, while he just held her tighter and tighter. Then he pushed her away slightly. "I've got to sit down," he growled, "before I fall down."

Laughing, Lesley led him to the long sofa that stood in front of the fireplace, its back to the door. They all but collapsed upon it and embraced again. "This is an exercise in frustration," Matt muttered. "I hope you realize that."

"I know."

"Very unsatisfying."

"I know," Lesley murmured against his mouth, "but we have tomorrow."

Matt stiffened. She pulled back and looked at him quizzically. "Don't we?"

He sighed. The expression on his face was apologetic. "I'm...afraid not. Vanessa called me this afternoon. She wants me in Dallas first thing Monday, so that means Sunday travel."

Lesley's sigh was even more pronounced. She sat back, not bothering to hide her disappointment. "If I believed in omens, I'd say we were receiving signs that you and I aren't ever supposed to be alone together."

He spread out his hands in a helpless gesture. "This . . . is just something I can't do a thing about. When Vanessa crooks her finger, I come running. We all do."

"Of course." *Of course,* Lesley thought bitterly. Hamilton House came first, always and forever. Maybe it had to be that way for a successful businessman, but she didn't have to like it. And if she was smart, she'd keep Matt's dedication to his work at the forefront of her thoughts at all times. She had no idea where she and Matt were headed; right now, nowhere seemed a pretty safe bet. But they were greatly attracted to each other, and they weren't babes in the woods. If they continued to see each other, they would make love. Once that happened, it was reasonable to assume they would want some kind of permanence in their relationship. Lesley doubted Matt was interested in an affair, and she knew she wasn't.

So caution would be the watchword. She had been through it before—the last-minute cancellations, the birthdays, anniversaries and holidays spent alone, the dropping of everything when a weary husband finally did come home. She had tried so hard to make Arturo understand that it wasn't worth it. She hadn't succeeded, and she wouldn't even try with Matt.

Matt wondered what she was thinking. He considered telling her what he thought might be behind the sudden summons from Vanessa, then decided against it. Vanessa might not be searching for her successor at all. She might have something entirely different on her mind. Matt didn't think so, but she might.

"How long will you be gone this time?" Lesley asked.

"I don't know. A couple of days, three, four. Vanessa didn't give me a reason for wanting to see me. She just said 'Come' and I said 'yes, ma'am.'"

Lesley nodded resignedly. "What time do you leave tomorrow?"

"Around two, four Dallas time. I'll get checked into the hotel, have dinner and hit the sack early. By the way, I'll be at the Anatole, in case you have to get hold of me. Maybe the time will fly for you. You and Carol seem so busy."

"Yes. I hope we don't have too many more days like today, though. She felt terrible about it, and so did I."

Matt frowned. "Sometimes I worry that you two push it."

"I'll tell you what I worry about. I worry that Carol depends on Eric too much, that she's flat when he's not around."

"No, I'll bet she just had an off day."

A minute of silence passed. Then Lesley asked, "Would you like to go downstairs and watch TV?"

His arm stole around her. "I was rather enjoying what we were doing."

"Do you really want to fumble with each other on the sofa?"

A suggestion of a smile twitched at the corners of Matt's mouth. "I...I guess not. It's too frustrating."

"My feelings exactly." She got to her feet and held out her hand. "Come on. Surely we can find something to watch. And if Vanessa turns you loose by next weekend, who knows, maybe we can start this all over again."

CHAPTER EIGHT

LESLEY SMILED at Garson Morman across the expanse of the game room's bar. She had been glad to see Arturo's old friend; she'd felt edgy and restless since she'd awakened. Normally she cherished her quiet Sundays, but today was an exception. Eric's phone call the night before had been to inform Carol he would be home today, and his mother wanted her to come for the Zitos' gigantic Sunday dinner. After Carol's ballet lesson, the two young people had driven off in Eric's new BMW. It was raining again, which precluded outdoor activities. So Garson's visit was like a ray of sunshine.

"This is what you've decided to do with your life, Lesley?" he asked in astonishment when she told him about Carol.

"I'm not saying I'm going to devote the rest of my life to it, but the next two years, yes."

"Athletics? Sweat?"

Lesley laughed. "We're not talking track and field here, Garson. Figure skating is a beautiful sport, and Carol is going to be its appointed darling."

Garson pulled on his chin. "I suppose you've missed it. I thought it was very wrong of Arturo to insist you quit when you had so much free time to kill.

Perhaps I should have intervened and tried to persuade him to leave you be."

Lesley turned serious. "Arturo was never influenced by another person in his life. Once he decided he wanted me to quit, that was it."

"Didn't you even try to convince him otherwise?"

"I had less influence with Arturo than anyone. When he married me, he envisioned taking this child and guiding her through life. He simply never realized that I'd grown up."

Both were uncomfortable with the turn the conversation had taken, so the subject was changed. They discussed some mutual acquaintances and a show Garson was mounting, things Lesley no longer had any real interest in, but the company was nice and a pleasant hour was spent. But when Garson left, the restlessness took over once more.

She would have given anything if Matt was there. Carol and Eric weren't due back for hours. Clarice had gone to visit relatives in Oakland. They finally could have had something that so far had eluded them—time alone together.

But, no, he had to be off bettering the fortunes of Hamilton House, and she was left to spend a rainy Sunday alone.

Lesley gave herself an impatient shake. If there was a more useless pastime than this, she didn't know what it could be. Matt was an important man with important things to do, but she had something important to do, too: make sure that by 1992 Carol was the odds-on favorite to capture the gold. She had to devote all her energies to that.

An hour later the rain stopped. Lesley decided to go to the drugstore for a few things, among them, a fat, juicy book she could lose herself in. Then she would stop for take-out Chinese food. Anything to keep from wandering through all those empty rooms.

IT WAS ALMOST SEVEN Dallas time, when Matt checked into the hotel. The first thing he did when he got to his room was call Vanessa to let her know he had arrived. The second thing he did was call Lesley. She wasn't home. Nobody was. Matt felt strangely dejected when he hung up the phone. All his thoughts should have been on tomorrow's meeting with Vanessa, but they weren't. Far too many of them lingered on a redhead in California, just as they had when he'd been in Phoenix. Something very odd seemed to be happening to him. His thought processes no longer were predictable.

He was restless. The best thing he could do was go down to the bar, have a drink, listen to some music, then have dinner where there were other people around. But he didn't leave the room. Instead, he ordered a drink from room service and sipped it slowly while he perused the copy of the *Dallas Morning News* he had picked up at the airport. It wasn't long, however, before he realized he was just looking at words, not comprehending them. Lesley's face swam in and out of his vision.

She had invaded his life and laid siege to his every thought, and she'd done it with such incredible swiftness that Matt couldn't believe it had happened. He very quickly blessed Sondra for deserting Carol and making a new coach necessary. He also blessed Joe

Hylands for telling him about Lesley. Then he turned around and cursed the demands of his and Lesley's respective jobs. She was committed to Carol, which seemed to mean two years of an afternoon here, an evening there, moments snatched away from other obligations—more like a long-standing affair than a real relationship...nothing protracted enough to begin to satisfy his craving.

Matt stirred. He reminded himself that he couldn't possibly know at this point if he wanted a prolonged, permanent relationship with Lesley. He of all people knew how superficial instantaneous attractions could be.

But this wasn't instantaneous, was it? It went back sixteen years. And Lesley wasn't anything like Olivia. His marriage had been based on pure physical attraction. As hard as he tried, he could not recall that he and his ex-wife had even once seriously discussed their feelings, hopes and dreams. On the other hand, Matt genuinely enjoyed talking to Lesley and sometimes they would do nothing else for hours but simply talk. Other times, he thought, he could simply look at her. Ridiculous for a sensible man his age, but a lot of what he thought and felt and did lately was ridiculous.

Like sitting in his hotel room, moonstruck and brooding. Feeling uncertain about what he wanted for the first time in his adult life. Always before, the adrenaline pumped like mad when he got within sniffing distance of the home office. Getting to his feet, he called room service again and ordered a hot roast beef sandwich and a cold beer. He had to get on track, had to stop thinking about home and start thinking about the meeting with Vanessa in the morning. It could be momentous.

A sheer wave of panic hit Matt just then. It was brief, fleeting, but it shook him. What if it did turn out to be momentous? What if Vanessa had something in mind that would completely alter his life? It would mean moving from the Bay Area, where he had spent his entire life. It would mean following Carol's progress long-distance, and worse, it would mean that circumstances once again would conspire to keep Lesley from him.

THE FOLLOWING MORNING Matt planned to take a cab the short distance down Stemmons Freeway from the hotel to the Hamilton House Building, but an early call informed him that Mrs. Hamilton was sending a car around for him. It was nine o'clock when he stepped into Vanessa's plush private office. As always, the company matriarch rose from her desk and went to meet him in the center of the room.

She wore a simple navy-blue dress, its severity softened by the strands of perfect pearls at her neck. When Matt had first joined Hamilton House, Vanessa's beauty had been breathtaking. Himself a young man in those days, he had been astonished to learn that a woman of some years could be a stunning beauty. Now that she was nearly eighty, that beauty hadn't waned. If anything, it had become more aristocratic. Whenever Matt entered her presence after a long period of time, he experienced an urge to bend on one knee and kiss her ring. Instead, they embraced, and he placed a light kiss on her translucent cheek.

"Hello, Vanessa. You look lovely, as usual."

"Matt." She held him at arm's length, drinking in every detail of his appearance. Seldom, if ever, had she known a man of such impeccable good taste, with so much savoir faire. Long ago she had decided that Matt Logan was a throwback from some distant age when manners, breeding and taste counted for something. How splendid he would look sitting behind her desk. "I trust you had a pleasant trip."

He chuckled lightly. "As pleasant as can be expected. You and I remember when airline travel was luxurious. It no longer is. Mostly it's an endurance run."

"How is Carol?"

"She's doing fine, thanks."

"Still questing for that Olympic gold?"

"Oh, yes."

"I hope I'm still around and have my faculties in '92. I would so love to see her win it."

"Of course you'll be around."

"Matt, no one lasts forever, not even me. There are those who will tell you I've lasted far beyond my usefulness as it is." Her eyes twinkled with merriment spiced by malice.

Instead of asking him to take a seat and returning to her own, Vanessa made a move toward the door, indicating that he do the same. "Come. Let's take a walk. There have been some changes since you last were here. I know you read all about them in those endless memos I sent you and the others, but that's not quite the same as seeing them."

In the corridor outside her office, Vanessa led the way to the elevators. Matt noticed that they passed Dolph Wade's office without stopping to have a word with the man, a first. Normally, Dolph would have been the second person he saw. Vanessa had not even mentioned Wade's name yet. So the rumors were more than rumors. How the mighty had fallen!

Vanessa took Matt on the grand tour, and she had been right—there had been a lot of changes. Hamilton House was a big, vital corporation that employed a lot of interesting people who did interesting things. Their first stop was a room that housed a control board that looked as though it belonged in a metropolitan airport. This one, however, enabled the controller to track every refrigerated eighteen-wheeler the corporation owned. In the data room, enormous computers, their printers clacking away, allowed Vanessa to see at a glance every meal served at every restaurant every day. She reached out and tore off several sheets of one printout, scanned them quickly and looked at Matt in exasperation. "Look at the green salads we served yesterday. You can get a green salad at a fast food joint. Why would anyone go to a Hamilton House and order a green salad for lunch? Why not that lovely eggplant terrine?"

That morning Matt renewed his acquaintance with an employee he hadn't seen in some time, a vivacious woman named Karen Holtz. Karen's job entailed traveling the country and studying eating trends and changing tastes. There were fads in food just as there were fads in clothes, and it was Karen's responsibility to spot the trends early enough to allow Hamilton House to go with the flow. She had correctly predicted the new Southwest trend, the Cajun craze and the grill-everything phenomenon.

"Rough work," Matt commented.

Karen just smiled. "Isn't it, though. My mother can't believe I actually get paid for traveling and eating out."

"So let me in on the next fad."

Karen didn't hesitate. "Real food."

"Real food?"

She nodded. "Look at this, our newest entrée. California beef braised in cabernet sauvignon, flavored with herbs and served in a rich sauce made from pan juices."

"Sounds wonderful," Matt said.

"It is. But any way you slice it, it's pot roast. Next thing you know we'll be serving chicken and dumplings. We just won't call it that."

A man named Bob Ferriday did nothing but ferret out new chefs in North America and Western Europe. "It's such a problem," Vanessa told Matt. "Once chefs establish a reputation, they become celebrities and want to open their own restaurants. We have to keep the young ones coming, literally pounce on them the minute they complete their apprenticeships, before they get set in their ways. The good ones become prima donnas very quickly. It's the biggest personnel problem we have."

Matt and Vanessa spent the morning poking in and out of offices and chatting with various men and women at various levels of the operation. He was beginning to see the Dallas office as one huge control center that tentacled the country. It was a far cry from the middling-size company he had gone to work for all those many years ago. The one thing that seemingly hadn't changed was Vanessa. Her energy astonished him.

Yet, even Vanessa was not completely tireless. Sometime around midday, she and Matt returned to her office. "Matt dear, I'm going to turn you over to Clark Jenkins for the remainder of the afternoon." Clark, Matt knew, was in charge of marketing. "As much as I hate to admit it, I find I can't operate at my optimum without an afternoon rest. But I want you to have dinner with me tonight at my place. A car and driver will pick you up at the hotel at . . . say, six-thirty?"

"Of course. I'm looking forward to it."

"There'll only be the two of us, so please don't feel you must dress."

If Matt had harbored doubts about the reason for his summons to Dallas, he no longer did. He was being given a crash course in the home office operation. He was beginning to see firsthand what he vaguely had always understood—that his bailiwick in San Francisco was only a small part of a very large jigsaw puzzle. Here was the very heart and soul of Hamilton House. There could be only one reason for the indoctrination: he was being considered for the top spot in the company. No doubt others were, too. Curiously, the excitement he expected to feel, thought he ought to feel, was tempered by uncertainty. It had nothing to do with doubts about his ability to handle the job; of course he could—there wasn't anyone better qualified.

But it hit him like a bolt of lightning that he wasn't sure he wanted it. He, the epitome of the dedicated company man, had found something else.

WHEN MATT RETURNED to his hotel room that evening to shower and change, he once again called Lesley, and once again she wasn't home. Clarice informed him that she and Carol had left for Carol's workout. Damn! How many nights a week were devoted to that now? he wondered. Was this the way it was to be, then? And it would get worse as 1992 neared. There would be no relationship at all if he moved to Dallas. Damn! A month ago if anyone had told him he would find even one unpleasant aspect about being the company's C.E.O., he would have laughed uproariously.

But surely he was putting the cart before the horse. He hadn't been offered anything but dinner with Vanessa tonight, and he was running late. By hurrying, he was waiting in the lobby when the car and driver called for him.

Matt seemed to recall that the beautiful estate Stuart and Vanessa had built north of Dallas was far out in the country, but if that ever had been true, it no longer was. The Metroplex had marched relentlessly toward it. Only the vast amount of acreage surrounding the place had kept it from being surrounded by development.

Refinement and good taste were the words that came to Matt's mind as he was ushered down the front hall of the house by an aproned servant. Vanessa's home was understated and unpretentious, yet its simplicity was deceiving. Its owner had spent a lifetime acquiring the very finest in furniture and accessories, and all were artfully displayed.

His employer waited for Matt in her paneled study, and she smiled at him fondly when he entered the room and crossed to her. "You're prompt," Vanessa said.

"Your driver is prompt," he corrected her. "I probably would have wandered aimlessly for hours. The traffic is horrendous."

"Isn't it, though. I loathe it. I poured a sherry for you, but if you prefer something else . . ."

"Sherry's fine. Thank you."

"Sit down, Matt. I want to talk to you."

They sat facing each other in front of the fireplace. "How was your afternoon with Clark?" Vanessa asked.

"Informative. He's a bright young man."

"Yes, he is. And tomorrow I'm turning you over to Harrison Roberts in restaurant operations. Wednesday you'll spend some time in planning and development. You're going to meet a lot of bright young people. I like being surrounded by them." Vanessa paused to sip her sherry. "But, of course, there are positions where a little age and a lot of experience are vital."

"Thank God. For a minute there I was afraid you were putting us old folks out to pasture."

"Quite the contrary." Her smile was secretive. "Tell me, Matt, what is your private life like?"

That took him somewhat aback. He didn't think Vanessa had ever asked him about his life away from Hamilton House—except for inquiries about Carol. Either she wasn't curious along those lines or she, like so many others, assumed he had no life away from Hamilton House. "Quite satisfactory, thanks."

"Is there a woman?"

"As a matter of fact, there is. One I'm quite fond of. She's Carol's new coach."

"You've just met her, then?"

"Actually, we first met sixteen years ago, but I was married then. It's a rather complicated story."

Vanessa's eyes twinkled. "I'd love to hear it."

As succinctly as possible, Matt told her how Lesley had come back into his life. When he finished, Vanessa clapped her hands. "How delightfully romantic. Is it serious?"

"It's too soon for that, but...I have every reason to hope it will be." Matt sipped his sherry, then leaned forward. "Vanessa, you know I always love coming to Dallas and seeing you. I would drop everything and fly here to do nothing but take you to dinner."

"I know that." Coming from anyone else, Vanessa would have suspected blatant apple-polishing, but she knew Matt meant it.

"But I've been around too long not to know this is no ordinary summons from on high. These questions about my private life are a bit out of character. What in the hell are you up to?"

She laughed lightly, then sobered. "Many years ago, long before you were born, my father gave me a sage bit of advice. Be careful of who you trust, trust very few and be suspicious of the rest. Oh, how right he was!" She paused thoughtfully for a minute. "How long have we known each other?"

"About twenty years."

"And you've never disappointed me. Not once."

"Good. I've certainly tried not to."

"Others, however, have...greatly. You heard about the offer from Barrington International, of course."

"Of course." Matt took another sip of sherry and watched her carefully.

"I never considered accepting it."

"I never thought for a minute you would."

That seemed to delight Vanessa. She flashed him a dazzling smile before turning serious again. "Dolph, on the other hand, urged me to accept BI's offer. Urged me so vehemently that it made me suspicious as the very devil. I investigated. Snooped might be a more accurate word. One afternoon I stayed at my desk long after everyone else had gone, and I...well, I cased Dolph's office. He did something so incredibly stupid that I still find it hard to believe. He taped a conversation between himself and the BI reps. To protect himself, I'm sure, in case they wanted to renege later. But I found the tape."

Matt frowned. "Obviously it was incriminating."

Vanessa uttered an unpleasant little laugh. "I'll say! It seems Dolph stood to come into a great deal of money if Hamilton House sold out to BI. A bonus of sorts. I can't begin to tell you how the news affected me."

"You don't have to, Vanessa. I can imagine. Is Dolph aware that you've heard the tape?"

She shook her head. "No, so nothing said here tonight must leave this room. Dolph and everyone else knows I'm miffed at him. Naturally they think I'm peeved because he favored the buy out. Everyone, including Dolph, assumes I'll get over it, but they're wrong. Too much of me—and of Stuart—has gone into what we built. We gave our youths to the business, and I cannot take the chance that it will fall into the uncaring hands of people who will systematically tear it down. The changes that Barrington wanted to make in the restaurants were deplorable. Stuart would have been horrified."

Her eyes narrowed slightly. "I could forgive Dolph for being stupid and greedy. I might even forgive his misjudging me. But I can't forgive his disloyalty. My God, when I think how Stuart took care of that man! Obviously, Dolph won't be taking over Hamilton House when I'm gone. I've seen to that. My attorney and I have spent weeks getting my personal and business affairs in order."

Matt sucked in his breath, but he was careful to keep his expression from showing the sudden acceleration of his heartbeat. He had thought about almost all of this, but he hadn't expected Vanessa to be so candid.

"Which rather leaves me in a quandary, doesn't it?" Vanessa continued.

"I guess it does."

"Who will mind the store when I'm gone? Lately I've regretted, for the first time, that Stuart and I never had children, and that's absurd. Blood ties no more assure fidelity than fifty years of friendship. But enough of that. The point is, I have to choose my successor. I'm considering several people for the position, and you're one of them. I'd like to know how you feel about that." She raised her glass to her mouth and looked at him over its rim.

Matt chuckled. "Do you have to ask? I'm flattered as hell."

"And would be more than happy to move to Dallas?"

There was a slight hesitation. "You'd know I'd be lying if I said I would be more than happy to leave San

Francisco. That would mean leaving Carol, too. Of
course there would be pangs of regret. But to run
Hamilton House, to be president? Naturally I'd like
that."

"Thank God you're honest. It's one of the things I
most admire about you. You love position, and you
don't waste time pretending otherwise. It's refresh-
ing. I've often thought that you and I are a great deal
alike. I doubt I could have had a son who reminded me
more of myself—and Stuart. But then, Stuart and I
were such peas in a pod we could have been twins."

Vanessa reached out to an end table and picked up
a small framed photograph, then handed it to Matt.
"Have I ever shown you that?"

He looked at the picture and smiled. It was a very
old snapshot of a small café with striped awnings and
a neon sign, the kind of place patronized by neighborhood regulars. "Once," he said, "a long time
ago."

"That was taken in 1939. It was our first venture
into the restaurant business, on a side street in south
Dallas. The place is still there. I have my driver cruise
by it occasionally. It's a barbecue joint now. Oh, how
I loved that cramped, noisy little café! I can't tell you
how many times Stuart and I walked into it at dawn,
not to straggle home until almost midnight." She
smiled wistfully at the recollection. "When *News-
week* did that article on Hamilton House a few years
ago, the reporter who interviewed me asked how the
business got started. I told him with five-cent coffee
and thirty-five-cent plate lunches."

Matt stared at the snapshot another second or two before handing it back to Vanessa. "Did you ever dream in those days that it would get so big?"

She shook her head. "My imagination wouldn't stretch that far in 1939. Stuart was the visionary. I just worked hard." She leaned forward then and spoke earnestly, fervently. "Nothing must be allowed to happen to Hamilton House, Matt. It's a strong, vital organization now, but the wrong people could destroy it in a matter of a few years. I want to extract a promise from you. If you occupy my office, promise you'll keep the company intact and pass it on to others who'll do the same."

"That goes without saying, Vanessa. I'll go you one better. Even if I'm not sitting in that office, I'll fight any attempted buy out or takeover with every conceivable means at my disposal. Take it to court, if necessary."

Vanessa sat back, looking enormously pleased. "Thanks. I rather imagined you would say just that."

IT WAS PAST TEN when the driver deposited Matt at the Anatole. He and Vanessa had enjoyed a beautifully prepared dinner and had reminisced about almost everything but business. Then, just as he was leaving, Vanessa had said, "I intend on giving myself plenty of time to choose my successor, Matt. Maybe a year, I don't know. Sooner if I take sick. And I do appreciate your loyalty. You, and a few others like you, have sustained me greatly since Stuart's death."

Throughout the drive into town, Matt's thoughts had churned. He hoped she took every minute of a year. A lot could happen in a year. Carol might be national champion in a year. He and Lesley might...

Again he was assaulted by confusion and uncertainty. He just hoped that by the time Vanessa finally made her decision, his own indecisiveness would have vanished.

When he got up to his room, he went straight to the phone and called Lesley. Her voice came over the line, and Matt sank onto the edge of the bed, smiling. "How was the workout?"

"It went quite well." she said. "Clarice said you'd called. I called the hotel, but you didn't answer."

"No, I had dinner with Vanessa."

"Is everything going all right there?"

"Yes, fine."

"When will you be home?"

Matt sighed. "Not for at least two more days, I'm afraid. Maybe longer."

"Oh." Her disappointment was obvious, something that pleased him no end. "I hoped you were calling to say the trip wouldn't last as long as you'd thought."

"No, I... If you want the truth, I called because I wanted to hear the sound of your voice."

Halfway across the country, Lesley's heartbeat quickened. When she hung up the phone some five minutes later, her eyes were as bright as diamonds. From across the room she heard Carol ask, "What did Dad want?"

Lesley turned. "Oh...nothing really. He just wanted to know how things were going here."

"Mmm," Carol murmured with a twinkle in her eye. "I'd have to say you've accomplished something no one else ever has, Lesley."

"What's that?"

"Managed to make Dad think about you while he's in the august presence of Vanessa Hamilton herself."

Lesley hoped her smile wasn't as foolish as it felt.

CHAPTER NINE

ON TUESDAY MORNING Carol woke suffering from an allergy that plagued her from time to time. She sniffled and sneezed all through breakfast.

"Honey, you just look awful," Lesley said.

"I'll bet. I feel awful, too. My nose is all fizzy, and my eyes are watery. It feels like a cold, only this doesn't get any worse or any better. It just hangs around a couple of days and then goes away."

"You'd better stay in today. We'll forgo practice. I don't think a day or two will hurt. I might use the day to run some errands that have needed running for a couple of weeks."

"Okay," Carol said listlessly. "I've got some medicine I can take for this. It really takes me out of it, but it does seem to help. Are you going to call Eric and tell him?"

"He wasn't going to be at the rink today, remember? He has an appointment with his agent and some television people."

"Oh, yes. Sometimes I forget what a busy man he is."

Lesley smiled. *Welcome to the club,* she wanted to say. "You'd better get used to it. If that television special materializes, you and I are going to have to muddle along without Eric for a long time."

"Yeah," Carol said with a morose sigh. "I'm afraid you're right."

Confined to quarters, Carol found the day dragging interminably. She read, she dozed, then read some more. Clarice brought a portable TV up to her room, but there wasn't anything on that interested her. Enforced idleness was not something she took to well, but the allergy medication always made her so groggy that she couldn't do much even if there had been something to do.

Promptly at noon Clarice came in with soup and a sandwich, which Carol picked at. She had fidgeted so much that the bed was a rumpled mess, so she got up and straightened it. Time crawled by. Just when she was wondering where in the devil Lesley was, Clarice stuck her head in the door again.

"Eric's here," the maid said.

"Oh, God!" Carol raised herself up to look in the mirror across the room and was appalled by the sight that greeted her: red eyes and nose and scraggly hair. She was probably the most unattractive thing she'd ever seen. But there wasn't much she could do about it, and she didn't want Eric to leave. He just might make the rest of the day bearable. Shrugging, she said, "Okay, Clarice. Tell him I'll be down in a minute, but warn him I look like the wrath of God."

Carol crawled out of bed and got a robe out of the closet. She tried to do something with her hair, but it was hopeless, so she simply cinched the robe tightly around her waist and went out into the hall to the stairs.

Later she wouldn't be able to tell anyone exactly what had happened. Perhaps she had been woozy from the medication and either misjudged the first step or lost her balance. Whatever, she took one step down and pitched forward, as though she had been tackled. Instinct made her grab for the banister, but she missed it. Tumbling end over end to the foot of the stairs, she landed with her right leg twisted under her. She let out a yelp of pain.

The noise brought Eric running. Finding her in a crumpled heap at the foot of the stairs sent shock waves through him. He hurried to kneel beside her. "Carol! What in blazes...?"

Dazed, Carol couldn't answer for a minute. Then she grimaced and said, "I...fell."

"Down the stairs?"

She nodded.

"Good God! What happened?"

"I...don't know. I just went down."

"Here, let me give you a hand." He noticed the robe, the uncombed hair, the face free of makeup. "Clarice said you weren't dressed for company, but were you in bed?" he asked incredulously.

"Uh-huh. My allergy's acting up, so Lesley made me stay in."

"I wondered why you two weren't at the rink."

"We didn't think you were coming today."

"I hadn't planned to, but I got through with that other business early. Come on, upsy daisy."

Carol reached and felt his firm grip, but when he tried to pull her up, she yelped again and fell back down. "Oh, God, it's my knee," she whimpered. Tears streamed down her face. "It hurts like crazy."

Eric's eyes widened. "Your knee? Geez, Carol, I... Come on, let me carry you back to your bed."

Effortlessly he lifted her into his arms and carried her up the stairs. In spite of the pain, Carol managed to notice how nice it felt to be cradled in his arms. When they reached the second floor, Eric paused. "Which is your room?"

She pointed, and he carried her to the bed. "See if you can stand up on your own."

He set her on her feet, but the knee gave way, and she clutched him for support. Then she looked up at him with eyes like a cornered fawn's and shook her head. "Eric, when I went down...I definitely heard a pop."

Her knee of all things. That was scary, damned scary. "Maybe you're just feeling reflected pain...or something."

"It's my knee. I know it's my knee."

"I hope you're wrong, but I guess we should be thankful you didn't break your neck. Where's Lesley?"

"She's out running errands. Oh, God, it hurts!"

"You'd better lie down." He eased her onto the bed. "Which knee is it?"

"The right one."

"Let me look at it." Carefully he rolled up her pajama leg, then let out a whistle. "It's swelling."

"Beautiful. Just beautiful."

"Well, I know one thing—ice first, then heat. And elevate that leg. Here, I'll do it for you. You lie flat." Taking both bed pillows, he gently placed them under her knee. "Where's Clarice?"

"I don't know. Maybe outside."

"I'm going to go find her and get an ice bag. Don't get up and hop around or anything."

Carol's chin quivered. "Very funny," she said. Any other time she would have been basking in the warmth of Eric's solicitous attention, but this wasn't any other time. She had hurt her knee, and that scared her more than she would have admitted to anyone.

She sneezed and groped for a tissue. At least her knee had taken her mind off her blasted allergy.

An hour later, Lesley and Eric hovered at Carol's bedside, looking good and worried. The knee had swollen to the size of a softball. "I'm going to call Dr. Bancroft," Lesley said. "This isn't something we should fool around with."

Carol sobbed. "I can't believe anyone could be so stupid. Who falls down stairs, for Pete's sake?"

"Hey, it was a freak accident," Eric said. "They happen all the time. Maybe you didn't hurt it as badly as we think." He swallowed hard and reached out to stroke her hand.

"I can't forget hearing that pop," Carol said. "I think I've done something bad to it."

Lesley went into her bedroom to call Ralph Bancroft. A sports medicine specialist who well knew what a knee injury could mean to an athlete, he insisted on seeing Carol immediately. A few hours later, after Dr. Bancroft had viewed the X rays, he faced Lesley, Carol and Eric. "First, I'm going to have to drain that knee. There's a lot of fluid on it. Then I want an orthopedic surgeon to have a look at it."

"Surgery?" Carol cried.

"You've torn cartilage and ligaments in that knee. That's going to have to be fixed," Dr. Bancroft said, confirming Lesley's worst suspicions.

"A scar?" Carol asked.

"Orthoscopic surgery doesn't leave a scar. There'll be three tiny pinholes in your knee that only you will know are there. You'll be as gorgeous as ever."

"Oh, I don't believe this! How long will I be out of commission?"

"Not long," the doctor said. "You'll probably be up hobbling around on crutches in no time. And you'll have to wear a brace for a while."

"Hobbling on crutches? A brace? Doctor, I can't hobble! I've got to skate."

"First we get the knee fixed. The surgeon can tell you far more than I can. I'm going to try to get him to see you right away."

Carol looked at Eric, her face a portrait of despair. "Why did this have to happen? I can fall on the ice a hundred times without hurting myself."

He smiled and made an attempt at levity. "But you were taught how to fall on the ice. No one ever taught you how to fall down stairs."

She pulled a face. "Do you know something? You're a regular comedian."

DR. HILLMAN, the orthopedic surgeon, told Dr. Bancroft to send Carol right over. He turned out to be a diminutive man who had a ready smile and exuded confidence. He more than anyone made her relax. He agreed that she needed surgery, the sooner the better. "But I've done hundreds of these things. I'm the best knee fixer west of the Mississippi."

Naturally Carol wanted to know how long it would be before she could skate again.

"Hard to say," the doctor told her. "You'll be up and about in no time after the surgery, but it'll be on crutches, and you'll have to wear a brace, then go to physical therapy. No one can predict how you'll mend, Carol. The knee is not a very stable joint to begin with. Some athletes bounce right back from this kind of injury and never have any trouble again. Some never come back. I wish I could give you some sort of guarantee, but I just can't."

"I'll come back," Carol said with a lift of her chin. "I have to."

"With that attitude, you probably will."

The surgery was scheduled for Friday morning. In the meantime, she was to keep the leg elevated, and when she moved around it had to be on crutches. She was also given a prescription for her pain, which was intense. It was a very unhappy young woman whom Lesley and Eric drove back to the house.

When they had gotten her settled on the sofa in the game room, Lesley picked up the phone to try to contact Matt. She didn't hold out much hope she would be successful, but because of the two-hour time difference, he had already returned to the hotel and was changing for a night out with several Hamilton House executives. The news about Carol shook him.

"Should I cut this short and come home?" was his first question.

"When were you planning to leave?" Lesley asked.

"Thursday afternoon."

"Then don't change your plans. Carol checks into the hospital at three on Thursday. Surgery is scheduled for Friday morning."

"Tell him not to worry about me," Carol called from across the room. "I'm fine."

"She says not to worry about her," Lesley told Matt. "She's fine. Well, not fine exactly, but pretty good, all things considered."

"Lesley, she . . . is going to be all right, isn't she?"

"There's . . . every reason to think so."

The slight hesitancy in her voice alarmed him. "You know what I mean. The knee. Skating."

"The chances are good. Matt, I haven't called her mother yet. I suppose I should as soon as I hang up."

There was a pause. Then Matt said, "Better let me do it. As strange as it seems, I can handle Olivia better than anyone. She doesn't take life's bumps in the road very well."

"All right," Lesley said offhandedly. Actually, she was enormously relieved. She had not yet had the pleasure of meeting Olivia Bannister, and she didn't think a phone call informing her of Carol's injury would be the best way to get acquainted. "Whatever you think is best."

"Lesley, how are you?"

"Me? I'm all right. Upset about Carol, of course, but other than that, I'm fine."

"I miss you."

"I miss you, too."

"It seems longer than three days."

"Yes, it does."

"Tell Carol to keep her chin up, and I'll see both of you Thursday."

"I'm sure we'll be at the hospital when you get in. Come as soon as you can."

"Sure. Goodbye, Lesley."

"Goodbye, Matt."

Lesley replaced the receiver and glanced across the room. "Your dad thought it best if he was the one to call your mom," she told Carol.

"He's probably right." Carol rolled her eyes. "Anything involving doctors sends Mom into full swivel panic. I hope she isn't going to go into a dither over this."

It was a useless hope. An hour or so later, Clarice ushered a very distraught Olivia into the game room. Carol's mother was dressed to the nines in a beautiful turquoise suit. Lesley didn't imagine she was the type of woman who ever got caught in jeans and a floppy shirt. "Oh, baby!" Olivia cried, rushing to Carol's side and ignoring everyone else. "I got here as soon as I could. Your father had to track me down at the club. I'm so horrified over all this."

Carol lifted her cheek to accept her mother's kiss. "I'm okay, Mom, really I am. Don't worry."

"'Okay'? 'Don't worry'? How can I possibly not worry when you're going to have to undergo surgery?" She studied her daughter's knee. "I thought it would be swollen."

"It was. Dr. Bancroft drained it."

"Oh, my poor baby! Did it hurt?"

"Sure it hurt, but just for a minute."

"Are you going to be disfigured?"

"No. Orthoscopic surgery doesn't leave a scar."

"Thank God for that, at least." Olivia dabbed at her eyes, then finally took notice of the other two people in the room.

Eric had gotten to his feet. "Hello, Mrs. Bannister."

"Oh . . . hello, Eric," Olivia said distractedly.

Lesley stepped forward. "Mrs. Bannister, I don't think we've ever actually met, but I remember you from a weekend gathering here many years ago. I'm Lesley Salazar."

"Yes, yes, the Kellys' daughter. Matt told me who you were. Can you please tell me what actually happened here?"

"Well, I wasn't at home when it happened, but—"

"No one can tell you what actually happened, Mom," Carol interrupted. "I don't even know what happened. My allergy was acting up, so I was staying in bed today. Lesley had gone out to run some errands. Eric stopped by, and I was coming downstairs to see him, and . . . I fell. It's as simple as that."

Olivia put a hand to her temple. "I knew I shouldn't have let you move out of the house. I don't know how I let your father talk me into it."

Lesley stiffened. She and Eric exchanged pointed glances.

"Mom, it could have happened anywhere," Carol said quickly. "It was an accident."

Olivia sighed dramatically. "Well, I'm certainly sorry it had to be this way, but I suppose this puts an end to the skating."

"No!" Carol, Eric and Lesley all exclaimed in unison.

Lesley hastened to explain. "Mrs. Bannister, there's every reason to believe Carol will be able to return to the ice. Athletes suffer injuries like this all the time. Dr. Bancroft says—"

"That's something else," Olivia said. "I really would prefer that Carol see our family physician."

"But Dr. Bancroft is a sports medicine specialist, Mom," Carol said, "and I really like him. I like Dr. Hillman, too. He's the one who's going to do the surgery. I couldn't get better care. Please, everything's going to be just fine. Let's just . . . leave things as they are. Lesley and Eric are looking after me real good, and I'd . . . like to stay here."

Olivia seemed to have a hard time accepting that, and Lesley understood. What mother would like hearing that her daughter preferred another household to her own? It would have been easier on Olivia, Lesley reflected, if she had made some attempt to learn more about the life of a skater. She recalled the years she had lived with her own coach, how liberating it had been to be around people who were as interested in her career as she was, who understood its ups and downs and even its injuries. She suspected her mother had actually been relieved that the household could stop revolving around her demanding schedule. But Olivia just wasn't bent along the same lines as Alicia Kelly.

Olivia stayed about half an hour, and it was an uncomfortable half hour. Lesley was only too glad to see it end. She knew, of course, that Olivia disapproved of the skating, but she had a feeling the disapproval also extended to her, to Matt, to Eric, to everything that currently made up Carol's world. Her manner implied that the accident wouldn't possibly have happened if Carol had been living at home, which was absurd, but still it bothered Lesley greatly.

As soon as Olivia had left, Carol breathed an audible sigh of relief. "I know, I know, I shouldn't let Mom get to me, but she does, she just does. She always has. I'll be so glad when Dad gets back. I always feel better able to cope with Mom when Dad's around."

"She's concerned about you, Carol," Lesley said. She wasn't sure why she felt the need to defend Olivia. The woman had stopped just short of being downright rude to both herself and Eric, but she was Carol's mother, and that counted for something. "How's the allergy?"

"Not too bad. I'd almost forgotten about it."

"For the next two days you've got to baby that knee, beginning right now. I'm going to go get your dinner and bring it to you on a tray. You, too, Eric."

Eric jumped to his feet. "Thanks, Lesley, but I'm going to have to pass. My mom and dad have been nagging me about never coming over, so I promised I'd have dinner with them tonight. I've really got to go." He turned to Carol and took one of her hands in his, rubbing it gently. "You behave yourself, and I'll see you tomorrow." Then, in a surprising move, he bent and placed a very light kiss on her very startled mouth.

Lesley walked him to the door. When she returned to the game room, she found a bemused Carol with her fingertips pressed to her lips and a dreamy look on her face.

"Carol?"

Carol looked up, wide-eyed. "Did you see that? He actually kissed me, just like I was female or something."

Lesley chuckled. "I'm quite sure Eric knows you're female. And I know he sympathizes with you about the knee. He probably feels very close to you right now. I'm sure he knows how he would have felt if the same thing had happened to him in his amateur days."

Carol digested that for a minute, and a slow smile spread across her face. "I probably shouldn't say this because the thing with the knee really is a bummer, but if Eric keeps being so nice to me, it might almost have been worth it."

"Don't say that, Carol!" Lesley exclaimed. "Please, don't say that."

She was thinking of something Dr. Hillman had told her earlier when she managed to have a private word with the surgeon. He'd said, "All athletes fear a knee injury and for good reason. I once had patient who was a football player. The man looked as though he could bench press the team bus, but he burst out crying when I told him his knee would require surgery. And those tears weren't unfounded. He never played again."

That couldn't happen to Carol. It just couldn't!

FROM THE TIME he got out of bed Thursday morning until his plane touched down at San Francisco International, Matt operated at a dead run. He didn't bother going home or to the office but headed straight for the hospital. When he arrived, Carol had already been admitted and was getting settled in her room. Lesley and Eric were there, too, and a minute later Dr. Bancroft showed up. There wasn't much Matt could do but give his daughter a hug and a few sympathetic words, though his impulse had been to hug Lesley first.

Fifteen minutes later, after the doctor had left, Matt seized the chance to talk to Lesley in semiprivacy.

"Eric, are you going to be sticking around for a while?"

"Yes, sir. The invalid apparently needs her lackey at her side."

"Lesley, will you come downstairs and have a cup of coffee with me?"

"I'd love one."

A minute later they were alone in an elevator, and between the fourth and third floors he managed to embrace her tightly and give her a sound kiss. "God, I'm glad to see you!" he exclaimed.

"And I you." During the remainder of their downward trip, they giggled like a pair of teenagers, overcome with delight at being with each other again.

But in the basement coffee shop, Matt turned serious. "God, I hate these places! I hate the whole idea of doctors and surgery and anesthetic. I don't even like bandages!"

Lesley smiled. "I don't guess anyone likes hospitals, particularly not when someone you love is in one."

Matt reached across the table and took one of her hands. "Tell me the truth about the knee. Is it going to be all right?"

"I've told you everything I know, Matt, but you have to be realistic. When I was skating, I saw so many skaters with injuries. Some comebacks were dramatic, almost unbelievable, but there were other injuries that meant the end of careers. You just never know. We'd be foolish not to consider the possibility that Carol might not compete again." She looked away, then back at him. "There! I said it."

Matt shook his head. "I don't know what she would do. I honestly don't."

"She wouldn't wither away and die, you can be sure of that. Of course it would be difficult for her—heartbreaking—but the human constitution is a wonderful thing. We do what we have to do."

"I don't know, Lesley. Maybe Olivia was right all along. I might have done Carol a disservice. She missed growing up like a regular kid, having dates, all the things that other kids take for granted. Maybe I should have encouraged her to begin college last fall, to pursue other interests along with her skating."

"If she had pursued many 'other interests,' she wouldn't be an Olympic contender. You wouldn't have been able to dissuade her, anyway, not after a certain point had been reached. Remember, I lived the same life Carol has. Do you find anything wrong with the way I turned out?"

His gray eyes warmed. "You know the answer to that, but this accident has really hit me. In all the years Carol has been skating, it never once occurred to me that she could get injured anywhere but on the ice. Not once. I'll admit I'm worried as hell."

"We're all worried, Matt, but let's not conjure up monsters. The possibility that this will be damaging to her career exists, but chances are a lot better that she'll be back on the ice one of these days. Let's think positively."

"You're right, of course. It's not like me to look on the dark side of things, but I've been so tied up in this skating for so long now."

Lesley sipped at the coffee, which she didn't want to begin with. She set down the cup and asked, "How was Dallas?"

"It's still there."

"Was your meeting with Vanessa successful, or whatever?" She really didn't know enough about his corporate life to ask intelligent questions. To date their chief link, other than their mutual attraction, had been Carol.

For reasons he didn't completely understand, Matt wasn't yet ready to tell Lesley about Vanessa's search for her successor. "Yes, it was . . . informative."

"You look awfully tired."

"I am."

"And it's a long drive home."

"That it is, but I have to go. If surgery's scheduled for ten tomorrow, that'll give me time to stop by the office before I come back here."

Lesley glanced down at her hands for a minute. Ah, yes, the office. It had been on the tip of her tongue to ask him to spend the night at her house, to spare him the drive tonight and another one in the morning. She honestly didn't think she'd had romance on her mind. Matt looked too tired to manage a passionate kiss, much less anything else. Now she was glad she hadn't issued the invitation. He wouldn't have accepted anyway, and she certainly wouldn't have wanted him to miss an opportunity to stop by the office. . . .

Don't be bitchy, Lesley. The man is the boss, and he's been gone all week. There are probably a thousand tiny details that only he can take care of. Matt's devoted to his work. You've never known a man who wasn't.

Lesley pushed her cup away. "More?" Matt asked, and she shook her head.

"Why don't you run up and say good night to Carol, then be on your way? If anyone ever looked like he needed a good night's sleep, you do. I'll hang around until the nurses run me off."

Matt nodded, stood and held her chair. "I'd like to hang around, too, but in another hour I won't be worth killing. Damn, it's still hard for me to accept that this has happened to Carol. When I left last Sunday, this certainly wasn't the way I envisioned my homecoming."

"Same here." She got to her feet and felt the comforting pressure of his hand on the small of her back as they left the coffee shop. "This has been such a setback for Carol, and young people don't take setbacks well. You and I have been around long enough to have learned to roll with the punches. I'm just sorry it was Carol who got punched."

ON THE FOURTH FLOOR Eric paced restlessly outside Carol's room. A nurse had come and politely requested that he leave for a few minutes while she did whatever it was she had come to do. The young man felt agitated and exhausted, mostly from the strain of keeping up appearances for Carol's sake these past couple of days. Under no circumstances did he want her knowing how worried he was. She was worried enough for both of them, though she was making a valiant effort to disguise it behind that trademark sassiness of hers.

Eric wondered if Carol's dad had any inkling of how serious the injury could be. Surely Lesley did, although the two of them hadn't discussed it. The minute Carol had told him she thought she'd hurt her knee, his heart had sunk to the pit of his stomach. He'd immediately thought of Kevin Riley, for years his younger, friendly rival. As far back as 1985, rinkside gossips had it that "Zito would get his medal first, then Riley four years later." But 1992 would be just another year for Kevin, thanks to a freak collision with another skater. Two knee operations later, Kevin had been told to hang up his skates. Eric had seen so damned many careers ended by injuries, almost always ankles or knees, and Carol was just too good to have to be put out to pasture.

He walked to a window and stared out. A light rain had begun to fall. He thought it was odd that in all the years he had known Carol, all those years of training under the same coach, he'd never fully realized her potential until he'd begun working with her on a personal basis. Now he could see that she was pure pleasure to work with—bright, eager and skilled. She listened to instruction and learned from it. She seemed to hang on his every word as though they were carved in stone on a mountaintop—Lesley's, too. Carol absorbed, reached, grew. Beyond that, she was the most pleasant person imaginable to be around. No temper, no stomping off the ice in a fit of pique when things weren't going right.

Many times in his life Eric had experienced a twinge or two of guilt that the lion's share of Sondra's attention had been reserved for him, but Carol had been such a quiet little thing with years ahead of her, while he had been heading toward the now-or-never point. The press had liked to call him "focused." Looking back, he thought there were times when "self-centered" might have been more accurate, but maybe it had to be that way when one was going for the gold. Still, in some vague, nebulous way, helping Carol get her medal was his way of apologizing to her.

If she never got her chance, he knew he would regret it the rest of his life.

He heard high heels clicking along the polished corridor, and he turned to see Lesley and Matt walking toward him. "There's a nurse in there with her right now," Eric told them. "She said it wouldn't take long."

Lesley touched Matt on the arm. "Just go on. I'll give Carol your excuses. I don't imagine they're going to let us stay with her very late."

Matt hesitated for a second, then relented. He was dead on his feet and wanted to be rested and alert tomorrow. "I think I will. I'll see both of you here in the morning."

"Good night, Matt."

"Good night, Mr. Logan."

He waved as he strode away from them. Just then the nurse came out of Carol's room, smiled and nodded to them. Almost simultaneously the meal wagon came to a halt in front of the door, and an orderly carried a tray into the room. Eric turned to Lesley. "When we have to leave, would you have dinner with me? I want to talk to you—about Carol and the knee."

"Okay, come to the house, and we'll have Clarice fix us something. I want to talk to you, too."

"About Carol?"

"Of course. What else do any of us have on our minds right now?" But Lesley cast one longing glance in the direction of Matt's departing figure.

CHAPTER TEN

IT WAS VERY LATE when Eric left Lesley's house that night. She expected to sleep like a rock; instead, she slept fitfully and woke unusually early the next morning. Sitting up in bed, she pulled her knees to her chest and hugged them. It seemed almost unconscionable to be thinking of anyone but Carol, but she had the utmost confidence in her student's doctors. And the accident, the upcoming surgery, all of that was totally out of her hands.

So at the moment her thoughts were all on Matt. Caution be damned. She could live with his devotion to duty. She wanted him, and he wanted her. It was time to get their relationship off dead center, and sometimes that required a strong push.

Carol, darling, I'm sorry you're hurting. I'm very sorry you're in the hospital, you know that, but you are, and that means you won't be home for a few nights, so please forgive me for taking advantage of your misfortune by finally attempting to seduce your father.

Attempting? She really didn't anticipate having any difficulty.

Jumping out of bed, Lesley stripped off the linens and replaced them with fresh ones of sea-foam green, then dropped the used ones down the laundry chute as she made her way downstairs. Clarice was already in the kitchen.

"Good morning, ma'am," the maid said, her expression registering surprise. "You're up and about awfully early."

"I couldn't sleep." Lesley momentarily had second thoughts about what she was doing, then dismissed them. "Clarice, Carol won't be coming home until Monday morning. There really won't be much to do around here—I won't even be here most of the time, and the house is already almost antiseptic—so I'm thinking that this weekend would be a perfect time for you to go visit your sister in Bakersfield. I know you don't get to see her very often. Would you like that?"

"Well, yes, of course, I'd like that, and so would she—" Clarice stopped and shook her head. "No, no, I don't want to leave you alone."

"Oh, don't be ridiculous. I'm not in the least afraid. You really should grab at this chance, Clarice. It may be the last you'll have for some time." Lesley prayed the woman wasn't going to take her role as the family retainer too seriously.

"Well, I . . . If you're sure. . . ."

"Of course I'm sure. It's settled, then. Why don't you call her? Now, I think I'll bathe and dress before breakfast this morning. I want to be sure and get to the hospital early enough to see Carol before she goes into surgery."

"Yes, ma'am. I guess I'll leave shortly after breakfast. Will you be sure to tell Carol that I'm thinking about her?"

"I'll do that, and I hope you and your sister have a wonderful weekend." *And I hope I do, too.*

Her plan formulated, Lesley went back to being concerned about Carol.

AT A QUARTER TO TEN they all filed into the surgical ward's waiting room, a worried, anxious lot. Each of them had been able to have a word with Carol earlier, but she had been pretty out of it, blessedly so. Matt, who hadn't undergone surgery or even been admitted to a hospital since he'd had his tonsils out, could think of nothing worse than just lying there, waiting to be wheeled off on a gurney. He was grateful that Carol had been sedated.

Now there was nothing to do but wait. Lesley crossed the room and took a seat in front of a window; Eric and Matt sat down on either side of her. Olivia and Louis chose to sit on the other side of the room. Louis looked very starched and dapper in his three-piece business suit. Olivia was wearing a stunning red outfit with a fur-trimmed collar. The Bannisters seemed uncomfortable, and when a decidedly untidy man in dirty jeans and a T-shirt sat down only one chair away, Lesley saw Olivia flinch.

On Lesley's left, Matt propped an ankle on one knee and picked up a copy of *Business Week*. On her right, Eric was already engrossed in *Sports Illustrated*. She discovered that nowhere on earth could time drag more interminably than in a surgical waiting room. Everyone in the place wore the dazed expression that fear and worry elicit. She stared straight ahead, dwelling on her scheme for tonight, even enjoying the anticipation. Then she remembered where she was, what was transpiring, and was immediately ashamed of herself. With considerable effort, she forced her thoughts along a different line—to last night's conversation with Eric.

They had arrived at her house far later than she had thought they would. Clarice had put together an impromptu supper for them, which Lesley had served at the bar in the game room. Without much preamble, the talk had turned to Carol, the knee, and what if. What if the worse happened?

"I'll tell you what I'm not going to do," Eric had said. "I'm not going to give her all that garbage about skating not being the most important thing in the world. It is the most important thing to her right now, just as it was to me when I was two years away from my medal. I'm not going to insult her intelligence, and if she needs to wallow in self-pity for a while, she's earned that right. I'll give her a week or two."

"And then?" Lesley wanted to know.

"And then…then I'll find something for her to do. Don't ask me what it will be, but I'll think of something. For some reason, she seems to listen to me."

For some reason. Lesley thought how incredible it was that Eric apparently had no idea that Carol's feelings for him went beyond friendship. She was a great little actress, exuding all that casual camaraderie when Eric was around, but to Lesley, who knew her true feelings, it seemed that adoration positively oozed from Carol's pores. Sooner or later something would have to give. Carol wouldn't be satisfied with simply worshiping him from afar, and skating wouldn't always be the grand passion of her life. No matter how brilliant her career turned out to be, someday she would probably want to be a wife and mother. If Eric never returned her feelings, Carol would find some-

one else. It was inevitable; the hormones demanded it.
Lesley thought how sad it would be to see the end of
what truly was a remarkable relationship.

But for now, Carol was very fortunate to have Eric.
He would be someone to lean on if, heaven forbid, Dr.
Hillman had to tell her that her competitive days were
over.

The surgeon said no such thing, however. After
what seemed an eternity of waiting, Matthew and
Olivia were summoned by a nurse. Carol was out of
surgery, and Dr. Hillman wanted to speak with her
parents. To Lesley it seemed that the conference with
the doctor took far longer than Carol's surgery had.
When Matt finally returned to the waiting room, she
and Eric jumped to their feet. Lesley's pent-up breath
was released at last. He was all smiles, so the news had
to be good.

"Carol's fine, and the surgery went off without a
hitch," he told them.

"Thank God!" Lesley exclaimed.

"Amen," Eric said. "When can we see her?"

"She'll be in recovery awhile. The doctor suggested
we have lunch, then come back. She'll probably be in
her room by then."

At that moment, Olivia entered the waiting room,
and Carol's mother's eyes were flashing. She immediately accosted Matt. "I can't believe that the first
thing you asked that doctor about was the skating."

"Not the first thing, Olivia," Matt said patiently.
"The first thing I asked him was how Carol was, if the
surgery had been successful."

"I do believe skating is all you people think about."
Then Olivia fastened the three of them with an icy

stare. "I certainly hope I can depend on all of you to proceed with caution and keep Carol off skates until the knee is completely mended. Come on, Louis." She swept out as haughtily as she had swept in.

Matt uttered a sound of disgust. "That woman tries my patience to the snapping point. My God, does she think we don't want Carol's knee to be like new?" He took Lesley by the arm. "Let's go have some lunch. I could barely choke down coffee and toast at breakfast, but now I could eat a horse."

LESLEY, MATT AND ERIC devoted the day to Carol, who seemed grateful for the attention, but by the time the dinner wagon rolled to a stop at her door, it had occurred to Matt that his daughter would be even more grateful if he and Lesley left her alone with Eric.

There had been a subtle change in the relationship between the two young people. Matt thought he had detected it the previous afternoon and was sure he had today. They seemed to have established a deeper rapport than had existed before. The prelude to something more profound? It was hard to say at this point. They still teased and exchanged wisecracks, but something had changed. He wondered if Lesley had seen it.

Thinking her name made him look across the room at her. There had been a subtle change in her, too. He hadn't noticed anything last night, but Lesley sure as hell had been acting funny all day. Once they'd been told that Carol was all right, she'd seemed preoccupied, as though her thoughts were far removed from her surroundings. What was on her mind?

Then it came to him. This was one night when neither of them had other obligations or other people to consider. They could be alone! That thought brought him to his feet. He crossed the room to Carol's bedside.

"Honey, will you be offended if Lesley and I leave now? I think I'd like to take the lady to dinner."

"No, of course not, Dad. You two run along. Eric's staying." Her eyes flew to the young man seated in the chair next to the bed. "Aren't you?"

Eric nodded. "Until they run me off."

Matt bent and placed a kiss on Carol's forehead. "We'll see you in the morning. You do everything they tell you to do, hear?"

"Sure. Good night, Dad. 'Night, Lesley."

"Good night, Carol," Lesley said. "Is there anything I can bring you from home when I come tomorrow?"

"I don't think so. I won't be here long, thank God. You guys have a good time."

Matt took Lesley by the arm and led her out of the room, closing the door behind them. "Was I being presumptuous in assuming you'd have dinner with me?"

"Not at all." She took a deep breath and set her plan in motion. "But wouldn't it be so much nicer to have dinner at home?"

He wasn't much interested in a noisy restaurant, either. "Yes, it would. Your place or mine?"

"Mine. It's closer."

"Fine. I'll meet you there. I had to park at the far end of the lot." Matt punched the Down button at the elevators.

"If I'm not there when you get there, just wait. I have a stop to make."

"That's all right. Clarice will let me in."

"Clarice... isn't there. She's spending the weekend with her sister in Bakersfield."

Gray eyes locked with green ones. Lesley offered him a beguiling smile. "I thought it would be a good time for her to take a few days off. She... works so hard, you know."

All of Matt's senses soared. His pulse hammered so frantically in his temples he was sure she could see it. "What a thoughtful gesture."

"I wondered if you would approve."

"Indeed. Yes, indeed I do."

The elevator doors opened with a whoosh, and they stepped inside the crowded conveyance.

ON THE WAY HOME Lesley stopped at a favorite take-out gourmet shop, where she bought bread, wine and cheese, some slices of their delicious country pâté, chicken kiev and a generous wedge of a sinful chocolate torte. Knowing Clarice, there would be plenty of salad makings in the fridge, and even Lesley could boil rice to serve with the chicken. Gathering up her precious purchases, she headed for home, where she found Matt seated on the front steps.

"A feast fit for a grand occasion," she announced, indicating the sack she carried.

"Oh?" His smile was warm and engaging. "What's the occasion?"

"The success of Carol's operation, of course."

"Of course." He relieved her of the sack so that she could unlock the door. Matt had never been in the kitchen, but it went with the house—spacious, with a large island in the center of the room and every conceivable built-in appliance. Lesley put everything but the loaf of crusty bread into the refrigerator, then turned to him. Her eyes were as bright and alive as he'd ever seen them.

"Wine?" she asked.

"No, I don't think so."

"A drink, then?"

"No."

"It's a bit early to eat, don't you think?"

"Yes."

For a long, tantalizing moment they did nothing but stare at each other. Finally one of them—Lesley wasn't sure who—moved, galvanizing the other. The space between them disappeared. Lesley's arms crept up his chest, and her hands locked behind his neck. Their kiss was searing. When Lesley stepped back slightly, Matt reached behind him for one of her hands and brought it to his lips. "You went to some trouble to arrange this. I can't thank you enough."

"It was no trouble, I assure you."

"Tell me I'm not jumping to one hell of a conclusion."

"You aren't."

"We're alone for the first time. No one on earth but you knows where I am tonight. I am...unreachable. I think we should take advantage of that, don't you?"

Lesley melted against him again. "Two great minds with but a single thought. I'll bet you and I would even agree on what time to leave a party and where to set a thermostat."

Matt cupped her face tenderly and rained a shower of kisses over it. Lesley gloried in the onslaught. Then, when he lifted his head, she took him by the hand and led him out of the kitchen to the stairs.

The blinds in Lesley's room were open, the drapes drawn aside. Outside it was dusk. The room was bathed in soft shadows, but Matt could see that it was very like her. Everything in it was incredibly feminine and small-scale, everything but the bed, which was a huge brass affair covered with a thick comforter. She immediately crossed to it and pulled down the cover, folding it neatly at the foot of the bed, then held out a hand to him. Without a word, he walked to her, and they embraced.

"Lesley." He said her name reverently as he nuzzled her neck. "Do you believe in fate?"

"If I didn't before, I do now."

"I still find it incredible that I met you sixteen long years ago and never entirely forgot you. How you insinuated yourself in my subconscious."

"You have no idea how long I thought about you after that weekend. I even got good at pretending you weren't married. I'd never met an exciting man before."

"And you thought I was exciting?"

"Very. I still do." With an assertiveness she had displayed few times in her life, Lesley kissed him in a way that eliminated all but one thought. "I want you," she said huskily.

"Well, you can have me," Matt crooned in her ear, "because, God knows, I want you, too."

Lesley sighed in utter contentment, molding herself against him while he caressed her. His hands were gentle and his mouth roamed over her face. She felt weak, pliable and moist, growing ever softer against his hardness. They held each other for several minutes, sharing kisses, each one hungrier than the last. Then they stepped apart and helped each other peel off their clothes until there were no barriers between them. Matt never took his eyes off her as his hands once again became sensuous and commanding instruments. Silently, they began the pleasurable ritual of discovering how to love each other.

It was always exciting, Matt thought, to discover what pleased a woman. And this time the excitement was even more pronounced because the woman he longed to please was Lesley. Her breasts were very sensitive, he noticed, and he took advantage of that new knowledge until her entire body seemed to throb. He searched his brain for all the hot, erotic phrases, all the sensuous moves a man perfected during the course of the years. Nothing seemed adequate to convey the desire he felt. He was desperate to have her, yet he forced himself to settle for kisses and caresses until she was ready.

Lesley thought how wonderfully intriguing his utter masculinity was—his broad chest, narrow hips and muscular legs, the dark hair matted in brushy clumps. He was an admirable, fascinating physical specimen. Her restless hands roamed over his body; whatever she touched she wanted to kiss. From the sounds he made deep in his throat, she knew she was driving him senseless, and it seemed she had only begun exploring his mysteries when he gently lifted her and placed her on the bed, then moved over her.

Hot and hard, Matt proceeded with an exploration of his own, using not only his fingers but his lips and tongue. Lesley tingled from head to foot. The texture of her skin changed. No longer silky smooth, it was on fire with aroused sensitivity. She gasped and moaned, inspiring him to discover new ways of pleasuring her. He kissed and stroked every inch of her—nipping, biting, teasing, sucking. Her body rose and fell, and just when she thought she was as close to ecstasy as it was possible to get, he entered her, and the natural rhythms took over. Lesley ached for release but couldn't bear to have it end. It was only when their passion bordered on agony that they gave in. One final thrust was all it took. The resulting explosion was violent.

Lesley lay weak and sated in his arms, savoring the feeling of release. Never before had she felt such a sense of completeness after lovemaking. "That was won-der-ful," she cooed.

"Something else we agree on," Matt said lazily. "It was like we were made for each other. You fit real good."

"Fit or felt?"

"Both. But I knew you would."

Lesley sighed. "I didn't want it to end."

"Well, I'm quite sure we'll find ourselves similarly occupied many times."

"That gives me something to look forward to." Lesley raised up on one elbow. The room was quite dark by now. She smiled down at Matt. "How many times did you think about me while you were in Dallas?"

"Lord, Lesley, there was hardly a minute when I wasn't thinking about you."

She glanced across Matt's prone form at the clock on the bedside table. "It's past the cocktail hour, and I spent a tiny fortune on our dinner tonight. I wanted to impress you to death, which I never could have with my own cooking."

"You could have opened a can of soup. I didn't come here for food for my stomach, just food for my soul."

She lay down again, this time with her head on his chest. She could feel the steady thumping of his heart, and she smiled against his skin. "I've wanted this since that first night we had dinner together."

"So have I."

Lesley sighed. "It's age, I guess. Sixteen years ago I would have been shocked to know I would deliberately send a servant packing for the express purpose of luring a man into my bed. But *tempus fugit*, and you have to seize the moment."

"This is no moment. This is the beginning of hours, days, weeks, years."

Lesley wanted to believe that. She wanted to believe it wasn't pent-up frustration on either's part. She had to believe that this was the beginning of a relationship that went beyond this room, this night.

"I was afraid I might have rushed you," Matt confessed.

She chuckled. "Funny. I was thinking the same thing . . . that I might have rushed you."

Silence descended for a minute. Then Matt tucked her against him and stroked her hair. "Lesley, I want to ask you a question. If you don't want to answer it, just tell me so. It probably isn't important to what we've found together, but I'm curious."

She was puzzled. "Of course, Matt. Ask me anything."

"Not long ago I said something to you that got the most unusual response. I told you that you'd done all right, or something to that effect, and you..."

She sighed. "And I froze. I know."

"You said you took the easy way out. I've wondered many times what that meant."

"It's complicated. It has to do with Arturo."

"I figured as much."

"I met him not long after you and Olivia were here. He was a guest at another weekend soiree—a very important guest. He'd just won his first Pulitzer, and my mother was impressed out of her mind. He was so suave, so debonair. When you looked at him you thought of a Velázquez portrait. He came on to me strong, and nothing like that had ever happened to me. He even sent me flowers. I'd had hundreds of flowers thrown to me after a performance, but no one had ever sent me flowers."

She paused. "Odd that something so insignificant could have impressed me so, but I'm sure you remember that I was not a very sophisticated twenty-four-year-old. You also have to remember that he came along at a bad time... or a good time, depending on the way you want to look at it. All my life there had been someone to take care of me. My parents, of course, then my coach and his family. I didn't know how to relate to other people my own age, except other skaters. When Arturo asked me to marry him, I suppose I thought he was someone older who could look after me. The easy way. And, too, he promised excitement. At least it seemed he did. But I was pitifully out of place with his worldly, artsy crowd. Too late I decided that I should have stayed in skating in some capacity, because that's where I felt at home. When we moved to Denver, I grabbed at coaching like a lifeline. But away from the ice..." She sighed. "However, my choice had been to marry a man who could take care of me, and Arturo did, handsomely. The conflict came when I decided to look after myself a little."

Matt brushed at her hair and kissed her forehead. "You simply learned what we all do sooner or later—that we live with our choices a very long time."

"Yes. It's been hard-won, but now I can take care of myself. That's a good feeling." She raised herself again. "Are we going to lie here philosophizing the night away, or are you going to eat some of that delicious food I bought just for you?"

Matt stirred out of his languor. "I suppose we can resume the philosophizing and...other things after dinner."

AN HOUR LATER, dinner was finished, the dishes were in the dishwasher and the dining room lights were turned off. They carried their coffee down to the game room and sat at opposite ends of the sofa, half turned to each other. Lesley sat with her head on a cushion, her feet tucked under her.

"If we didn't have to go to the hospital tomorrow, what would we do with our first Saturday alone?" she asked.

Matt pursed his lips thoughtfully. "Oh...drive down the coast and have a delicious meal somewhere. I don't know."

"But we at least have some time alone, so it seems a shame to waste this tiny interlude of privacy."

"I couldn't agree more."

"And it seems silly for you to drive home tonight, only to come back in the morning. You'll stay, won't you?"

Matt gave her his uneven smile. "I was definitely thinking about it. There's only one thing—I don't have a razor or a toothbrush with me."

"I have lots of both."

"Then I guess it's settled."

Lesley smiled and buried her head deeper into the cushion. "We've all been so caught up with Carol that we've hardly talked about you at all. Tell me about Dallas."

Matt wondered if it was a good time and decided there probably never would be a better one. Besides, she meant a lot to him, and he wanted to share his news with her. First he explained about Dolph Wade. Then he said, "So Vanessa's on the prowl for her successor, and it seems yours truly is being considered." Try as he might to sound casual, he wasn't able to mask the note of pride in his voice. In spite of his ambivalent feelings about the promotion, he was pleased at being in the running.

A tiny ping went off somewhere in Lesley's head. "President of Hamilton House?"

"Yeah. The top spot. Isn't that something?"

"Yes, it's...really something. That means living in Dallas, right?"

He heard the fear in her voice. "It hasn't happened yet, Lesley. Others are being considered for the position."

Lesley opened her mouth to ask if he would accept the position if it was offered to him, then quickly closed it. Of course he would. Hamilton House would always come first. A heaviness developed in her chest. She knew she should say something upbeat and congratulatory. He had worked hard all these years and deserved to be rewarded for it. But the promotion would mean the end of something that had barely begun. If she congratulated him, it would sound hollow. She had never learned the art of pretending emotion she didn't feel.

"You . . . must be proud of yourself."

"I guess anyone would be."

"Yes, I guess so. When will the decision be made?"

"Vanessa told me she'd decide within a year. Sooner if she took sick."

"And when will that be?" Lesley wouldn't have thought it possible to experience such a drastic mood swing within the space of a few minutes.

"Her birthday's in January." Matt didn't know what he had expected her reaction to be, but it wasn't this, that was for sure.

Lesley was aware that her lack of enthusiasm had put a damper on the earlier mellow mood, and she could have kicked herself. Hadn't she vowed to seize the moment and worry about tomorrow tomorrow? They had months and months ahead of them, so many possibilities, and things would work themselves out. They almost always did.

Removing one leg from beneath her, she stretched it out and touched his thigh with her stockinged foot. "I believe we were discussing your spending the night here."

Matt shook away his thoughts and moved toward her. He curved an arm around her shoulders and pulled her to him so that her head now rested on his chest. Then he tilted her head up and kissed her mouth. "So we were."

"I think I'll take a shower. We might be a bit rushed in the morning."

"Sounds like a splendid idea. Mind if I join you?"

Lesley stirred, getting to her feet. "Turn out the lights. I'll make sure everything's locked up."

Matt followed her up to the bedroom. Within minutes she was in the shower. Quickly he stripped off his clothes, slid aside the glass door and stepped in. Lesley was standing with her face up, her eyes closed and water streaming down her lithe body; she was already soaping herself. He moved behind her and gently pulled her against him, then cupped her breasts and nipped her neck. Suddenly she turned to face him and began lathering him from shoulders to feet. By the time they had rinsed, their desire had reached the boiling point. When Lesley turned off the water, they stepped out and took turns drying each other. Then, wrapped in towels, they dashed into the bedroom and fell upon the rumpled linens.

Though the excitement of discovery was absent this time, the lovemaking was even more satisfying for its familiarity, leaving them spent and exhausted. Lesley curled contentedly in the warm circle of Matt's arm and fell instantly asleep.

For Matt, sleep was more elusive. Earlier they had talked about choices, and for the first time he took a long, objective look at the choices he had made in his own life: ending his marriage, choosing not to remarry, devoting himself to his career and encouraging Carol to do the same. As he had told Lesley earlier, he'd lived with those choices a long time. He was galloping toward the half-century mark, and his proudest possessions up until now were his talented daughter and the title after his name.

He kissed the top of Lesley's head, nestled so comfortably on his shoulder, and pulled the coverlet up over her. For a long time he lay awake, overcome by new thoughts and feelings. Lesley, with seemingly no effort at all, had made him suspect that there might be more to life than Carol's career and his job.

IT WAS A WEEKEND TO REMEMBER. Lesley would always think of it as a time of awakening, as though she had been half-asleep—or half-awake—for far too much of her life. All of her senses seemed to have sharpened, and she was keenly aware of things she'd never bothered to notice before. She and Matt woke late, breakfasted leisurely, then dressed for the drive to the hospital.

An astonishing array of bouquets and plants had been delivered that morning. It was amazing how news got around. Matt had told no one but Helen, but his secretary was a one-woman telegraph service. Hamilton House, San Francisco, had sent a stunning arrangement. So had Hamilton House, Dallas. Joe Hylands, Helen and her husband, Eric's parents and two of Carol's perennial competitors were represented. Apparently Eric had done some word spreading, too. And Vanessa had sent an azalea and a card with a personal note.

As heartwarming as the outpouring of good wishes was, the patient's mood wasn't exactly sunny, which wasn't surprising. Carol had not had a good night, and her knee was giving her a fit. That she was in pain was obvious. "The doctor says I can't go home until I can do without such heavy pain medication," she said, "so I told them to give me only half as much today."

Matt frowned. "It might be too soon, honey. Let them decide what's best for you."

"The doctor also says I'm going to have to wear that brace eight to ten weeks. Can you believe that? Eight to ten weeks!"

"If you have to wear it that long, you'll wear it that long," Lesley said firmly. "We're going to do this by the book."

"Then I have to go to physical therapy." Her face twisted. "At least three months. At least, maybe longer. Everybody heals differently."

That surprised Matt. He hadn't thought she would be off the ice nearly so long. And though he was relieved and grateful that Carol was all right, that the surgery had been successful, he couldn't avoid thinking that she couldn't possibly be ready for next year's nationals. And if the pain and the medication allowed her to think at all, Carol had probably thought that, too.

"What time is it?" Carol asked.

Matt glanced at his watch. "Ten-fifteen. Why?"

"Eric said he'd come have lunch with me. He asked for an extra plate when they came by last night. But that won't be until eleven-thirty."

"Does this mean that Lesley and I aren't enough company for you?"

Carol tried to laugh but couldn't. "Sondra came to see me last night after you and Lesley left."

"Oh? I hope you were nice to her."

"I was. I just went on and on about how great Lesley is. Eric thought I laid it on a little thick." That brought an impish smile to her face. "Then Mom and Louis came by."

"Sounds like you didn't lack for company," Matt remarked.

"No, it was pretty nice. Did you two guys have a good time?"

Lesley had to look away, but Matt kept a perfectly straight face. "Yes, we did."

Somehow the morning passed. Eric showed up shortly before the meal cart did, and the difference in Carol when he was present was dramatic. The pain on her face didn't completely vanish, but it definitely softened somewhat. Matt and Lesley stayed around until they began eating, then took advantage of Eric's presence to slip away for lunch themselves. Neither of them heard Eric's remark to Carol after they'd left.

"Now there is a romance looking for a place to happen," he said, staring at the closed door.

"Dad and Lesley?" Carol asked.

Eric nodded. "Unless the vibes I'm getting are all wrong, they're crazy about each other."

"I wondered. Funny, I can't imagine Dad being crazy about any woman. There's just never been one around who I knew anything about. I guess he was crazy about Mom at one time, but I don't remember it. Now they just seem to have established an uneasy truce because of me."

Mr. Logan being "crazy" about Mrs. Bannister was not a picture that readily came to Eric's mind. He liked Carol's dad real well, but her mom made him jumpy as hell. Every time he'd called at the Bannister house, Olivia had behaved as though he were there to kidnap the princess and hold her for ransom.

"If I were you," he told Carol, "I'd give some thought to maybe having a stepmother."

The medication she was being given every four hours had Carol feeling a bit tipsy...or at least what she imagined being tipsy would feel like. Otherwise, she probably wouldn't have said what she did. "Since when did you become such an expert on developing romances?"

"Hey, I'm not blind. You can see the signs."

"Oh? What are the signs?"

"Just...the way people look at each other. Their body language. They give off an...aura or something."

"'Aura'? Aura? What do you know about romantic auras?"

"I wasn't raised in a cave. And I'm not stupid. Eat your lunch."

"I...guess you've probably had a lot of girl-friends."

He shot her a peculiar look. "Carol, you've known me for eleven years. When would I have found the time to have a lot of girlfriends?"

Carol thought about that and decided he was right. Neither of them had had time to devote to establishing relationships. But it was different for him now, wasn't it? He had time and freedom and money. "What about Elke?" she asked, referring to the Swede he had been rumored to be seeing.

"What did you hear about Elke?"

"Oh . . . just that the two of you are sorta . . . you know."

Eric rolled his eyes. "I don't believe it! A photographer got a shot of us talking to each other backstage at the Challenge of Champions, and suddenly we're an item."

"One of the pitfalls of fame," Carol sniped. "I guess that's what happens to big stars who also happen to be outrageous flirts."

One corner of his mouth lifted in a lopsided grin. "Are you referring to Elke or to me?"

"Guess. You always flirted with the women backstage."

"There's a difference between flirting and being friendly. Since when did you get so interested in my love life?"

"Do you have a love life? I hadn't noticed."

"Seems to me you've been giving it a lot of attention."

Carol realized she had probably said too much. She tried to cover up. "Oh . . . go call your agent or something."

Eric just laughed.

CHAPTER ELEVEN

FOR LESLEY AND MATT, Saturday night was a replay of Friday, with the added thrill of variations played on a theme. He was so skilled, Lesley thought dreamily—tender and demanding all at once. He had taught her that, at forty, there was a great deal about life she had missed. She felt as though she had only been hovering on the brink of womanhood and finally had been released to know its full joys. At last she knew what it was like to touch someone else's soul.

After the lovemaking, they roused themselves sufficiently to go downstairs and think about dinner. While Lesley made a salad and heated up some of Clarice's delicious moussaka, Matt uncorked a bottle of wine.

"I just can't believe it!" Lesley said as they were sitting down to eat.

"Can't believe what, sweetheart?"

"We've had an entire day together, and tomorrow is yet to come."

"I like to think there will be hundreds of such days ahead of us," he said with a smile.

Nice words, but Lesley wondered how valid they would prove to be. He was so busy and no doubt would be even busier now that he had been away from the office so long. She would be busy, too. Getting

Carol back to the top of her form wouldn't be easy after such a long layoff. It seemed more likely that she and Matt would have to content themselves with an evening here, an afternoon there, some broken dates, some missed opportunities.

But perhaps that was the price people paid for success, and Lesley definitely considered them both successful. She was a coach with a potential gold medalist on her hands; he was being considered for the presidency of the company he'd been with for more than twenty years.

She put the brakes on her thoughts; she didn't want to think about Hamilton House, and she fervently hoped Matt wouldn't either.

He didn't. At least he didn't mention it. They talked the night away, and not once did he say a word about business. Instead, he told her about his college days, when Matthew Logan had been considered something of a hellion. She, in turn, related anecdotes from her days on the circuit. Later they made love again, and again it was wonderful because they had something they'd never had before—plenty of time alone. Nestled in the circle of Matt's arm, Lesley stretched along the length of him, certain she had never been so happy.

Sunday was a long, lazy day devoted entirely to each other, except for the three hours spent at Carol's bedside. Neither of them felt the least bit guilty about the time they spent away from the hospital. As long as Eric was there, they suspected that their presence was neither needed nor wanted.

It was a short-lived idyll, however. By Monday, Matt was back at work and so was Clarice; Carol was out of the hospital, and Eric was out of town. Still, the whole pattern of Lesley's life was changed. No longer did morning bring the necessity of heading for the rink. Days that once had been filled to the brim now were rather empty and not just a little boring.

The knee brace meant Carol was totally out of commission, and she was impatient, restless, edgy. Never having been forced to pass away idle hours, she had no idea what to do. She felt like a caged tiger. The only time she forced some sunniness into her voice was when she talked to her mother on the phone. Then she tried very hard to be upbeat. A tacit agreement existed among Lesley, Matt, Carol and Eric: no matter what, Olivia was always to be told that everything was just fine.

Carol's mother had presented something of a problem initially. When Olivia had realized that Carol would be off the ice for many weeks, she had hoped her daughter would return home to convalesce. Carol hadn't wanted to, so once again Matt's powers of persuasion had been called upon. He'd explained to Olivia that Carol's doctors were close to Lesley's house, as was the physical therapy clinic. It would be some time before Carol could drive. Did Olivia really want to make that long drive several times a week? Daily when the therapy sessions began? That did the trick. Carol was restless but far more content at Lesley's than she ever would have been back in Pacific Heights.

Lesley took advantage of the lull to dabble in some of the hobbies she had taken up over the years, but Carol had no such outlets. Finally Lesley insisted she at least give needlepoint a try because of its relaxing effect. To her surprise, Carol found that she rather enjoyed it. When the weather turned benevolent in late March, Lesley and Clarice attacked the garden, while Carol stayed on the patio with her needlework.

During all this time, Eric flitted in and out of their lives with increasing irregularity. When he was in, Carol was a delight to be around—she even joked about her knee. The two young people would banter back and forth and laugh a lot; Lesley would watch their developing relationship from the sidelines and feel a faint uneasiness stir. Now that Carol wasn't practicing, practicing, practicing, Eric had all but become her main interest in life.

And that, Lesley feared, could mean potential heartbreak waiting just beyond the horizon. So far she had seen no sign that Eric regarded the relationship as anything but a platonic one. And when he was away from home he led a high-charged, sophisticated existence filled with gorgeous Hollywood-type women. Lesley couldn't bear to think how Carol would be affected if he became seriously involved with one of them ... or with any woman, for that matter. She was afraid she'd find herself faced with something far more complicated than an injured knee.

Lesley's own love life, on the other hand, was so satisfying it was heart-thumping. Of course, she didn't get to see as much of Matt as she would have liked. Something was always coming up at work that meant a quick dash off to Seattle or Boise or Salt Lake City, but with Lesley's work temporarily limited to keeping Carol occupied, they almost always had the weekends, from Friday night until Sunday night. They had attended enough parties together for Matt's acquaintances to now think of them as a couple, but Lesley always begrudged having to devote any of their precious hours together to what he called his "social IOUs." Probably their nicest evening out had been the night he took her to the San Francisco Hamilton House for dinner. They had arrived unannounced and without reservations, but once word got around that Matt was there, they were treated like visiting royalty. Lesley could honestly say she'd never had a more memorable meal.

Most weekends, however, found them having dinner at his house, making love in his bed and, Lesley suspected, shocking proper Horace down to his toes. Then they would drive back to her house, where Matt often spent the night in the guest room. Decorum was the watchword. Lesley would have loved the luxury of waking up beside him on Sunday mornings, but both of them had some old-fashioned, conventional ideas about what constituted acceptable behavior. Under no circumstances would they have flaunted their intimate relationship, certainly not in front of Matt's daughter.

Sometimes, when she wasn't functioning in a dreamlike daze, Lesley would wonder what next week or next month would bring for them, but mostly she appreciated every minute they had together. She hadn't experienced many really special moments in her life, so her times with Matt were especially meaningful for her.

Finally Carol's brace came off, and the physical therapy sessions began. Suddenly Lesley was busy again. Since Carol had been in superb physical condition before her accident, her progress was remarkable. Desire and determination, Dr. Bancroft had said, constituted half the battle. And though it seemed to Carol that her recovery period lasted forever, the day finally came when Dr. Hillman released her as a patient and turned her over to Bancroft, who pronounced her fit to return to the ice, but with restrictions. In his office they had a private talk.

"I know how anxious you are, Carol, but you're going to have to do as I say. No jumps and no spins. Just take it nice and easy. No matter how great the temptation to hurry back into the swing of things, you're going to have to do it my way. You think the knee feels pretty strong now, but there might be times when it feels about as strong as a wet tissue. And it's liable to be very sensitive to cold. When it feels vulnerable, stay off the ice. You're the only one who really knows how it feels, so it's up to you. Another fall could be disastrous. Can I trust you?"

"Don't worry, Doctor. With Lesley and Eric riding herd on me, there's not much chance I'll be able to do anything but follow your instructions to the letter," Carol assured him.

"HOW'S SHE DOING, Lesley?" Matt asked during one of the rare weekday evenings they were alone together. Carol and Eric had gone to a movie after which they were going to grab some Chinese food; and Clarice had retired early to her room to do some sewing. Since by now the maid was aware that more than friendship and an interest in Carol's skating existed between the mistress and Mr. Logan, nothing short of a blazing inferno would have prompted her to interrupt them.

Lesley was sitting on the sofa in the game room, very close to Matt, her head resting on his shoulder. She stirred when he asked about Carol. "She's doing very well, better than I would have dared hope. But, oh, she's rarin' to go, and she tries her dead level best to get me to let her try things I know she shouldn't be doing. I notice she never tries that with Eric."

"Then take this Saturday off."

"What?"

"Forget practice this Saturday, or let Eric take over if he's available. Let's get away for two days."

Lesley raised her head to look at him. "Sounds nice. Where do you suggest we go?"

"I have a friend named Ted Shanks who keeps a houseboat at a marina in Marin County. I have carte blanche to use it anytime it's available, and he and his wife are leaving for New York this weekend . . . so it'll be available."

"I didn't know you liked boating."

"I don't especially. Sweetheart, we are talking about a boat that's sixty feet long if it's an inch. I wouldn't dream of taking it out. It's just a place for us to get away and be by ourselves, a place where no one knows us. We won't have to dress up or go out or do a damned thing but enjoy each other."

She smiled. "It's sounding better by the minute."

"Then let's do it."

Lesley hesitated. "Your daughter might have a fit. As impatient as she is, missing Saturday isn't going to sit well with her. But, of course, if Eric's here . . ."

"She still listens to her old man, believe it or not, and I'm sure she'll understand if we've been invited to a weekend party. She doesn't need to know that we'll be the only guests...and the hosts will be in New York."

"You don't mind if I go off and leave Carol?"

"Lesley, she's almost nineteen. There are plenty of nineteen-year-old women who are out on their own."

"I'm sure there are, but I doubt if many of them have led the sheltered life Carol has." Lesley smiled sheepishly. "I don't know why I worry like I do. Lack of experience in parenting, I suppose. Carol's a very sensible, levelheaded young woman. And I'd trust Eric with my own life, so I guess I can trust him with Carol's. Definitely yes, Matt. Let's go houseboating this weekend. Wonderfully lazy days, just the two of us. It sounds heavenly. I can hardly wait."

IT WAS SEVERAL HOURS later when Eric eased his BMW into the driveway of Lesley's house and switched off the engine. He noticed that Matt's car was gone, and there was a light on upstairs. Lesley would be waiting for her charge to get home. He glanced at his watch. It was ten-fifteen, and he had promised to have Carol home in time for her to be in bed by eleven. No problem. Instead of opening the door, he half turned to face his passenger.

"That was fun," Carol told him. "I'm wonderfully stuffed. I love to eat Chinese. It's the only kind of food I can pig out on and not worry that Lesley will be all over me."

"I enjoyed it, too. I've been going to the Blue Moon since I was a kid—ever since Sondra told me I was going to have to curb my insatiable hunger for fatty foods. Can you imagine what it was like growing up with my Mom's cooking and having to watch what I ate?"

Carol could imagine. Rosie Zito's table always seemed to groan under enormous platters of food. Of course, the woman usually had a small army of people to feed, especially on Sundays, but no one ever went away hungry. Carol was silent for a minute before asking, "Did you ever resent all the restrictions? Ever? Even once? Did it ever burn you up when you were constantly told to eat this, not eat that, get plenty of rest, get your hair cut or let it grow, don't wear red or yellow or blue or whatever color Sondra knew some dour-faced judge didn't like?"

He chuckled. "I don't think so. That's just the nature of the sport. You have to look your best. There's no finish line or home plate to cross, so you're judged."

"Maybe it's different for you guys. Maybe your lives aren't as sheltered as ours are."

"What brought this on?" Eric asked, reaching out to finger one of the springy curls framing her face.

She frowned. "I don't know. Maybe it was all that time I had to baby my knee, just sitting around the house going bonkers. I didn't have the slightest idea what to do with myself, and that has to be because I've never done anything but skate. I thought I was going to lose my mind. And I remember thinking, what if I've hurt the knee really bad, so bad that I couldn't ever skate again? What in the devil would I do?"

She would have cut out her heart before telling him about another thought that had recurred over and over during those long, idle days: if she couldn't skate again, what would keep him in her life?

Eric's fingertips continued playing with the curl. Then he brushed her hair away from her nape, and in so doing grazed the back of his hand along the side of her neck. It was the simplest gesture in the world, unconscious on his part, but it spawned a thousand tiny goose bumps over her skin. She forced herself to stare straight ahead instead of looking at him. She was sure her longing was emblazoned on her face.

"You'd do something," he said thoughtfully, removing his hand, barely aware that he'd touched her.

"That's easy for you to say," she reminded him. "You've had the whole ball of wax—the amateur career, the Olympic gold, now a pro career. 'Skating's leading man'—isn't that what you're being called? Without so much as a scratched finger."

"Oh, I imagine I've had a scratched finger once or twice. But you're right—it is easy for me to say. Still, if you had to give up skating, I doubt you'd curl up in a corner and die. I wouldn't have."

Carol felt sufficiently recovered to turn and face him squarely. "Again," she said softly, "that's easy for you to say. You never had to…and now you have what the rest of us dream about."

"You're forgetting something, Carol. In '92 there'll be a new star."

"But all your life, whenever your name is mentioned, 'Olympic gold medalist' will precede it. All your life."

"Maybe someday it will precede yours, too."

Eric felt a peculiar tingle in the pit of his stomach. Carol was staring at him with such intensity, her lips slightly parted. For the first time he became aware of how really pretty she was. She'd always just been around, someone he knew and liked and worked with, but he'd no more taken the time to really look at her then he had to study the chairs in his parents' living room.

Now he took note of Carol's features, one by one, and decided that they were arranged in a particularly beguiling fashion. When had she stopped being a little girl and become a young woman?

His eyes finally stopped their roaming and came to rest on her mouth. It was a very appealing set of lips. For one wild moment he experienced the urge to bend his head and cover them with his.

The urge had no more formed than his good sense took over. God, she didn't need amorous advances from her choreographer, of all things. No complications in their relationship, no distractions for her. He knew the score, for he'd heard it all his life. No serious involvements; focus, focus, concentrate, concentrate.

He straightened, looked at his watch again, then reached for the door handle. "I'd better get you in, or Lesley'll raunch all over me."

Carol's pent-up breath fluttered out. Her heart was knocking against her ribs. For a minute he'd had the strangest look on his face. For a minute she'd been so sure he was going to do or say something...

"Yeah, I guess so," she said, and opened her door. Eric rounded the car to take her by the arm, and together they walked through the iron gate and up the flagstone walk. They had almost reached the front steps when Carol suddenly fell against him. He reacted quickly, putting a strong arm around her waist and righting her.

"Carol?"

"Sorry. I . . . just stumbled. I think my heel caught a stone."

"Sure?"

"Yes, it was nothing."

He let out a sigh of relief. "That's good. Can't have you falling again."

They continued on up the walkway, and Eric waited until she was safely in the house before returning to his car. Inside, Carol closed the door and leaned against it for a minute. Taking two deep breaths, she covered her trembling mouth with a hand. Her eyes were frightened.

She hadn't stumbled over anything. Her knee, her wretched, traitorous knee, had simply given way without warning and for no apparent reason, just the way Dr. Bancroft had said it might.

She was shaking all over when she reached the top of the stairs, so instead of stopping for a word with Lesley as she normally did, she called "I'm home" as she passed the door and hurried to the privacy of her own room. Sinking onto the edge of the bed, Carol struggled to control her rapid breathing. *Don't overreact,* she cautioned herself. *It might have been an isolated incident. It might never happen again.*

But what if it did?

ON FRIDAY EVENING, once they were across the Golden Gate Bridge in Sausalito, Matt and Lesley followed a sinuous road along the waterfront. The sun was setting rapidly. Lesley wouldn't have attempted to describe the view to anyone. Breathtaking would have been inadequate. It was enough to say that the Sausalito waterfront offered the single element missing from every vista in San Francisco—a full view of the entire city.

They drove past the piers lined with sleek yachts, sloops and motorboats until Matt found the one he was looking for. He parked in the slip's assigned space and unlocked the gate leading to the boat ramp. Ted Shank's houseboat was the fourth one down, and it dwarfed the boats on either side of it. Lesley gaped when she saw it. She thought calling it a boat was doing the vessel an injustice; floating condominium was more like it.

"Shades of Donald Trump!" she exclaimed.

"Wait'll you see the interior," Matt said. "It's really something."

It really was. Matt opened the sliding glass doors at the side of the boat, then stood back and let her enter. She stepped into a stunning main salon, with a red and blue color scheme. A sofa and two overstuffed chairs faced the captain's console, upon which sat a TV set, VCR and stereo. "Looks like we have all the comforts of home," Lesley remarked.

"Ted and his wife spend weeks at a time on this boat, so I'm sure it's the last word in comfort. Look around while I unload the car."

"Need any help?"

"No, there's not that much."

Northern California was going through a period of unusually warm weather, so they couldn't have picked a better weekend. Lesley walked through the vessel, marveling at the efficient, compact galley and the head that was almost as large as her bathroom at home. At the rear was the master bedroom. It had the usual built-ins and a queen-size bed covered with a vivid print spread. When she heard Matt return, she went back to the salon to help him put everything away.

They had brought only a few items of clothing but lots of food and drink; they didn't want to have to go out to eat, nor did they intend to do any sight-seeing or shopping, even though Sausalito supposedly was a shopper's paradise. They only wanted to enjoy each other. Frankly, Lesley hoped they wouldn't see another living soul the entire weekend.

Groceries were stashed, clothes were hung in closets, and Lesley's makeup bag and Matt's shaving kit were placed in the head. Then he poured some wine, and they went topside to the rear deck to enjoy the warm evening air. All was still and hushed. They sat side by side in deck chairs, sipping the wine and holding hands.

Lesley was awash in contentment. She didn't have to feel guilty about making Carol miss practice—Eric had been more than willing to take over—so she and Matt had an idyllic weekend stretching ahead of them. "Oooh, this is nice," she murmured. "I wish there wasn't another person for miles around."

"There might not be," Matt said. "It's awfully quiet."

"I know. I haven't seen anyone. Isn't that nice?"

The words were no more than out of her mouth than lights began going on all over the marina, and suddenly it wasn't dark and quiet anymore. Walkways were illuminated, as were the parking lots. As if that were some kind of signal, there was a sudden increase in activity all around them. Lights came on in boats; from somewhere came the sound of music and laughter. On the boat next to them a deck light came on, and it was only slightly less bright than an average spotlight. Lesley smiled at Matt ruefully. "I should have kept my mouth shut."

"Hey!" they heard a voice call. Matt looked to the right but saw no one.

"Ahoy there!" the voice called again.

Matt's head swiveled in the other direction, and he saw a man standing on the deck of the adjacent houseboat. In one hand he held a drink; the other was raised in greeting.

"Good evening," Matt said politely.

"Name's Harve Whitestone," the man said jovially. "You folks must be friends of ol' Ted's."

Reluctantly, Matt stood. "Yes. My name's Matt Logan. This is Lesley."

"Good to meet you," Harve said. "Is Ted here?"

"No, he gave us the use of the boat for the weekend."

"That's great! Nice to see some new faces. You're just in time."

Matt frowned down at Lesley, then returned his attention to their neighbor. "In time for what?"

"The party!" Harve said. "This whole marina is just one big party, party, party from Friday until Sunday or pass out, whichever comes first." He laughed lustily. "Let me freshen up my drink, and I'll be right over."

Lesley placed a hand over her mouth to stifle her groan. "I don't recall inviting him," she muttered.

Matt's shoulders rose and fell. "What could I do?" Dismay was written all over his face. "Maybe he won't stay long."

"Hold that good thought."

True to his word, Harve was right over, agilely negotiating the slight leap from his deck to theirs, though his too-full drink sloshed over onto what looked to Matt like brand-new deck covering. The men shook hands and Harve nodded to Lesley, then pulled up another chair and sat down. He was a nondescript-looking man of roughly fifty-five or sixty. He wore cutoffs, a T-shirt and sandals. A baseball cap sat atop a head of gray hair that desperately needed cutting. But he was as friendly as a puppy and apparently thought everyone else in the world was, too.

"Boy, us River Rats have been waiting a long time for weather like this. The place will be jumping tonight." To underscore that, Harve pointed to the parking lot at the end of the pier that was swiftly filling up.

"River Rats?" Lesley asked, not wanting to appear deaf and mute.

"That's what we call ourselves, the bunch that owns the boats along this pier. Oh, a few are outsiders who live over on the next pier, but mostly it's this bunch." His hand swept out to include the long line of luxury boats moored on either side of Ted's. "Some of us live here all the time—retired you know—but the others come in on Fridays. That's when things start poppin'." Harve took a hefty swig of his drink. "What line of work you in, Matt?"

"The restaurant business."

"Guess folks are always going to eat out, right? Now me, I was in the culvert business. Sold out a couple of years ago. That's when I found out what a dirty rotten scoundrel my brother-in-law is. Don't ever bring your brother-in-law into the restaurant with you.''

Matt couldn't help smiling; the man was too outrageous. ''Not likely I will since I don't have a brother-in-law.''

''Boy, are you lucky. Come to think of it, don't even let your brother in your business. Or your sister. Or your mama and daddy. Just stay away from kinfolk when it comes to business. I should have come out of my company with five or six million, but I had to settle for three, all because of my rotten brother-in-law. I won't bore you with the details of how I got royally shafted.''

Thank you, Lord, for small favors, Lesley thought, still stunned by the news that this man who looked like a refugee from the Beat Generation had three million dollars.

''Oh, by the way, Matt,'' Harve said. ''Sarah will be right over.''

''Who's...Sarah?'' Matt asked, almost afraid to find out.

''My wife. She's washing her hair. She's always washing her hair, but I never can say it looks any different after she washed it than it did before. She's real excited about somebody new, and, of course, she wants to meet your missus. It's Lesley, right?''

''Yes, it's Lesley.'' Matt and Lesley exchanged glances. Harve obviously wasn't leaving right away.

Just then their neighbor spotted something in the water. He jumped to his feet and started waving his arms like a berserk cheerleader. A man cruising by in a small powerboat cut the motor. ''Hey, Paul,'' Harve called. "Tie up over at my place and come on board. Got some new folks I want you to meet."

Lesley heard Matt actually growl. And from out on the water came Paul whoever's voice. "Great! Let me get a fresh beer."

"Don't bother," Harve called. "Ted'll have plenty of beer."

That brought Matt to his feet. "Ah, listen, Harve... this isn't my boat, as you know, and I don't think Ted's hospitality extends to my giving away his beer."

Undaunted, Harve just grinned. "Aw, Matt, you don't understand how the River Rats operate. All for one and one for all. What's yours is mine and vice versa. Just one big happy family, and the gathering of the clan is upon us. Hell, Ted's our ringleader. He's not going to begrudge ol' Paul a beer."

While Harve and Paul were greeting each other like long-lost relatives, Matt sat back down and leaned toward Lesley, speaking confidentially. "I find it impossible to believe that Ted and Harve have anything in common. Ted Shanks is one of the most distinguished men I know."

"Apparently the water is a great equalizer." Lesley covered her face with her hand, and her shoulders shook. Matt thought she was crying, and he didn't blame her. He felt like crying, too. Their lovely evening, shot to hell. Then she removed her hand. What she was doing was laughing hysterically.

"I fail to see how you can laugh about this," he fumed.

"What else can I do? Can you believe we went to all the trouble to come here to be alone? We would have been far more alone at home. Sh, here they come."

Harve brought Paul over to meet them. The new arrival was about Harve's age and was similarly dressed. Paul announced that he was going to get his wife, Cindy. They lived three boats down, so he would be right back. First, though, he was going to help himself to a beer. By the time Paul and Cindy arrived, a man named Roger and his wife had heeded Harve's summons and come on board, and Sarah had shown up, wet hair and all. "Aren't you a pretty little thing!" she exclaimed when introduced to Lesley, then proceeded to talk nonstop for twenty minutes, telling Lesley far more than she wanted to know about Harve and herself.

The boat drew people like a magnet, and soon there were so many people on it that Matt was becoming slightly claustrophobic. No one seemed interested in staying out on deck; everyone wanted to be in the cabin, where the liquor and beer were. Matt worried about the way Ted's rations were being depleted—no one asked, everyone just took. More times than he cared to remember he was told "that's the way the River Rats do things." He had to bite his tongue to keep from saying, "Well, I'm not a River Rat, and I'd appreciate it if all of you would get the hell out of here."

Lesley had never been particularly fond of boats, and now she remembered why. There were always too many people in too little a space and there was never any place to sit. She found a relatively uncrowded corner and spent the evening studying the oddest assortment of humanity she had ever encountered.

And yet, looks were deceiving. They all might look like aging hippies, she reflected, but they were affluent people. Beside Harve and the other retirees, there was a bank president whose wife had her own real estate firm, a man in the import-export business and an oral surgeon. Only one person aboard was younger than Lesley. That was the oral surgeon's third wife, who didn't look much older than Carol. The woman had on a swimsuit that covered just enough to keep her from being arrested, and she did not sit down the entire evening. To preclude the possibility, Lesley assumed, that someone might miss seeing a shocking amount of her delectable body.

There were far too many names to remember, but by ten o'clock, Lesley didn't care who anyone was. By eleven, she was genuinely afraid that Matt might systematically begin throwing everyone overboard. He looked as close to genuine anger as she had ever seen him.

But by eleven-thirty, Ted Shanks's liquor supply had been wiped out, and that had the effect of clearing the boat faster than a cry of "Fire!" would have. The party was moving down to the oral surgeon's boat, and naturally everyone wanted Matt and Lesley to come along. With some difficulty they managed to beg off.

When the last of the revelers had stumbled off, Matt locked the door, all the windows and pulled the blinds. He turned off every light except a small one over the galley's sink. Hopefully from the outside it would appear that they had turned in for the night. He was starving and so was Lesley. Except for three cans of peanuts, none of their "guests" had seemed interested in food. They made sandwiches and ate them in semidarkness at the counter that separated the salon from the galley.

"How do we keep them from coming back tomorrow?" Lesley wanted to know.

"I've been giving that some thought," Matt said seriously. "One, everyone's going to have a crashing hangover, so that ought to keep them at bay until midafternoon, but that's not good enough. Then it hit me. Did it seem to you that Ted's liquor supply was more of a draw than our sparkling personalities?"

"Definitely."

"You couldn't mix a Shirley Temple with what's left. Obviously I'm going to have to go out tomorrow and replenish it, but the booze stays locked in the trunk of the car until we get ready to leave Sunday." He tapped his forehead with a finger. "Always thinking."

"You're a genius."

Lesley stood to carry their plates to the sink, but Matt grabbed her around the waist and pulled her down onto his lap. "You're gorgeous, and the night is young."

"No, it isn't."

"Pretend it is. We don't have to get up until noon tomorrow if we don't want to. I hope you aren't sleepy."

"Not especially. What do you have in mind?" she asked playfully.

"I think I'm going to make love to you for...oh, two hours."

The plates went down on the counter. "Forget the dishes. Let's go."

TWO HOURS LATER they lay entwined, their bodies limp and glistening with a musk-scented moisture. Matt's leg was thrown possessively across her stomach; one of her hands lay on his chest. Lesley felt the satisfying thumping of his heart. Her lips felt swollen, her skin actually tingled, and her bloodstream coursed with life. Each and every sensation was marvelous. It was so wonderful to feel so much.

"You're as good as your word," she said with a sigh. "It was so... Sorry, words fail me. It was indescribable."

"I hope you're not going to expect that kind of performance out of me very often."

"But you're so accomplished."

"And not as young as I used to be."

"I'll help you stay young."

"Not at this rate, you won't. You'll have me in the hospital, a mere shadow of my former self."

Lesley wiggled beside him, seeking a more comfortable position. "In spite of the River Rats, tonight has been magical." Suddenly she grew serious. "Matt, don't let Harve and his friends on this boat tomorrow, not for a second. I don't care if you have to threaten them at gunpoint. We'll stay locked inside."

"Don't worry. I think an empty liquor cabinet will do more than a loaded gun could. Now, go to sleep, sweetheart. I'm wiped out."

"Matt."

"Hmm."

"I love you."

He smiled sleepily. "I love you too, Lesley. Very much."

CHAPTER TWELVE

"ERIC, WHEN are we going to get this show on the road?" Carol complained. "I've been waltzing around this rink for weeks. I'm never going to make it to the nationals at this rate."

It was Saturday morning, and they had the arena to themselves. He skated out to her in the center of the ice. "Face it, babe. You might not . . . but there's the next year. Don't rush it."

"Rush it? You're worse than Lesley. You've got me making moves I could do with my eyes closed when I was ten years old."

"God, you're a pain in the posterior this morning. What's the matter, anyway?"

"I just don't feel like I'm getting anywhere."

Eric thought about it a minute. "How does the knee feel?"

"Fine, really."

"Well, okay. Do something simple. Maybe a camel spin. Remember, you're not trying to impress any-one. No jumps." Eric skated off to the side to watch her. He was encouraged. As far as he could see, Carol was coming along great. She looked much stronger than she had the week before. He hated it that he was leaving on tour Monday because it meant he couldn't watch her for another month. And he sympathized with her impatience. If he was in her shoes, he probably would have been chewing nails by now.

He watched her go through her paces for a minute, charmed by her grace and poise. For some reason he thought of the first time he'd seen her, when she'd shown up for her first lesson with Sondra. He'd been a big shot of twelve with a junior championship under his belt, probably too full of himself. She'd been a knobby-kneed seven-year-old with two front teeth that looked too big for her mouth. He smiled. Who would have thought that graceless little girl would grow into the dazzling charmer out there on the ice?

Just then Eric's peripheral vision caught some kind of movement. He turned to see what it was—the custodian had just walked through—and when he turned back, Carol was in a heap in the middle of the ice. He rushed to her, kneeling beside her.

"Carol? What happened?"

She was sobbing. "Nothing...h-happened. The k-knee just...gave way."

"Gave way?"

"You know...b-buckled."

"Oh, geez..." She looked so patently miserable that he put his arms around her and pulled her head to his chest. "Don't cry. You didn't hurt yourself, did you?"

"N-no." Carol clutched him so tightly that he found breathing difficult. "But, Eric...you know the other night when we were walking up to the house and I stumbled?"

"Yes."

"I...didn't stumble. The knee just gave way, like right now. Dr. Bancroft warned me it might."

Eric sat back on his heels, releasing her. "Oh? This is news to me. I'm sure it would be to Lesley, too. Why didn't you tell us that?" His tone was accusing.

"I . . . I don't know."

"Suppose you tell me what else he said that Lesley and I don't know about."

"He said the knee would be sensitive to cold for a long time."

"Is it?"

"Yes."

"Dammit, Carol, you shouldn't have kept anything from us!" he barked.

"I'm sorry. He told me so many things. I couldn't remember everything. Don't fuss at me."

"You need to be fussed at. What did you think you would accomplish by not telling us everything? We're trying to help you."

"I just didn't think it was all that important."

"Well think now. Did he tell you anything else we ought to know?"

"Not that I remember." She began to cry again. "Oh, Eric, I'm so s-scared."

He wanted to be mad as hell at her, but anger wouldn't come. He pulled her to him again and stroked her hair. "Yeah, babe, I know. I am, too."

They continued clinging to each other for several wordless minutes, until her sobbing subsided. Then Eric got to his feet and pulled Carol to hers. "You okay? Can you stand?"

"Yes. It doesn't hurt. Most of the time it feels fine, but then it just crumbles."

"Maybe we need to give it more time. I shouldn't have let you do that spin. Lesley's going to kill me."

"Oh, Eric, it wasn't the spin! I was out of the spin before I fell. It was the knee!"

"You're still doing your exercises, aren't you?"

"Of course. Religiously."

"And you haven't missed any therapy sessions?"

"No!" She almost screamed it in her frustration.

"Okay, don't yell. Let's call it quits for the day. I don't suppose there's a chance of getting Bancroft on the phone today, but I'll try. I want to talk to him."

A dejected Carol followed him off the ice. She had told him she was scared, but that wasn't true. She was terrified. Missed jumps and screwed-up spins were one thing. She could work at making herself sharp again. She could even handle taking it easy awhile longer. But a knee that buckled at will, without cause or warning? Would she worry every time she landed that this was the time it would give? She couldn't handle that.

The thought of the long weekend alone in that house with no one but Clarice for company depressed her further, as did the knowledge that Eric was leaving on a lengthy tour Monday.

"What are you going to do?" she asked him. "I mean, for the rest of the day?"

He shrugged. "I don't know. Hadn't given it any thought. Why?"

"I . . . I don't want to be alone."

Eric regarded her with sharpened awareness. The sassy scamp he'd known for eleven years was gone. During the months since her accident, he had come to appreciate the subtleties of Carol's personality, and he had discovered she had a quiet charm all her own. There had been a time in the not-too-distant past when he wouldn't have thought to mention Carol and charm in the same breath, not with that quick mouth of hers. Now he wondered if all that flippancy hadn't been an act designed to cover up...what? Insecurity? Self-doubt? He didn't know, but she definitely was a far more complex person than he'd realized. "Okay. I guess I can understand that. We'll do something together. What would you like to do?"

Carol brightened. "I don't care. Stare at the walls. Just as long as I'm not alone."

Eric thought a minute. "I'd considered giving Mom a thrill and having dinner with her and Dad tonight. I'll bet they'd love to see you, too. Want to come along?"

"I'd love to."

She looked so pleased that he experienced a great rush of warm feelings toward her. In fact, all his feelings about Carol seemed to be going through a strange metamorphosis. That possibly could be attributed to the change in their relationship—from co-students to teacher and student. Every time she fastened that rapt expression on him, as though what he were about to say would be regarded as the absolute gospel, he felt some odd stirrings in the pit of his stomach. Whatever it was, he definitely felt closer to her than he ever had before, and he was worried as hell about that knee.

But he wasn't about to let her know that. Slipping his arm around her waist, he said, "But that's tonight. There's the rest of the day ahead of us. I'll take you home so you can change and I can call Bancroft. Then we'll stop by my place so I can change. I have some shopping to do and we'll have to have lunch. I'll bet we find a way to pass the time."

Carol hoped she didn't have stars in her eyes, but she feared she did. She never ceased to wonder at his effect on her. It had been profound enough before, but now that they spent so much time together, that effect seemed to have intensified. Her girlish crush had not turned out to be naive fantasy, after all. He really was Zeus . . . and he was going to spend the entire day with her.

After she changed clothes at Lesley's house and Eric left a message with Dr. Bancroft's answering service, they headed for his apartment. He'd lived there only a few months, so it was Carol's first glimpse of his new digs. Located not far from the Stanford campus, the flat was small, uncluttered and completely masculine.

"Do you like living alone?" she asked Eric as she browsed through the place.

"I love it," he called from the bedroom where he was changing.

"I guess it would be nice for a while, but I wouldn't want to do it forever, like Dad has."

Eric reappeared. "He might not be living alone much longer, not as thick as he and Lesley are getting."

"You might be right. It would seem strange—Dad with a wife—if that actually happens." She glanced around the apartment once more. "I think if I had a place like this, I'd want a roommate, someone to talk to at the end of the day."

"From what I've heard, you have to be damned careful about roommates. Be sure it's a real good friend. I've heard some tales of horror about the wrong kind of people trying to live together."

"In my case," Carol said, "it would be super hard to find someone. I guess you're the only real friend I have, and I think people might talk if you and I lived together."

"Yeah. Your mom and dad, for two." It occurred to Eric that Carol might be one person he actually could live with. Of course, no one would believe the arrangement was platonic, and being honest, he wasn't sure he'd be able to keep it platonic. Just thinking about having her in the other bedroom made his insides grow warm. "Come on, let's get some lunch. I'm starved."

He took her to a restaurant located in an old-style movie palace, and after lunch they went shopping along University Avenue, with its door-to-door boutiques, galleries and knickknack shops. That consumed the remainder of the afternoon. It was after five when they headed for the Zitos' house.

Like Lesley, Eric's parents lived in one of the affluent bedroom communities strung along the bay side of the peninsula. The similarity ended there. Lesley's house was a mansion; the Zitos' was merely large—an old-fashioned, two story structure that a couple with five children would buy. Carol loved the place. It was the kind of house that invited you to come in, sit a spell and visit. And it always smelled of good cooking.

Whenever one of her children came for dinner, Rosie turned it into a special occasion. Tonight was even more so. Not only was Carol along, but Eric's sister, Amy, her husband, Bob, and their two children were there. The evening turned into a party. After being served more food than anyone could or should

eat, Eric's father, Angelo, played the piano, and
everyone sang and danced. Eric danced with his sister, and Rosie danced with Bob. Then Bob took over
at the piano while Angelo danced with Carol. It was
the sort of thing that had so endeared the Zitos to her.
She wished the evening could go on and on.

Only one incident marred the evening. Eric mentioned it while he was driving her home. "I watched
you while you were dancing with Dad," he said. "You
were favoring your right leg."

"Your imagination."

"Bull! It hurts, doesn't it?"

"It's . . . just a little sore," Carol hedged. "I might
have bumped it hard when I fell this morning."

"I wish you'd level with me."

"I am! It's going to get better, Eric. You wait and
see."

He sighed. "Sure it is, babe. Sure it is."

LESLEY AND MATT returned to her house Sunday
evening, laughing uproariously over their secluded
weekend. It had been secluded, all right, because they
hadn't dared venture out of the boat for fear of being
swallowed up in the hilarity that ruled supreme at the
marina. Lesley had never seen so many adults con-
duct themselves in such an uninhibited manner.

Fortunately, Matt had been right about the empty
liquor cabinet. Harve and Paul had come to see them
Saturday afternoon, but when confronted by a non-
existent booze supply and the news that Matt suffered
from an ulcer and wasn't allowed more than an occa-
sional glass of wine, they departed and weren't seen
again. Blessedly, neither was anyone else. Harve and

Paul would have spread the word, and apparently the River Rats weren't interested in a couple of party poopers.

So even though their weekend hadn't been exactly as they had envisioned it, Lesley and Matt had had a wonderful time—they'd simply held their own very private party. Everything Matt knew about men and women and love and sex told him that a man his age couldn't perform in bed with the vigor of a twenty-year-old stud, but damned if he hadn't come close.

That was all Lesley's doing, of course. He'd met his match. She liked lots of kissing and touching and stroking, plenty of foreplay, just as he did. She liked to talk to him while they made love, and he liked that, too. She didn't think lovemaking should be restricted to a bed, and neither did he. There were sofas, bath-tubs, floors, and they had tried them all.

In fact, Lesley seemed to instinctively know just what to do and when to do it. Her arms were like a charmed circle; and when he was in them he felt younger and freer than he had since he was a kid. Their magical weekends had transformed him. What once had been merely a pleasure for him had now become a need, and he knew beyond a shadow of a doubt that he was in love with her. He doubted he could function any longer without periodic transfusions of Lesley's love. He couldn't allow anything to happen to something so special. Soon, very soon, they were going to have to talk about the future.

And that was the sole aspect of their relationship that brought on pangs of uneasiness. He couldn't forget Lesley's reaction to the news that he was being considered to fill Vanessa's shoes. That was one reason he hadn't brought it up again. He couldn't shake the nagging fear that he might not want to hear how she felt about it.

There was no uneasiness when they reached Lesley's house Sunday night, however. They both were in high spirits as they walked into the game room and found Carol and Eric, but one look at their faces and Lesley's smile faded.

"What's wrong?" she demanded sharply.

Eric got to his feet and shoved his hands into the pockets of his jeans. "Carol fell at the rink yesterday."

"Fell?" Lesley and Matt exchanged anxious glances.

"It wasn't a bad spill," Eric hastened to assure them. "She didn't hurt herself, but her knee just gave way. It seems it's happened before."

All eyes went to Carol. "Just once," she said in a small voice.

"That's one time too many," Lesley retorted.

"I called Dr. Bancroft yesterday and left a message on his answering machine," Eric went on. "He got back to me about fifteen minutes ago. He wants to see Carol tomorrow. I'm leaving town in the morning, and I thought I ought to stick around tonight to tell you this myself." He looked down at Carol, and a private glance passed between them. "I wasn't sure I could depend on our friend here to give you the straight scoop."

Matt sank onto one of the bar stools. "We appreciate your concern, Eric," he said inadequately, but his gaze rested squarely on his daughter's downcast eyes.

"Yes, yes, we do," Lesley agreed. "Yesterday when you fell, Carol—you two weren't cutting up on the ice or anything like that, were you?"

Carol shook her head vigorously. "Ask Eric. We were just doing simple stuff. The other time when the knee crumpled, I wasn't doing anything but walking."

"Bancroft warned her this might happen, something she neglected to pass along to us," Eric said. "He also told her the knee might be sensitive to cold, and it is."

Lesley didn't like the sound of any of this. It was a real setback. Maybe they had been moving too fast, she thought, then dismissed the thought. They had done everything by the book. She was sure of that because, except for yesterday, Carol had not skated onto the ice without her having been right there with her.

So that left the real possibility that Carol was one of the unfortunate ones whose knee would never again be strong enough for competitive skating.

Eric removed his hands from his pockets. "Well, I guess I'd better be going. I've got to get up pretty early in the morning."

Lesley shook away her dismal thoughts. "Thank you so much, Eric."

"Don't mention it. Good night." He turned and gave Carol a thumbs-up gesture, then left the room. Only a second passed before Carol was on her feet, following him to the front door and out onto the steps.

"How long do you think you'll be gone this time?" she asked.

"Probably a month. This is a major international tour. But I'll call tomorrow night to find out what the doc had to say."

A month? An eternity. "Okay. Have a safe trip."

Eric had never seen a sadder face. She tugged at his heartstrings. He wished he could think of something upbeat and encouraging to say, but his mind went blank. So he acted rather than spoke. He bent to give her a light kiss. Suddenly her arms went around his waist, and she clung to him desperately. The move was so surprising it caught him off guard, and he stumbled backward a few steps before regaining his balance.

"I'm going to miss you so much," Carol said, her voice muffled in his shirtfront.

Oh, God, he thought, *that's the change I've been wondering about. I've let her become too dependent on me.*

He hadn't meant to. At least he hoped he hadn't, but maybe her dependency had been irresistible to his male ego. Certainly he'd done nothing to discourage it. Eric wondered how well his motives would bear up under close, hard scrutiny.

One thing was certain: Carol didn't need that kind of dependency. He couldn't make the knee stronger any more than he could go out and do her triples for her. Her strength had to come from within.

He allowed her to cling to him another minute, then gently disengaged himself from her tight embrace. "You take care of yourself, and I'll see you just as soon as I can." Dropping a light kiss on the top of her head, he turned and disappeared into the darkness.

THE FOLLOWING AFTERNOON Carol waited in Dr. Bancroft's examining room, her stomach churning. The doctor was scowling over her x-rays and medical records. Why did they have to scowl? she wondered. They always looked as though they were going to tell you your case was hopeless.

The minutes ticked by. Finally he looked up. "Well, the pictures please me, but the inescapable fact is you've fallen twice. The knee isn't strong enough to allow you to do the things you want to do."

"Maybe it's too soon. I'll work twice as hard. It'll get better."

"Maybe." He closed her folder and smiled, folding his arms across his stomach. She had learned that look by now. They were going to chat. "Have you ever seriously considered that it might not?"

"Not really."

"You know, last night after I talked to Eric, I got out my videos of the last Olympics and watched all the skating. Some of that stuff you people do takes legs of steel."

Carol watched him warily, wondering what he was getting at.

"And that little girl who did the triple axel in the last world championships," the doctor went on. "The first for a woman in a major competition, wasn't it? Now I suppose every woman skater is going to want one in her repertoire."

Carol laughed lightly. "That's just the way it goes. It wasn't that long ago that a woman could win a competition without a triple jump of any kind, but now they're here to stay."

"Can you do a triple axel?"

"I have in practice, but it wasn't anything I would want captured on film for posterity."

"How many times do you suppose you'll fall before you perfect that jump?"

Carol lowered her eyes. Now she knew what he was getting at. "Fifty or sixty, I guess."

Dr. Bancroft chuckled. "You're honest." Then he sobered. "And out of fifty or sixty falls, what do you suppose are the chances you'll not hurt that knee again?"

Carol said nothing; she stared at the hands in her lap.

"I'd hate to see you have to live the rest of your life with a bum knee. I have patients who do, and it's not something I'd wish on anyone. Please be aware of your limitations. Skate all you want to, but if I were you, I'd have second thoughts about ever competing again."

Carol's eyes grew moist. "I'm going to work on the knee, Doctor. It's going to get stronger—I just know it is."

"I hope so, Carol. I really do. But don't push it. Don't do anything you're not sure you can do."

"I won't."

Carol meant what she told the doctor, and for a time after that visit, she concentrated more on her exercises than on skating, although she and Lesley still went to practice every day. She skated school figures until she wanted to scream. Even though they had recently been phased out of competitions, Lesley insisted on them because she honestly believed the ones who were good at figures were the best overall skaters.

But Carol quickly grew bored and impatient again. It was never far from her mind that her competitors were making progress daily while she was stagnating. Besides, her knee felt fine.

Her natural optimism and exuberance warred constantly with her more cautious side. Occasionally, when Lesley went to make a phone call or to see about lunch, she would try a little jump—nothing difficult. Her confidence grew as the days passed, one after another, without incident. It was easy for her mind to take another turn. After all, she would think, there had been only two falls, and neither of them had been serious. She probably had placed too much importance on them. She had to stop thinking about the knee and get back to working on her program. The real program, the one she would skate in the Olympics. Easy routines and cautious skating did not win major competitions, and she had lost so much valuable time.

"We've got to pick up the pace, Lesley," she complained one day. "I'm going nowhere fast. I'm fine, really. I'd know if I wasn't. My knee feels great."

Lesley still had doubts, but before she could say anything, Carol underscored her point by skating onto the ice and executing a double axel. Lesley thought her heart had stopped for a second when she saw her student launch herself skyward, but Carol landed the jump cleanly and looked in top form.

"How'd that feel?" she asked when a pleased Carol skated back to her.

"Solid."

Lesley chewed her bottom lip. She was as anxious as Carol to get her skating back on track, and hadn't Dr.

Bancroft said Carol was the only one who really knew how the knee felt? "I guess we could start working on the short." The short program was jazzy, with visually engaging moves but without the difficult technical ones of the long.

For days afterward, Carol looked wonderful, and the enthusiasm she displayed was contagious. She was reluctant to leave the arena every afternoon. She slept soundly at night and was up at dawn, eager to get started, every morning. At last Lesley decided it was time to work on her long program.

Carol's spirits soared. If things continued to progress this nicely, she would be ready for the nationals, after all.

CHAPTER THIRTEEN

ALL WEEK LONG Matt had promised himself he would take Friday afternoon off. He had been getting some glowing reports from Lesley on Carol's progress, and he wanted to watch her skate. Now, as he sat at his desk, he kept looking at his watch as one telephone call after another kept delaying his departure. At two-thirty, Helen came through the door.

"I know you want to leave, Matt," the secretary said. "I'll take all the calls from now on."

He looked at her gratefully. "Thanks, Helen. I'd appreciate that."

"I'll straighten your desk and lock up, too. How's Carol doing?"

"From the reports I'm getting, she's doing great. That's where I'm going when I leave here. I want to watch her."

"Give her my love." Then, instead of turning to leave the office, Helen sat down in one of the chairs facing Matt's desk. "I won't keep you but a minute more, but I wanted to ask you about something I just heard."

"Sure."

"I was talking to Mary Linden on the phone this afternoon. She called about something else, but as usual, I got an earful of some office gossip."

Mary Linden was Dolph Wade's secretary in Dallas. As Helen had said, she was also the company gossip. Matt guessed every big organization had one— someone who made it his or her business to know everything that was going on "backstage." He couldn't imagine how Mary ever got any work done. Keeping up with the public and private lives of everyone at Hamilton House, Incorporated, had to be time-consuming. He also couldn't imagine why so many people confided in her, but Mary was privy to an astonishing amount of personal information. "What did dear Mary have to say?"

Helen frowned. "Normally I don't put much stock in her gossip, even though she's been proved right more often than not, but today's tidbit is so disturbing. Mary thinks there's going to be fireworks in the upper, upper echelons of the company, and she's afraid her boss is going to be right in the thick of things. She says Dolph and Vanessa are definitely on the outs, and she wouldn't be surprised if he was in line for the ax. Have you heard anything like that?"

"No, not a thing," Matt lied. He'd never tell anyone else in the company one word Vanessa had said to him that night in Dallas.

Helen looked relieved. "That's good. I know Dolph called you this week. I thought he might have said something."

Matt wished she hadn't reminded him of Dolph's call. It had been the most difficult, uncomfortable twenty minutes he'd ever spent on the telephone. Ostensibly Dolph had called about a West Coast distribution problem, but five minutes into the conversation he'd begun milking Matt for information. The man was nervous, pathetically so, but the last person he'd ever learn anything from was Matthew Logan.

Strange what success did to some people, he mused. One exigent move and Dolph had gone from first in line of succession to possibly getting canned—all because of avarice, crippled judgment and an astonishing lack of foresight.

"No, Helen, Dolph called about that distribution snag."

"That's a relief. I guess Mary got some bad signals this time. If something was going on, I'm sure you'd know about it. Thank heavens! The minute Mary told me that, I thought—oops. Bye-bye, boss."

"I don't understand, Helen."

"Matt, think about it. We've all assumed Dolph would succeed Vanessa someday, and she's no spring chicken. If Dolph's out, somebody's going to be C.E.O. My money would be on you. Who else?"

"Well, for openers, there are five other vice presidents."

Helen shook her head. "No, I'm afraid you'd be a shoo-in."

"Thanks for the vote of confidence."

"I think if you had to leave, I'd just quit. I'd hate it. I've always planned to work until Steve retires, but I wouldn't know how to work for anybody else."

Matt smiled. "Let's neither one of us start cleaning out our desks just yet, okay?"

"Fine with me." Helen got to her feet. "Have a good weekend."

"You, too, Helen."

Not surprisingly, Matt's short conversation with his secretary prompted him to ponder his mixed emotions over the prospect of the promotion. He wasn't accustomed to ambivalence, and it bothered him. Every shred of common sense he possessed told him there should be no doubts. What had he worked for all these years if not to go as far as he possibly could? That was what the American dream was all about— starting at the bottom and rising to the top. He had earned the right to Vanessa's office, and the company would be in capable hands.

He recalled a question his friends in college had liked to ask one another when talk turned to the future: Would you rather be a big fish in a little pond or a little fish in a big pond? Matt had never hesitated with his answer. He'd always said, "I want to be big fish in a big pond." And he had meant it. So why all the soul-searching?

Yet, no matter how often he told himself these things, he always returned to one thought: *I have so much here.*

Those were the things occupying his mind during the drive from his office to the arena, but once he arrived and parked his car, he shook them off. He hadn't seen Carol skate in a very long time, and he was looking forward to it.

Inside the building, Carol's skates scratched the surface of the ice, making a sound that cut through the still air of the empty arena. Matt spotted Lesley seated in the stands, and he went to sit beside her. Seeing him, she broke into a happy smile.

"So you got to come, after all," she said. "I didn't hold out much hope that you'd actually get away from the office."

"I simply got up and left." He leaned toward her; they kissed. "How's she doing?"

"We've had a good day so far. She works so hard. She wants very badly to impress the heck out of Eric when he gets back."

Carol spotted her dad and waved. She was feeling very on, and Matt's presence, like Eric's, always inspired her to do her best. She had been itching to do a triple for days, but Lesley kept saying "not yet." Carol couldn't imagine what they were waiting for. Every day they waited was a day wasted, as far as she was concerned. It no longer was a year until the next nationals; they were counting down the months.

As she skated around the ice with her hands on her hips, she glanced over her shoulder. At the moment Lesley was far more intent on the man by her side than she was on her student. Carol began to work up some speed. The urge to do a little showing off was irresistible.

She always knew early on when a jump was in trouble or when it was perfect, and this one was perfect. The moment she set her left toe pick in the ice to propel herself upward, she knew she was going to nail it. Then...

Crun-k-k-k! Upon landing, her right blade cut deeply into the ice, and she went down. It was a violent fall, but it wasn't the fall that bothered her. She had taken worse spills. The fall was nothing. Her wretched knee had failed her again. And this time it hurt. A sob caught in her throat.

She righted herself but continued sitting on the ice, her bowed head in her hands, her legs stretched out in front of her. Depleted of energy, sapped of strength and filled with despair, she felt disoriented, dizzy and so miserable she wanted to die.

She couldn't fool herself any longer. She had a bad knee and would have it the rest of her life. The one support she'd had since she was seven had been jerked out from under her. The whole purpose of her life had crumbled like clay. She recalled Dr. Hillman's words: *Some athletes bounce right back.... Some never come back.* Painfully, she accepted that she belonged in the latter category. There wouldn't be an Olympic medal. She had hoped and prayed, lied to herself—and Lesley and Eric—but it was over. She didn't even want to fight it any longer. As of that minute she never wanted to see a pair of skates again.

Both Lesley and Matt were calling her name. Heaving a surrendering sigh, Carol pushed herself up and skated over to them. The expression on her face reminded Matt of a tragedy mask.

"Let's go home," she said listlessly.

"Carol!" Lesley cried, truly alarmed. Carol was the one who was never ready to leave the rink. "So you bobbled a jump. That's the first triple you've tried since the accident. Did you forget the adjustment we made in the approach?"

"It wasn't the approach! It wasn't the jump! I aced the jump. It was the knee. When I landed, my leg suddenly felt like a strand of cooked spaghetti. What good would it do me to be able to leap over the moon if I can't land without falling? Face it, it's hopeless. Let's go home, and I'm not coming back tomorrow." She headed for the dressing room, leaving Lesley and Matt to stare after her.

"I'm worried," Matt said.

"So am I."

"And I'm not only worried about her knee. Mainly I'm worried because she sounds like she's giving up."

"Maybe she has." Lesley's voice was none too steady. "Maybe she should."

NATURALLY, BOTH LESLEY and Matt assumed Carol would change her mind after she got over her initial disappointment. Lesley, especially, fully expected to have to deal with should she or shouldn't she, but she was spared having to make a decision. Carol remained adamant. She not only was through with competitive skating—she was through with skating, period.

"There's no need to wash your hands of it completely, Carol," Lesley told her. "Why don't we go to the arena today for a light workout?"

"I'm not going back," Carol said. "What good would a light workout do me? How good can I possibly be if I'm always afraid the knee is going to buckle? And I'd rather not skate at all if I can't be one of the best. Forget it. The career is history."

"Oh, how I wish Eric was here. You need to talk to him."

"Why? He's not going to change my mind, either. Besides, I don't have any idea how to reach him or even where he is."

"He's going to be very unhappy about all this," Lesley told her.

"He'll live."

"What are you going to do?" Lesley asked, wishing Carol would cry or kick a door or throw something. Her calm, resigned acceptance was one of the most disturbing aspects of the unhappy situation.

"You mean with the rest of my life?"

"Yes."

Carol sighed and shrugged, which was the nearest thing to emotion she'd displayed since walking off the ice. "Do what Mom's always wanted me to do, I guess. Go to college. Make something of myself. Maybe I'll get a doctorate, be a real brain. And . . . I suppose I'll move back with Mom and Louis."

"Oh, Carol!" Lesley had been too preoccupied with other things to have considered that.

"Aw, Lesley, I'm not blind. I know you and Dad have something great going, and I'm always in the way."

"You've never been in the way. How could you possibly think that?"

"There's just no reason for me to stay here any longer."

Lesley didn't press it. She knew there was no way Olivia would want Carol to stay now that she wasn't skating. "What about Eric?"

"What about him?"

"Are you just going to stop seeing him?"

"I . . . I guess that will be up to him. I really don't imagine he'll keep hanging around, though. Why would he? Skating's his life, and I'm not part of that now."

This was the first time since Carol had decided to stop skating that Lesley had seen a tear in those lovely gray eyes. "That's a shame. The two of you seemed to have grown so close."

"He's got about two thousand things to think about besides me. I doubt he'll miss me much."

"I wouldn't bet on that, Carol. I've been around a number of years, and I think Eric cares for you more than even he realizes at this point."

"Yeah, well . . . he's certainly mastered the fine art of hiding it from me." Carol looked down at the floor. "I . . . guess I'll go call Mom and start gathering up all my stuff."

"There's no great rush, is there?"

"Might as well get it over with."

"I'm going to miss you," Lesley said, amazed at the size of the lump in her throat.

"I'll miss you, too, Lesley. I really will." Carol turned and hurried out of the room.

The news came as a complete but welcome surprise to Olivia. Although she went through the motions of being sorry that Carol had to give up something she'd wanted so badly, no one took her seriously, and it was to her credit that she didn't overplay her "sorrow."

Carol was no more than settled back in her old room than her mother began arranging a busy social schedule for her. It was time, Olivia announced, to introduce Carol to polite society, and some of the affairs she had planned sounded worthy of a coronation. Carol finally had to put a stop to it.

"Please, Mom, I don't want to do any of those things. I'm not interested in parties at the club, or parties anywhere, for that matter. Haven't you ever noticed the way I sort of float on the edge of those things, never really getting into the spirit of the occasion? I don't want to meet Louise Hall's nephew who's going to be a neurosurgeon. I barely know

Cynthia Scott, so why on earth would I want to go to her birthday ball? Until the fall term begins, I think I'd just like to be left alone.''

And she was very alone. After years of giving her all to skating, she knew very few people. She had been rising at dawn since she was seven, but now she found herself sleeping later each morning in order to shorten the days. She read voraciously, took up needlepoint again and continued to do her barre exercises, but it all seemed pretty pointless.

She vowed to exorcise skating and everything associated with it from her mind. Unfortunately, despite better intentions, she thought about Eric incessantly. The first Saturday after returning to the Pacific Heights house, she caught a professional figure skating exhibition from Paris on *Wide World of Sports*. All of the big names were there—Witt, Orser, Boitano and, of course, Eric. So that's where he was. France this week, then heaven only knew where next week. Busy, busy. A real pro. A star.

Carol wondered at the masochistic tendencies that kept her attention riveted on the TV, her eyes filling with tears, her chest heaving. She was supposed to be forgetting all this. She didn't want to look at those pretty people in their gorgeous costumes skating to exciting music. Why didn't she turn off the set?

Her nineteenth birthday was just around the corner. Once she had thought that would be her year, the time when she would finally break away from the pack and begin to make a name for herself. Instead, she was the most miserable person alive. Everything had come unglued all at once.

Olivia, gregarious soul that she was, fussed and fretted for a while, then gave up. She'd never really understood Carol and conceded that she wasn't apt to begin doing so at this late date. Carol, it seemed to her mother, had always been more Matt's daughter than hers.

"HAVE YOU TALKED to Carol recently?" Matt asked Lesley.

"Only once. She called—when was it?—Tuesday, I think. Funny, I thought she'd call every day, at least for a while. I called her yesterday but she had gone shopping. I left a message, but she didn't return my call."

"That doesn't sound like Carol."

"Oh, Matt, I think I understand. She must be feeling wretched, and I think at this point she just wants to divorce herself from anything and anyone that reminds her of skating. I'm sure we'll be close again one of these days."

"That's no excuse, and I plan to tell her that when I talk to her."

"Please, don't. Let her work it out her own way."

It was a Friday night. Carol had been gone for more than a week. Earlier that evening, Lesley and Matt had enjoyed dinner at the restaurant where they'd had their first date. Now they were back at Lesley's seated on the sofa in the library. Both of them had removed their shoes and had propped their feet on the coffee table. Soft music came from the stereo. A warm, good feeling engulfed Lesley. It was the kind of evening she loved best, when they were free from anything demanding.

It was also the first she'd seen of Matt since the previous weekend. He had spent most of the week in British Columbia, returning only that morning, while Lesley had spent the past four days on, of all things, spring cleaning. She and Clarice had scrubbed every inch of the big house, no small feat. Normally she would have called a cleaning service, but she had needed the activity. She missed Carol and Eric far, far more than she had thought she would.

"What was the purpose of this trip?" she asked idly. She seldom inquired about Matt's work, which was remiss of her, she supposed. Didn't all men love talking about what they did for a living? But up until now, when they weren't thoroughly engrossed in each other, they mostly had talked about Carol's skating. Lesley still found it hard to believe that was over. She missed it, too, so she could imagine the void it had left in Carol's young life.

"Vanessa said 'Go,' so I went," he said with a grin. "She's considering putting a restaurant in Vancouver, so I went to scout locations, talk with the city's movers and shakers, check out the business climate—that sort of thing. She's long harbored a desire to expand into Canada. First one thing, then another always kept her from it, but now she's calling the Canadian expansion her swan song. It might very well be."

A minute of silence ensued. That casual remark turned both their thoughts in the same direction. "Lesley," Matt said finally, "we haven't talked about this except that one night, but I think it's time we did. As far as I know, nothing's changed. I'm still being considered for the presidency. I have to know how you feel about that."

She said exactly what she thought. "I don't know. When I think about it, and lately I've thought about it quite a lot, I mostly think how different everything would be. Do you want the job very badly?"

"I deserve it," he said simply.

"I'm sure you do."

"But there are others who deserve it, too."

"You still haven't told me if you really want it," she reminded him.

He pursed his lips thoughtfully. "It's strange. I think I do, and yet . . . I also think of what I'd have to give up. My home, the city I've lived in all my life, people I've known for years, my daughter. You don't realize how solidly set in concrete your life can become over the years. I no longer have any burning desire to see new places, meet new people, have new experiences. I like what I have now, and it would be difficult to give it up." He paused and looked at Lesley. "The one thing I couldn't give up is you. You know I love you."

"Of course."

"I didn't expect that to happen to me. Through the years, whenever I thought of the future, I never considered falling in love. I suppose I thought if it was going to happen, it would have happened long ago. But if I moved to Dallas, I'd want you to come with me."

And that, she knew, was her out. All she would have to do was tell him she didn't want to go, that she wanted them to stay the way they were, and he would probably ask Vanessa to remove him from consideration. Lesley was sure she had that much of a hold on him.

But how grossly unfair to Matt. As he'd said, he deserved to be president.

"Is this a proposal?" she asked.

"Damned right. It can't be much of a surprise."

She smiled at him adoringly and planted a solid kiss on his mouth. "That's my acceptance. And doesn't a wife go where her husband goes? 'Whither thou goest' and all that."

"Not necessarily, not anymore, and besides, that's not the kind of answer I want—that you'll do whatever's required of you. I don't want you waking up in the morning and thinking, oh, God, today I have to be nice to so-and-so, or I have to go to such and such affair. Life's too short to spend it doing things you don't want to do, especially when you're as old as we are. I have to know how you honestly feel about it."

Lesley gave some thought to what she was going to say. "Matt, do you know what I like to do more than anything in the world?"

"I hope it's make love to me."

"After that."

"Well . . . maybe I don't. What do you like to do more than anything in the world?"

"This."

Matt looked around. They weren't doing anything, just sitting and talking and listening to music. Earlier they'd had a quiet dinner and shared a bottle of wine, hardly the kind of thing that wound up in the society pages.

Now that he thought about it, the times Lesley had been at her happy, animated best were when it was just the two of them. She withdrew from crowds, noise and hilarity of all kinds, which was pretty funny because she caused a stir wherever they went. Her arresting beauty was so unique that men stared at her and women envied her. Still, she shunned the limelight and tended to keep to herself. She actually was rather shy. Charmingly so, but shy, nevertheless.

Once he had asked her how on earth someone with her retiring nature ever performed in front of thousands, and she had replied, "I simply blotted out the crowd and skated as if I was the only one in the arena."

But how did one "blot out" two hundred people at a cocktail reception or dinner dance? "I guess I know what you're telling me," he said quietly.

"I wonder how many evenings like this the wife of the president of Hamilton House would get to spend."

"Maybe more than you think."

Then Matt recalled the Vanessa Hamilton of years ago, when she had been younger and Stuart had been alive. He'd spent some weeks with them in Dallas that had him, a much younger man, drooping. When the business hadn't been occupying their time, social, civic or political functions had. He couldn't count the times he had heard that Senator so-and-so *needed* the Hamiltons, this or that charity *needed* the Hamiltons, the Dallas Symphony *needed* the Hamiltons.

That required an awesome economy to their lives in which not a minute was wasted and every action contributed to the whole. Nothing was left to chance, and nothing was allowed to interfere. They'd even had to schedule their times alone together. Had they left intimate moments to chance, to spontaneity, they simply might never had happened. Matt had no doubts about being able to lead such an existence, because he had taught himself how to do it. Years earlier, when it had become apparent that his career was going to be a spectacular one, he had even used Vanessa and Stuart as role models.

He tried to envision Lesley living that way and found he could not. Above all, he wanted her to be happy. If being his wife made her miserable... He shuddered. It wouldn't be worth it.

An unnamed fear swept through him. She would marry him and go anywhere he chose, but would her love last if she was forced to live a life she not only didn't want but was woefully unprepared for? In spite of popular sentiment, love did not always conquer all.

"Carol's a great deal like me," Lesley said, as if she could read his thoughts. "I don't know if you've noticed that. She's a private person, too. I have to think the life a skater leads is partly responsible. Sometimes it's glamorous, but more often it's just filled with work and aloneness and very few friends. I used to see the life my mother led—benefits, the symphony, fashion shows, entertaining or being entertained, numbering her 'nearest and dearest' in the hundreds—and think, thank God I don't have to do all that. Now I'm not too sure it wouldn't have been good for me to learn a little something about that kind of life, but I wasn't interested, and neither is Carol."

"I thing you sell yourself short," Matt said, taking one of her hands and rubbing it between his. "I've watched you at social affairs. You're gracious and charming, and I have a feeling you could be an accomplished hostess."

"There's a big difference between being able to do those things and wanting to do them, enjoying them."

She had him there. *A big difference,* he silently agreed. "I'd never demand that you do things you didn't want to do," Matt said solemnly.

"I know that, darling, but you might resent it. A man in the lofty position you're being considered for needs a wife who's a partner in every respect."

"What are you telling me, Lesley?"

"No deep message. You asked me how I felt, and I told you."

He drew her into his arms, and for several minutes they embraced and did not speak. Then Matt stirred. "How did we let the mood turn so somber? I just asked you to marry me, and you accepted. We should be dancing for joy."

"So we should." Lesley struggled to her feet and held out her hand to him. "Come upstairs with me. Perhaps we won't dance, but I'll bet I find a way to properly thank you for that proposal."

Lesley switched off lights as they went, then she preceded him up the stairs. She wondered if she was being terribly disloyal to Matt by thinking what she was thinking—that maybe, hopefully, Vanessa would choose someone else. She was going to be his wife, and loyal wives wanted the moon for their husbands, didn't they? Some wives worked harder at their husbands' success than the husbands did. Why was she harboring such selfish thoughts? How could her heart be so full and her mind so troubled?

You want too much, Lesley, an inner voice said. *You want to call your days your own. You want Matt all to yourself, and that isn't possible.*

Then they stepped into her room, which had increasingly become their room. She felt him come to stand behind her and slip his arms around her waist to give her a comforting squeeze. With his nose he parted her hair and kissed her nape. She turned and sought the solace she always found in Matt's arms.

Yet, even with his warm mouth grazing her cheek, her troubled mind recalled something he had said the first night they had made love: *We live with our choices a very long time.*

As THE WEATHER grew milder, Matt began doing something on weeknights he hadn't done in years—taking long walks after dinner, past Grace Cathedral, Huntington Park and the city's finest hotels, all perched atop the nest known snidely by local folks as "Snob Hill." The doorman at the Fairmont now waved to him each evening. The walks might have been good for his physique, but they weren't successful at clearing his mind. Nightly he walked and pondered.

He didn't know what he wanted. There was Lesley, of course. No confusion about that. He wanted her with the kind of intensity he had thought was reserved for much younger men, and she wanted him, too. There was no question in his mind that she would go wherever he wanted, do whatever he wanted. But . . . what did he want?

Last weekend they had decided to be married at the end of the summer. Then it had become a question of "your place or mine." His town house was convenient but her house was her home. Forget that it was fifty percent more house than they needed. They ten-

tatively planned to live in the city during the week and
at her place on the weekends and holidays. In a couple of years, perhaps he would turn the town house
over to Carol. She'd probably be ready to cut the
apron strings about then.

Thinking of Carol brought to mind the call he'd
made to her to give her the news about the marriage.
"Oh, Dad, that's wonderful!" his daughter had exclaimed, then promptly dissolved into tears. He and
Lesley had invited her out to dinner to help them celebrate, but that had been a mistake. Misery did not
want the company of two blissfully happy people.
Naturally, Carol had refused, and Matt admitted he
understood.

But, thankfully, Carol would not remain unhappy
forever, not at her age, so he didn't brood too much
about her present frame of mind. His brooding, if it
could be called that, centered squarely on his own
inner turmoil.

Never before in his adult life had Matt questioned
his devotion to work. What difference did it make that
he could count on the fingers of one hand the real
vacations he'd taken during the past twenty-odd
years? Moreover, he'd never seen anything wrong with
regarding social invitations as major IOUs that he
would collect on one day. He was a successful businessman, and he operated accordingly.

But a lot had changed since Lesley had happened,
and those changes had him feeling less restricted, far
freer than before. Now he could see that too much of
his life had been ordered around obligations that in
retrospect seemed meaningless. Now he could leave
work early without feeling he had committed a major

crime. He could keep his weekends free without a trace of guilt. He found it easy to turn down invitations to tiresome events he knew Lesley would hate. He doubted the president of Hamilton House, Incorporated, would be allowed such small luxuries.

He guessed what it boiled down to was that he wasn't sure he wanted to go back to being the old Matthew Logan, so intensely dedicated to his work that he inspired awe in his peers and fear in his subordinates. The new one was a much nicer guy.

But the old one would be more effective as the company's C.E.O.

Plus, he knew what Lesley wanted, and it wasn't to move to Dallas.

But is it in me to say 'No, thanks' to Vanessa?

Matt's mind whirled. He descended from Nob Hill's gilded heights, past the Mark Hopkins and the Stanford Court, and went home, as confused as ever.

CHAPTER FOURTEEN

PHILADELPHIA WAS the last stop on the tour. Eric had never been so glad to see anything end in his life. Not even Paris had been fun this time, and it was his favorite foreign city. He couldn't imagine why he felt so restless and unfulfilled. The tour had been a huge success. Attendance had been great, the audiences receptive, and he'd been the headliner. Still, instead of exhilaration after the applause, he felt only relief that another show was over and he was one day closer to home.

He wondered if disillusionment had set in. He had expected to enjoy performing more than he did. Representatives from one of the big ice shows had contacted him, offering him a record amount of money to sign, and he'd experienced a fleeting moment of temptation. It had passed quickly, however. A month on the road had been bad enough. Nine of them would be intolerable.

For the first time in his life, he didn't know what he wanted to do tomorrow or the next day or the next. Obviously it wasn't to perform night after night. The TV special was okay because it was a one-shot, but a seemingly endless string of one-nighters? No, thanks. There had to be something else his training would allow him to do, something satisfying, something meaningful.

Coaching? That wasn't one of the options he'd seriously considered when he was just coming off the Olympics, but he'd enjoyed working with Carol more than anything he'd done since turning pro. However, he had to consider the possibility that it was working with Carol, rather than coaching per se, that had made it so enjoyable. During the past month of traveling by day, performing at night, giving interviews that required answering the same questions time after time, he had experienced his first brush with homesickness. And it suddenly dawned on him that what he mostly was homesick for was Carol.

He missed her. Admitting that had hit him with a jolt. How had she wormed her way into his thoughts? When exactly had he stopped thinking of her as that flip little kid? He didn't know, but he thought about her almost constantly. As he watched the other skaters in warm-ups, he found himself on the lookout for engaging new moves she might add to her program. A new piece of music automatically made him begin choreographing it for her in his mind's eye. He hadn't heard her voice since his first night away from home, when he'd called to find out what Bancroft had told her. "He told me to be careful," she'd said, and Eric hoped that was the truth. He longed to talk to her daily, but there was never a good time to call since the troupe was constantly on the move. Besides, phone calls were too unsatisfying. Sunday night—or rather, early Monday morning—he would be back home, back to her, and until '92 her medal would be his chief goal. After that . . . he'd find something they could do together.

He wondered if he should tell her that—all of it, some of it, any of it. Did he want to run the risk of complicating their relationship, maybe ruining a wonderful friendship altogether? She really didn't need complications at this stage in her career, and truthfully, he had no reason to think he'd get anything but a snappy retort if he suggested they might make beautiful music together.

He honest-to-God couldn't imagine when or how this had happened to him.

The door to the dressing room flew open just then, and Carl Walsh walked in. Carl was a pairs skater who, along with his partner, had won a long string of national and world medals. He also was the nearest thing to a friend Eric had on the tour. "We've got some time to kill," Carl said. "How about coming with me? I want to see my sister. She runs a clinic in South Philly, and she's after me to come see it."

"A clinic? What is she, a doctor or something?"

"Nah, she's a skater, just like everyone in my family. It's a skating clinic for kids."

"Aw, Carl, I don't know...."

"Come on. Give my sister and the kids a thrill. Sign some autographs. What else do you have to do—hang around backstage?"

He had a point there. Eric shrugged. "Okay, I'll go along to keep you company."

"You might even pick up some pointers," Carl joked. "My sister says those kids are astonishing. I don't know what it is they do that's so remarkable, but she says I really need to see them."

EARLY MONDAY AFTERNOON, while Clarice was out doing their grocery shopping for the week, Lesley came into the game room carrying a cardboard box. Earlier, the maid had mentioned finding the box in Carol's closet, so Lesley had investigated. Its contents broke her heart. Carol's skates, the tapes of her music, her leotards and a couple of costumes—everything Carol had in the house that was associated with skating—had been left. And not by accident, Lesley was sure.

Even Eric's poster had still been tacked to the back of the closet door. That spoke volumes about Carol's frame of mind. Her precious poster, the first thing she'd put in her room when she'd come to stay here, left behind. Lesley had taken it down, rolled it into a tight cylinder and propped it in the box. She intended on giving the things to Matt, who could decide whether to give them to Carol.

It was sad really, but Lesley, more than anyone, could empathize. She'd been through something similar—coming off a disappointing showing in the Olympics, certain she was through with skating forever but at a loss to know what else she could do. One of these days, when Carol felt better, Lesley planned to discuss coaching with her. She had intended mentioning the two of them coaching together, but then she was reminded that they couldn't very well do that if she was in Dallas.

And that prompted a rash of unrelated thoughts. Dallas! She was beginning to hate the sound of the city's name, which was ridiculous. Several times she had found herself wistfully wishing Matt was in another line of work or wasn't quite so successful, which was even more ridiculous.

Your problem, Lesley, her inner voice said, *is that you resist change. Let go a little. You might have a wonderful time in Dallas.*

Not if I have to live on a social merry-go-round.

Well, then, you could always tell Matt no.

I couldn't! I don't want to live without him. Just thinking about it made her sick to her stomach. After a sheltered youth and a less than satisfying marriage, she was living, really living, for the first time in her life.

You'd better make some heavy decisions before you get married. Once Matt gets that promotion, he's outta here.

Well, I'll be outta here, too.

Then she wondered if her real worry was that she would do a lousy job as the president's wife and disappoint Matt. She could live with the benefits, the cocktail parties and dinner dances, but she couldn't live with Matt's disappointment in her.

Oh, how she hoped he wouldn't get the promotion! She knew how horribly selfish that was, but she couldn't help it. It was the way she felt.

The doorbell's ring interrupted her thoughts. Lesley answered the front door and found Eric standing there. "Well, hello, stranger. I heard you were in Paris. I was beginning to think you might be taking out French citizenship." She stepped back, holding the door wide, and he brushed past her.

"It was a grueling tour. I'm not anxious for another like it anytime soon. Are you guys goofing off this morning? I went to the arena, but nobody was there.''

Lesley took a deep breath. "You *have* been gone a long time. A lot has happened since we last saw you. I need to talk to you."

"Where's Carol?"

"That's why I need to talk to you."

She led him down to the game room, offered him something to drink, then told him the news. Eric was stunned by the unexpected turn of events.

"You mean, she really quit?"

Lesley nodded. "Just walked off the ice and hasn't been back. I've resigned myself to it. She'll never go back."

"Does she need to quit, Lesley?"

"Probably. Certainly she can't realistically hope to compete again. After that last fall, her knee was sore for a couple of days. She was running the risk of ruining that knee for good. I called Dr. Bancroft, and he said the same thing. Ultimately, however, it was Carol's decision."

"That's a damned shame." Eric sighed. "But maybe I've half expected it since the accident. Still, I'm surprised she quit. I thought she'd have to be carried off the ice on a stretcher. How long has she been gone?"

"About two weeks."

"What's she doing? How is she?"

"I have no idea. I've only talked to her once since she left. She really doesn't seem to want to have anything to do with anyone."

"I don't believe this! As close as you two were? I'm going to have a nice long talk with that young lady."

"Eric, I..." Lesley hesitated. "Don't be surprised or offended if she doesn't want to see you."

"Of course I'll be offended. Why wouldn't she want to see me? I think Carol and I...you know, sort of have this special thing between us. For Pete's sake, I've seen far more of her during the past eleven years than I have my parents or brothers and sisters."

"I know, but this is such a difficult time for her. You can understand that, can't you?"

"Yes, yes," he said impatiently. "I can understand how really rotten she must feel, but that's no excuse. We're her friends."

At that moment Clarice stuck her head in the door to tell Lesley that Matt was on the phone, so Lesley excused herself. Eric stood up and began pacing the room. The box sitting on the bar caught his eye. He glanced at its contents idly, then did a double take. In it were skates and several leotards that he thought he recognized as Carol's. Poking out of the box was a long paper cylinder. He unrolled it and found himself looking at the poster that had been made last fall. He was staring at it in puzzlement when Lesley came back into the room.

"Uh-oh," she muttered under her breath. Carol would die.

Eric turned. "What's all this stuff?"

"Things Carol left in her closet," she admitted.

He looked at the poster again, then rerolled it and stuck it back into the box. "That's Carol's?"

"Uh-uh."

Lesley noticed the way the corners of his mouth twitched, as though he were holding back a smile. He was genuinely pleased. So she'd been right. He cared for Carol, and in a way that transcended mere friendship.

"The photographer told me to look sexy," Eric said with a sheepish smile. "Does that look sexy to you?"

"Pretty sexy."

"Funny what girls think is sexy." Then he frowned. "Why would she leave her skates?"

"That's what I've been trying to tell you. Carol's trying to forget skating and anything or anyone associated with it. It's a self-defense mechanism."

"I guess that makes sense."

"I went through something similar when I came off the Olympics. I was expected to win, and I was lucky to wind up with the bronze. I cried every day for two weeks. I didn't want to compete. I didn't want to perform. I didn't even want to skate, and I didn't until I started coaching. I know how unhappy and lonely Carol must be right now, and that's why she's shutting us out."

"You can't just wipe people out of your life," Eric insisted.

"Be patient with her. Above all, don't take anything she says or does right now to heart. You, far more than Matt or I, can do her a world of good, and I'm sure you'll be able to one of these days. But if she doesn't want to see you just yet—"

"Tough," Eric said, already heading for the door. "She's going to see me whether she wants to or not." At the doorway he stopped and snapped his fingers, as though he'd forgotten something. Turning, he walked to the bar and scooped up the box. "I'm going to return these things to their rightful owner. Do you mind?"

"Oh, Eric, I don't think—"

"Trust me. I'll be in touch."

"What if she refuses to see you?"

"I'm not going to give her that chance."

THE MAID WHO ANSWERED Eric's ring informed him that Carol was in the morning room, wherever that was. Since she gestured toward the rear of the house, he headed in that direction.

The Bannister house was very quiet, almost eerily so. Every time he'd been in it he had noticed the absence of activity and noise. Didn't these people ever turn on a radio or TV? It always made him think of his parents' house, where the noise level often rivaled that of an average steel mill.

Eric walked into the den, looked around, then spotted Carol seated in a glass-enclosed cubicle overlooking a rose garden. Her back was to him, her head bent in concentration over a book. Soundlessly he crossed the den and was almost upon her before she sensed rather than saw him. Looking up, her mouth formed an astonished O.

She was wearing a yellow blouse that wrapped in front and was tied at the waistband of her jeans. Her mane of dark, springy curls had been tamed with a ribbon of the same color. She reminded Eric of one of the perky daffodils that were currently in bloom all over the city.

Then he looked into her sad, sad eyes and decided that perky was the last adjective he would use to describe her. She looked lost and frightened. He experienced a lurch in his heart, a lump in his throat and a tightness in his groin simultaneously.

God, she was lovely! And she had grown up right before his eyes. She'd be nineteen soon, not a bratty little kid any longer. And she no longer affected him like a bratty little kid. Sometimes his thoughts toward her turned dangerously lustful.

For several seconds they merely looked at each other. Eric stood searching her face for some sign that she was glad to see him, but she was expressionless. He set the cumbersome box down on the floor. Carol glanced at it but didn't react in any way. When Eric straightened, she still simply stared at him.

"Hi," she finally said.

"'Hi'? That's it? Just hi? You'd think we just saw each other yesterday. It's been weeks and weeks."

"Wh-what did you want me to do?"

"I don't know. Bat your eyelashes at me or something."

"All right." She batted her eyelashes at him.

He bent to kiss her cheek, then sat down. "I just came from Lesley's. Seems you ran off and left a few things. I brought them to you."

Carol looked at the box again but said nothing.

"It was quite a shock to learn that my services are no longer required."

Carol's face flushed. "I'm not worried you won't find work elsewhere. I had to quit. I had no choice."

"Maybe not, and I hate that, I really do. But apparently you did choose to wash your hands of Lesley and me."

"Who told you that?"

"Lesley."

Carol marked her place in the book and set it down. "I'm sorry she thinks that, but I haven't been very good company lately."

"We don't expect you to keep us entertained."

"I just haven't felt much like talking...about anything, actually, but especially not about skating."

"I imagine if Lesley and I tried real hard, we might come up with something else to talk about."

Carol looked away. How she wished he hadn't come. He was too forceful a reminder of what she had come to think of as her other life, the one no longer possible. And, too, as the days had passed without seeing him, she'd found it easier to go an hour or so without thinking of his soulful eyes, his sensuous mouth and that superb body in Lycra pants. Now, she supposed, she would have to start back at square one. Why had he come?

But, realistically, had she honestly thought he wouldn't? He wouldn't have any idea how desperately she wanted to forget skating. Once he knew, he would leave and not return of his own accord. They no longer had anything in common. When she looked back at Eric, she asked, "Did Lesley tell you she and Dad are getting married at the end of the summer?"

Eric's eyes widened. "No, she didn't. That's great!" That drew no response from Carol. "Don't you think so?"

"Sure. I'm happy for both of them."

"Yeah, you sound thrilled." Eric glanced around the room. It was an atrium of sorts, with dozens of plants scattered around. But the house was as quiet as a tomb. That would depress someone who felt pretty good to begin with, but for someone in Carol's frame of mind... "What do you do here all day, every day?"

"Oh ... read, do needlepoint, things like that."

"All day?" he asked incredulously.

"Of course not all day. I still work out with weights a little and do my ballet exercises."

"That sounds like fun. Is that the way you plan to spend the rest of your life?"

"No," she said through clenched teeth, "that isn't the way I plan to spend the rest of my life. I'm starting college this fall."

"To study what?"

"I don't know. It doesn't matter in your freshman year. You just have to take junk, anyway."

"Sounds like you're really looking forward to it," he said a bit sarcastically. Sitting back, Eric studied her. The one thing that had always struck him about Carol was her upbeat outlook. She could be sassy and flip, but she was always up. She'd never had much patience with doom and gloom. Now she looked as though she had lost her best friend, and in a manner of speaking, he guessed she had.

He tried putting himself in her shoes, but that was useless. He'd never been injured, never had to choose between skating and perhaps doing permanent damage to his body. How could he really know how she felt?

But he did know one thing: she had to find a new interest. And he thought he had just the thing. "I really don't think you should stop skating."

"I have to."

"Competitive skating, yes. But why stop altogether?"

Carol made a contemptuous sound. "Do it for rec-
reation, you mean? I'll never be able to regard skating as a diversion. I've gone way beyond that."

An uncomfortable silence passed between them. She
was in such a mood! Eric hardly knew how to relate to
Carol when she was like this. "I came over here to tell
you about a project, something I've been thinking
about getting involved in. I was hoping you might
want to do it with me."

"Does it involve skating?"

"Of course it involves skating. What else do I know
how to do?"

"Then I'm not interested." There was a stubborn
lift to her chin.

"How do you know? You haven't heard what it is
yet," he said rather harshly.

"Eric, I know I don't want to skate again, ever! I
wanted to be a champion. I wanted to be an Olympic
medalist. I'll never be either, so forget it."

He simply looked at her for a minute. Then he
shook his head. "Boy, have you got your head screwed
on wrong today."

"It might seem that way to you, but it makes perfect sense to me. Every time I'd step onto the ice I'd
think of all that money, all that training, all those
years of doing without friends and parties, of getting
up at dawn—for nothing. Zero! Zilch!"

"Carol, I know it's a damned shame, but you're not
the first person this has happened to, and you won't
be the last."

"Is that supposed to make me feel better?"

Eric raked a hand through his hair, then spread his
hands in a helpless gesture. "I don't know how to talk

to you when you're like this. You're like someone I don't even know."

Carol rubbed a hand over her eyes. "I know," she said, "and it'll get worse. Skating's your life, and...I won't be part of that world anymore. You'll be off competing, performing. I'll never see you. We'll drift apart. It's bound to happen."

"My God, do you think I only want you for a friend if you have an Olympic medal? Carol, we don't have to drift apart. It doesn't have to be that way." He reached into his hip pocket and withdrew an envelope. "That's why I wanted you to have a look at this. It's something we could do together."

She stared at the envelope but didn't reach for it.

"I got this when the tour was in Philadelphia. I went to this place, a clinic where handicapped kids are taught to skate. Even blind kids! It was the most exciting thing I've ever seen. You wouldn't believe the things those kids learn to do or how enthusiastic they are. But there aren't nearly enough of those clinics around the country, and I thought..." He stopped, seeing the lack of response on Carol's face. "Please, won't you at least read about it?"

For a minute he thought she was going to reach for the envelope. It seemed to him she wanted to but was fighting it. Finally, however, she clasped her hands in her lap and shook her head. "I'm...sorry, but I'm going to school. I'll be...too busy for the next four years to do anything else. I'll make new friends, have new experiences..."

Eric stared at her in disbelief. For weeks now he'd thought of almost nothing but getting back to her. During the flight back from the east, he'd planned and rehearsed how to tell her what he felt, how he'd come to care for her in a way that had nothing to do with their past relationship. Now she was behaving as though she wished he would leave. Suddenly he felt sick to his stomach . . . and not just a little afraid that something he wanted very badly wasn't going to happen. "Are you telling me to buzz off?"

"I didn't mean it that way."

"Then how did you mean it?"

"I thought I was making myself clear. I don't want to skate anymore, ever. It has nothing to do with you."

"Seems to me it does." Eric's chest heaved in agitation. He shot to his feet and kicked back the chair. "God, you're ticking me off!" He set the envelope on a nearby table. "If you can stop feeling sorry for yourself long enough, you might try reading that pamphlet one of these days. You'll discover there are a lot of people in the world with bigger problems than yours. I once told Lesley that if the knee thing turned out to be more serious than we thought, I'd never try to tell you that skating isn't everything. Well, I lied. I am telling you just that. It isn't. Some of those kids at that clinic would give anything if all they had to contend with was a weak knee. If you ever want to talk to me about it, you know how to reach me. You call me—I won't call you." Throwing up his hands in disgust, he angrily strode from the room, kicking the cardboard box as he passed it.

Carol remained silent until she heard the distant sound of the front door opening and closing. Then she began to cry.

CHAPTER FIFTEEN

MATT REGARDED the solemn-faced, earnest young man seated across from his desk. He had been surprised, to say the least, when Helen had announced Eric. He was sure the young man had never before come to see him at the office . . . or anywhere else, for that matter. One look at the expression on Eric's face had prompted him to tell Helen to hold all his calls. Now that he'd heard the story, he was as upset as Eric was.

"Is she really in such bad shape?"

"We are talking major blue funk here," Eric said. "I don't know if I'm more worried than I am mad, or if it's the other way around. I drove around for a long time before coming here, and I don't know what I thought this would accomplish, but . . . I guess I just wanted someone to talk to."

"I'm flattered you chose me."

"I never thought Carol would treat me like that. Lesley tried to warn me, but I figured it would take me all of fifteen minutes to have her back to her old self again. I sure never thought she'd treat me like an . . . an intrusion or something. I half expected her to tell me to get out of her life." He paused for a moment. "Come to think of it, I guess she more or less did."

Matt frowned. Carol's treatment of Eric stunned him, too. The young man she had worshiped blindly for eleven years? What could be going through her mind? Apparently Lesley's theory had been correct. Carol was serious about forgetting skating and everyone associated with it. Lesley seemed to understand, even to consider it a normal reaction to Carol's devastating disappointment. Matt tried to look at it that way but couldn't. He would have thought his daughter was more of the "pick yourself up and start all over again" school.

Eric got to his feet, shoved his hands in his pockets and walked to the window. "I always thought Carol and I were pretty tight. When you work with someone almost every day for years, the two of you end up either close or unable to stand each other. I guess you know which we were."

"Yes, Eric. I thought it had become a remarkable relationship," Matt said. There was a lot more he wanted to say, but for the moment he let it go at that. Eric, he sensed, just wanted to talk. He watched as the young man paced the room.

"It had changed a lot lately," Eric went on. "At least I thought it had. I don't really feel comfortable saying these things to you because I know how fathers are about their daughters. I had older sisters, and my dad hated every guy they ever dated. But I really care about Carol, in ways that have nothing to do with skating. I care about her as a person...a female person, if you get my drift."

Matt smiled. "I get your drift."

"I know she's pretty young, but she won't be forever, and I can wait. And I know she thinks of me as nothing but a big brother figure, but that could change with time.''

So, Matt thought, *Carol's a better actress than I gave her credit for. He really doesn't know.*

"Nobody, but nobody, feels worse about her accident than I do," Eric said. "I just knew she was going to be a champion someday, and I wanted to help her because...well, because I always felt bad about being Sondra's favorite. I know Carol got shortchanged a lot of the time." His voice rose, and frustration was etched on his face. "But that wasn't my fault, and neither was her accident, so why in hell is she treating me this way?"

Matt felt for the young man right down to his toes. How galling frustration could be when one was twenty-three. "Eric, I'm on your side in this. I'm not going to defend my daughter's actions, because there's no defense. There's no excuse for the way Carol's treating Lesley, who loves her and is deeply saddened that she never calls or comes by. There's no excuse for her giving you the brush-off. You're probably the best friend she's ever had. She can cry three times a day, and I think all of us would understand. She can sequester herself in that house—the worst thing she could do—but we might even understand that. She's suffered a stunning disappointment, the death of a dream. But none of that gives her the right to turn her back on the people who care for her most."

He'd gotten Eric's attention, so he pressed on. "Still, we've got to be patient. You know she's not going to stay in a blue funk forever, and when she snaps out of it, she's going to need all of us around again."

"I don't have all that much time," Eric said. "I'm going to do that TV special, and it's going to be filmed all over the country. I hate to tell you I'm doing it for money, but I am. I've got a project in mind, but it's going to take some cash. That's what I wanted to talk to Carol about. I wanted her in on it with me, but she wouldn't even talk about it, wouldn't even read the information I'd brought along."

"Project? What sort of project?"

"A clinic where handicapped kids learn to skate. I visited one in Philadelphia. I thought Carol and I could open one here in the Bay Area. Of course, I figured it would have to be a sometime thing for her until after '92, but now she could give it her all. And since we don't start shooting the special until September, I'll have some time to start laying the groundwork. I've been about to burst with excitement just thinking about it, but Carol took the wind out of my sails fast."

Matt's ears perked up. Again and again Lesley had said that the answer to Carol's problems was a new interest, something she could do well, something that would give her a sense of purpose. The clinic sounded perfect. Not only would she be doing meaningful work, she'd be doing it with Eric. What was wrong with her? She couldn't be thinking straight. "It sounds like just what she needs," he told Eric.

"Yeah, but the lady's not interested, thanks. I guess she'd rather sit in that house and mope. Well, I'm going to open that clinic one of these days, with or without Carol. If she won't have anything to do with it, I'll find somebody else." Eric's eyes clouded. "It's just that we work so well together."

Carol was making a terrible mistake, Matt knew. One she would regret the rest of her life. It was Lesley's contention that they ought to leave Carol alone to shake her despondency in her own way, but Matt wondered if perhaps it wasn't time for a little parental intervention. He got to his feet. "Come on, Eric, you and I are going to pay the lady a visit. It's time I went into my 'dear old Dad' number."

"Oh, no, not me. Not on your life. Not after she practically threw me out of the house."

"Trust me. By the way, did you say anything here this afternoon that you don't want to go further?"

Eric thought about it. "No, I don't think so."

"Then let's go. Just give me a minute for a word with my secretary. When I get through with Carol, she'll be begging to see you."

He just hoped to hell he was capable of being that persuasive.

ERIC FOLLOWED MATT back to the Pacific Heights house, but he balked at going inside again. "I'll just stroll around the neighborhood," he said. "It's fun to gawk at the mansions and see how the other half lives."

"Don't stray far," Matt called as he went up the walk. He rang the doorbell and tried to recall the maid's name. It came to him just as the door swung open.

"Good afternoon, Lucille," he said pleasantly.

"Good afternoon, Mr. Logan. It's nice to see you again." She stepped back to allow him to enter.

"I'd like to see Carol."

"I believe she's up in her room. I'll get her."

"Please, no. I'll just go up, if that's all right."

"Of course it's all right. She'll be so happy to see you."

Matt fervently hoped so. He started for the stairs, but the sound of Olivia's voice halted him. "Matt?" she called.

Turning, he saw her framed in the parlor doorway. She was wearing one of those braid-trimmed suits she was so fond of.

"Hello, Olivia. I was on my way up to see Carol."

"Would you come in here first? I want to talk to you."

"Of course."

He followed her into the room; then, to his surprise, she closed the double doors behind them. "Problems?" he asked, wondering why the need for privacy.

"It's Carol." Olivia nervously began twisting the massive solitaire she wore on her ring finger. "Matt, she's a mess. I doubt that she's poked her head out of this house three times since she moved back."

"So I understand."

"Lucille said that Eric came by to see her earlier. I can't imagine what he said to her, but she's been crying off and on ever since. She's driving me crazy! I simply cannot abide a gloomy person. I wouldn't be surprised if she's headed for a major depression and taking me right along with her."

"She's going through a very difficult time, Olivia," Matt reminded her.

"And making it difficult for the rest of us while she's at it." She sighed. "Oh, Matt, I know what a terrible time this is for her. For the life of me, I can't think why the skating was so important to her, but obviously it was. I, as you well know, would not have chosen that life for her, but it wasn't my choice."

The dig was gentle but aimed squarely at him. "It wasn't mine, either. It was Carol's."

"Yes, well ... something must be done about her present frame of mind."

"That's why I'm here. I'll do my best."

"I thought it might help her to talk to her coach ... that Lesley person, you know."

"Yes, I know," Matt said, trying to hide a smile.

"But Carol won't even call her. She won't do anything, and her attitude is upsetting the entire household. I'm worried about her, and that worries Louis, who takes it out on the servants."

Matt took her by the shoulders, patting her reassuringly. "I told you, I'll do my best."

Olivia sighed again. "For so many years now I've desperately wanted Carol to stop skating and to go to college. In spite of what you thought, I honestly believed that was the best life for her. Now it's happened ... and I find it isn't what I want at all. I wish she was still skating. I wish she still lived with her coach. I wish she would *smile*, for heaven's sake! I wish everything was the way it used to be! I didn't realize how nice things were until they changed."

Admitting she was wrong did not come easily for Olivia. For once, Matt could smile at her with genuine warmth. For once, their thoughts about Carol were on the same track. "Isn't it a shame? That happens too often in life. Aren't we told to be careful what we wish for? Carol's going to snap out of this, you'll see."

"You know, I truly hate myself for what I'm about to say, but I have to say it. *I told you so.* I told you the child was one-dimensional. Take away the skating and she has nothing! Everyone needs something to fall back on."

Matt took a deep, steadying breath. "Yes, Olivia, you told me so. Now, I'd like to go up and have a talk with her, if that's all right."

"Of course it's all right," Olivia said tiredly. "Good luck."

"Will I see you again before I leave?"

"I'm afraid not. I'm on my way to the club, and I'm already running late."

"Then I'll be talking to you. Give my regards to Louis."

Carol's room was at the top of the stairs. The door was closed. He tapped, waited for his daughter's summons, then opened it. Carol was sitting cross-legged in the middle of her four-poster, surrounded by stacks of photograph albums and scrapbooks. She brightened considerably when she saw her father.

"Dad! What on earth are you doing here in the middle of the day?"

"Hello, honey." Crossing the room, he bent to kiss her cheek before sitting down on the edge of the bed. "How are you?"

"Oh—" her shoulders rose and fell "—okay, I guess."

Matt searched her face. She looked less "okay" than anyone he'd ever seen. And he definitely saw signs of crying. "What's all this?" He indicated everything on the bed.

"The story of my life," Carol said grimly. "Since there's no need to preserve it for posterity, I'm trying to get up the nerve to just pitch it all."

"Pitch it!" Matt exclaimed. "Honey, nobody throws away memories." He opened one of the scrapbooks to a random page and looked at the yellowed newspaper clipping pasted on it. A radiant eleven-year-old Carol smiled back at him. The picture had been taken when she had won her first junior competition. It was hard to believe that happy little girl was the beautiful, sad-eyed young woman seated next to him. Closing the book, he said, "I understand you had a visitor earlier."

Carol's eyes widened. "Eric? How did you know that?"

"He came to see me, too."

"Whatever for?"

"He needed someone to talk to. You know, you cut him to the quick—you really did."

"Oh, Dad, he'll get over it. He's such a busy man."

"What about Lesley? Is she supposed to 'get over it,' too? She's going to be my wife, your stepmother. How can you continue to ignore her?"

He saw Carol's chin quiver. Lord, the last thing he'd come up here to do was make her start crying again. Feminine tears always made him feel helpless and inadequate.

"It's just..." Carol began, then hesitated. "It's just that every time I'd look at either one of them I'd be reminded of all the things I've lost, and—"

"So you just might as well lose them, too, right?"

Carol looked shocked. "Well, no, I... Not lose them. I just haven't felt like talking to anyone."

"How long do you think Eric's going to remain your friend if you continue to treat him the way you did this afternoon? I thought you cared about him—as in, a lot."

"Was I that obvious?"

"Not to the world, no. But to me and to Lesley, yes."

"There's not much mystery behind Lesley's knowing how I feel about Eric. I told her. We used to talk about him a lot. She called us an invincible trio. Guess I proved her wrong, huh?"

"And still you can treat them the way you have?"

"It's complicated. You wouldn't understand."

"Try me."

Carol took a minute to decide what she was going to say. "Lesley has you now. She couldn't give a flip whether she's into skating or not. And Eric? He's going to be a big star for years and years. There won't be a common interest, a bond. I'll just be a nobody."

"Carol!" Matt reached out and brushed a curl behind her ear. "You're somebody if you think you are. You're somebody when somebody else thinks you are. Eric's crazy about you. He admitted as much to me in my office."

Carol's eyes widened, then narrowed suspiciously. She didn't think her father was above telling a white lie or stretching the truth to get his point across. "Eric said that?" she asked, disbelieving.

"Uh-uh."

"Why would he tell you something like that?"

Matt chuckled. "I guess because I'm your father and he thought I might have some influence with you.

He had talked to Lesley earlier, and she told him you never call or return her calls."

Carol glanced down at her hands. "I just didn't know what to say to her."

"Anything. Lesley doesn't think of you only as a student. She thought you were friends." Matt scooted closer and put his arm around her shoulders. "Honey, I'm sorry you won't go to the Olympics—I really am. God knows, it's hard to give up a dream. Remember, it was my dream, too, for a lot of years. And Lesley's. And Eric's. We all hate it. But I'll tell you one thing— I don't hate that nearly as much as I'd hate another accident, another operation, the chance that you might be crippled for life."

"I know." Carol spoke just above a whisper.

"Not many of us get through life without some major disappointments. Adapting, going with the flow, changing with the circumstances are all signs of maturity. Life goes on ... or it should. Once, a long time ago, a very wise young woman told me something that had a big effect on my life at the time. She said that when something's over, it's over—that it doesn't make sense to cling to what's gone. When you think about it, that's about as sensible as anything you'll ever hear. We all love you. I've never been an athlete, so maybe I'm looking at it differently than you, but to me, all that love is better than a room full of medals."

Carol placed her fingertips over her mouth and closed her eyes, heaving such a pronounced sigh that Matt was afraid the tears were about to fall. This time, however, he did not think they would be from sadness alone.

"It seems to me that a lot of this stems from the fear that if you aren't skating, Eric will more or less disappear from your life, right?"

"Stands to reason, doesn't it? He'll be running all over the world, meeting all these fantastic people. Why would he remember me?"

"So you'll end the relationship before he can, is that it?"

"I guess . . . it's something like that."

"Then you weren't listening to him. Eric has some fantastic plans for the two of you, something that would have you working together for years and years. I wish you would at least let him tell you what they are. You can always say no then."

"Be sensible. When would he have time to run a clinic, for Pete's sake?"

"Why don't you ask him?"

"Well, I . . ." Carol cocked her head. "Dad, exactly what did Eric say to you that makes you think he's . . . crazy about me?"

Matt smiled. She was curious, and that was the first chink in the armor. "He wasn't exactly speaking in code. As I recall, he was fairly explicit. He said . . . now, let me think. He said he really cares for you in a way that has nothing to do with skating. He cares for you as a person . . . a female person."

"He did?"

"Absolutely."

"Oh my gosh!"

"Now, are you going to tell me that means nothing to you?"

Carol shook her head. "No, no, of course not. It means a lot, it really does. I just . . . never thought it would happen.'' Suddenly she slid off the bed. "I'm going to try to find him. If he's not at his place, maybe he'll be at his mom's."

Matt placed a restraining hand on her arm. "No need. He's downstairs."

"Eric?"

"Uh-huh. Actually, he's outside walking around."

"Oh my gosh." Carol's hand flew to her hair. "I'll bet I look awful."

"You look fine. Wonderful, in fact. Do you want me to tell him he can come in?"

Carol rubbed her palms on her jeans, then placed one hand over her heart, as though that could steady its beat. "Isn't it funny? I feel so flustered. I've never felt that way around Eric before. What...will I say?"

Matt got to his feet. " 'I'm sorry' might be nice to begin with. Then let him take the lead. Let's go."

Arm in arm they descended the stairs. Matt saw no sign of Olivia. Hopefully she had left for her engagement. At the foot of the stairs, Carol stood on tiptoe to kiss his cheek. "Thanks, Dad. You've always been the real champ in this family. I'll...uh, wait in the den for Eric, okay? Tell him to just come on in." She started toward the rear of the house, then stopped and turned. "Tell Lesley I'll call her later, okay?"

"Okay, hon." Matt opened the front door and stepped out into the afternoon sunshine. He spotted Eric standing with his rump propped against the front of his BMW, ankles crossed, hands shoved into his pockets. The young man looked up at the sound of the door opening, and Matt gestured to him. He bounded up the walk and the steps to the veranda.

"Carol's waiting for you in the den," Matt informed him.

Eric looked skeptical. "There'd better have been a major mood swing, or I'm not going in."

"There has been a startling change—you'll see."

"If that's true, you're a miracle worker."

"No, just ol' Dad, muddling along at this business of parenting."

Eric stuck out his hand. "Thanks, sir. Thanks a lot."

"You're welcome," Matt said, pumping his hand. "But, Eric, we've known each other a long time, and you're much too old to still be calling me sir. Could we just make it Matt from here on in?"

"Sure. Of course...Matt."

"I'll be talking to you, Eric. Don't make yourself scarce."

"I won't. Oh...I forgot something. Congratulations. You and Lesley. That's really great."

"Yes, it is, isn't it? Thanks, Eric."

Matt went down the steps, and Eric turned toward the door. Steeling himself, he grasped the knob and pushed it open. Inside, the house was as hushed as a museum. Earlier he had seen Mrs. Bannister drive away, so that meant Carol was the only one home, save for the servants. Soundlessly he moved down the hall toward the den.

Carol was seated on the sofa, her hands folded primly in her lap, her back ramrod straight and her eyes uncertain. She looked for all the world like a Victorian miss receiving her gentleman caller, except no Victorian miss had never worn stone-washed jeans and Reeboks. When he entered the room, her eyes flew to his. She jumped to her feet, and the hands that had been clasped in her lap locked behind her back. She sort of rocked back and forth, waiting.

"Should I say something profound and memorable or something snappy and witty?" Eric managed to ask.

"Oh!" His words opened the floodgates. Carol rushed across the room, threw her arms around his waist and buried her face against his shoulder. "Oh, Eric!" she cried. "I'm sorry! I don't know why I was—I was so glad to see you I wanted to cry.... I did have my head screwed on wrong. You were right— you're always right—I'm sorry—"

"Hey, it's okay." He wrapped his arms around her, and his hands roamed restlessly over her shoulders, down her spine to the small of her back. She smelled as fresh as a summer morning after a rain shower.

"No, it wasn't okay. I behaved horribly."

"Well, maybe a little. But it's okay now."

"I really am so glad to see you." She clung to him for what seemed like minutes. Finally, disentangling herself, Carol took him by the hand and led him to the sofa, then pulled him down beside her. "I watched the exhibition in Paris. That's a wonderful program. It shows off your skating well."

"Yeah, I thought it went pretty good." Eric shifted his position slightly to get a better look at her. "Carol...I am sorry about your knee. Sorrier than you'll ever know. And I don't mean it as pity. I'm sorry that the world will never know what a great champion you'd have made."

"Thanks. It was a blow, I'll admit, but after talking to Dad this afternoon I realized that I'm not hurting anyone but myself by moping around. I've got to get on with my life and accept the fact that ... there won't be any triple axels in it."

"But you can still skate, and you can teach others how to."

"The clinic you were talking about?"

He nodded. "Carl Walsh took me to it. Neither one of us had any idea it was for handicapped kids before we got there."

"Tell me about it."

Settling back, Carol buried her cheek in one of the sofa's cushions and listened while he went on about his experiences at the skating clinic in Philadelphia. She didn't think she had ever seen him so wildly enthusiastic about anything, not even on the ice. He'd always been so confident about his own skating that mastering a new move or jump didn't particularly elate him; it was simply what he was supposed to do. But this new project had him excited. And it was contagious. She could feel her own excitement building.

When he finally stopped speaking long enough, Carol said, "I just don't see how it's possible to teach a blind person to figure skate."

"I know. I didn't, either. But one of the instructors asked me to go out on the ice with her star pupil, a little twelve-year-old girl. I wish you could have seen her. She was wonderful. At one point she was skating backward, and I thought she was flat going to run into the wall. I'd just opened my mouth to tell her she was running out of ice when she put on the brakes. She said she could feel the wall coming up on her."

"Oh, wow!" Carol said, wide-eyed.

"Their other senses are just so finely honed."

"But, Eric ... are you and I qualified to teach kids like that?"

"We'll go to Philadelphia, and the staff there will teach us. We'll learn together."

We'll go to Philadelphia. Us. Together. Carol felt her heartbeat accelerate. "But what about your career? How are you going to have time for all that?"

Eric leaned forward slightly, his hands clasped in front of him, his arms resting on his knees. "Well, there's something I ought to tell you about that. You know, when you're a kid and dreaming about winning a gold medal, you think of all the glamour and excitement, of going this place and that, of meeting all these wonderful people. But you don't think of the hard work it takes, or how hectic all that travel can be, or that some of those wonderful people are trying to take advantage of you. I guess what I liked most about skating was the athletics of it, the day-to-day improvement. I never was all that gung ho about competing, and I've discovered I'm not much of a show biz type. Every time some big guy with a fat cigar in his mouth calls me 'Eric, baby,' the fillings in my teeth hurt."

Carol laughed. "You mean you're not going to perform anymore?"

"Oh, I suppose I will occasionally. I'll do the TV special, but visiting that clinic sure changed my priorities." He unclasped his hands and settled against the back of the sofa, turning fully toward her. Their noses were less than a foot apart. "You can still go to school, if you want. I'll spend the rest of the summer getting organized, finding out what we need to do. We won't finish shooting that special until mid-November, and then there's Christmas. It'll be after the first of the year before we can get started in earnest. Are you in?''

"Yes. I have really tried to get enthusiastic about going back to school, but this sounds so much more interesting.''

"Aren't you glad I brought your skates back? Those things don't come cheap.''

"Yes, thanks. It was silly of me to leave them at Lesley's in the first place.''

"It was especially silly to leave that great poster. I know you don't want to be without that.''

Carol's cheeks pinkened, and Eric grinned. "You should have let me know you had it. I would have scribbled a message on it.''

"Like what?''

"I don't know. Something bright, original and clever. Something like—'' abruptly his face sobered, and his dark eyes bore into hers "—like 'with love.' Could you have handled that?''

Carol swallowed hard. "I guess I could have handled it if... Would you have meant it?''

"You bet. I...thought about you a lot while I was on tour.''

"You did?''

"Yes—too much, probably. It's occurred to me that I might be a little bit in love with you.''

Carol was sure her heart had stopped completely. "Only a little bit?''

"Maybe more than that. Maybe a lot.''

The confession out, Eric breathed deeply. His eyes dropped to her lips; what raced through his mind had been kicking and bucking inside him for months. He wondered if she had ever thought about it, too. If so, she had done a good job of hiding it from him. But this afternoon she seemed so receptive. He allowed himself the pleasant thought that perhaps what he'd called dependency on her part had really been affection. He supposed there was only one way of finding out. Leaning forward, he closed the space between their heads and kissed her lightly, letting his mouth linger on hers far longer than he ever had before.

Carol sat as still as death, her eyes closed, her lips still, her breath held. Eric sat back and watched her eyelids flutter open. She looked stunned, as though she had been kicked in the stomach. But he saw her pulse beat fast at the hollow of her throat and knew she had been moved. Thus encouraged, he leaned toward her again, and this time his mouth was more ardent. His tongue automatically darted, but her lips remained closed. He toyed with their seam until they at last opened. The second his tongue made contact with hers, he felt her tremble. Her arms finally went around him, and they shared their first real kiss, their first intimacy.

Her initial response was so shy, but he persisted, and gradually she began to explore his mouth's wonders. This time, as her slender tongue hesitantly entwined with his, he was the one who trembled. He felt her hands massage his shoulder muscles, her body melt against his, and he deepened the kiss.

His open mouth sent a shock wave through Carol. She was sure nothing had ever felt as wonderful as this. For so many years, ever since she was old enough to think of such things, she had imagined kissing Eric. Now that her curiosity was being satisfied so expertly, she could see that her imagination had not done justice to the reality.

Everything had changed in the course of a few minutes. She'd never again be able to look at those rippling muscles under a tight T-shirt without wanting to feel them. She'd never again be able to look at those full, sensuous lips without wanting to kiss them.

Eric lifted his head by slow degrees and stared down at her upturned, awestruck face. His hands splayed across her back still held her tightly against him. He could feel her breasts pressed into his chest, a thrilling sensation. Her breath came in labored little puffs, fanning the underside of his chin. Her eyes were still closed, her lips still parted, moist from the kiss. Her body seemed to have warmed several degrees. He had expected her to be innocent about men since she'd never had a boyfriend, but it occurred to him that she might have just received her first real kiss. His heart made a tight fist in his chest. He hoped it was everything she had expected a kiss to be . . . and then some.

"Carol? Please . . . say something."

Her eyelids opened, then closed. Her voice came out on a suspended sigh. "More," she said.

CHAPTER SIXTEEN

IF MATT DID SAY SO, he had been marvelous. A deep sense of parental satisfaction was attained when one talked to one's offspring and said offspring actually listened.

So Carol and Eric would have their clinic, and there was no telling what the future had in store for them. The clinic interested Matt, too. It sounded like the kind of project he wouldn't mind giving some financial backing. And he hoped that this time Olivia would be more supportive of Carol's plans than she'd been in the past.

Thinking of Olivia brought a thoughtful frown to Matt's face. Normally, very little his ex-wife said had any lasting impact on him, but she'd hit a nerve or two this afternoon. *Now it's happened...and I find it isn't what I want at all.... I didn't realize how nice things were until they changed.*

Why, he wondered, did human beings spend so much time wishing, then even more time being disappointed when their wishes came true? He didn't have to look far to find a perfect example of that. The nearest mirror would do. For as long as he could remember, his aim had been to go as far and as fast as he could. Yet nothing in his life had ever shaken his equilibrium as thoroughly as the chance for the ultimate promotion. *Go figure it.*

Everyone needs something to fall back on. Olivia had hit the nail squarely on the head with that little gem of wisdom, too. He enjoyed his work far more now that it wasn't the only compelling interest in his life.

Suddenly Matt realized he was driving aimlessly, going nowhere in particular, certainly not back to the office. He got his bearings and spotted a convenience store on the corner. Driving in, he used the pay telephone to call Helen. No emergencies were in progress, no one was trying to get in touch with him, so he told the secretary he wouldn't be in until the following morning. Getting back in the car, he made a beeline southward. Abruptly, the need to talk to Lesley had overtaken him.

LESLEY HAD BEEN SURPRISED to receive a visit from Garson Morman later that afternoon, but no more surprised than he had been to find her home. He had simply stopped by to drop off some old photographs of Arturo's he'd found, examples of the famous photographer's earliest work. Garson had intended leaving them with Clarice, but when Lesley put in an appearance, he'd stayed for coffee and conversation. First they'd studied the photographs, mutually agreeing that their value was more nostalgic than monetary. Then she'd filled him in on the changes the past week had brought.

"So you're getting married," Garson said with a smile. "I'm happy if you're happy, Lesley. Are you?"

"Very."

"Tell me something about the lucky man."

"He's very nice. Very good-looking. Very successful." Describing Matt wasn't easy, she discovered. So much of his appeal and charm was indescribable, and she didn't want to come across like a lovesick teenager—even if she felt like one half the time.

"Is he anything like Arturo?"

Lesley laughed. "No, nothing."

"That's good," Garson said.

That brought Lesley's head around with a start. "Garson, what an odd thing to say. You and Arturo were such good friends."

"As a friend and colleague, Arturo was a great guy. As a husband..." Garson shrugged. "I must say, you were a mismatched pair. I hope you and this new man have a lot in common."

Do we? Lesley wondered. *We're crazy about each other. Maybe at our stage in life no one can ask for more than that.* "We mesh well" was all she said.

"So, what are your plans? Now that your little skater has quit, what are you going to do?"

"I really don't have anything on tap at the moment, Garson. Matt and I are getting married at the end of the summer, and there'll definitely be a honeymoon. Just where we'll go hasn't been decided. Then...to tell you the truth, I'm holding off on making plans. You see, Matt's up for a big promotion, and if he gets it, we'll be moving to Dallas."

Garson's expression altered slightly. "Dallas? What kind of promotion is it?"

"He would be president of his company."

"Hmm."

"Now, what does that mean?"

"Nothing, nothing. I was just thinking about the time Arturo packed you off to Denver, how unhappy you were for a while."

"Garson, I was a kid! I know I was twenty-four, but believe me, I was a kid. Of course I was homesick and blue. I didn't have any business marrying anybody, much less a restless globe-trotter like Arturo."

"True," Garson agreed. "Do you want to go to Dallas?"

"I want to go wherever Matt goes."

"Somehow the corporate life doesn't sound like you. And I suppose you've given a lot of thought to the life you'd be required to lead as the wife of a company president."

"A lot." It bothered Lesley that Garson, who had known her so long and knew her nature so well, had misgivings about the marriage. He did; she could see it. She had spent days convincing herself that she could and would do anything that being Matt's wife entailed. She had even convinced herself it would be good for her—something of an adventure, a whole new world. She could do nicely without Garson's doubts.

"I wish you the best," her friend said. "You know that."

"Yes, I know. Thanks. You're a dear."

"And I'm not making any money by frittering away the afternoon, so I guess I'll be on my way. I'm sure Sally will call when I tell her the news."

"Let me see you to the door."

Lesley followed him out of the house and stood on the steps watching until the iron gate clanged shut behind him. Then she sniffed the fresh afternoon air and glanced around the courtyard. It was a beautiful day, and the gardens were primed to put forth their riots of color. The daffodils and tulips had faded, but day-lilies and irises and daisies had taken their place. The year before, recently widowed and back in the Bay Area for the first time in years, Lesley had enlisted the aid of a nurseryman to restore the neglected court-yard. Together they had planned a garden that would bloom almost all year. At the time, the garden had been another badly needed hobby. Now that she was seeing the fruits of her labors, Lesley felt almost maternal toward it. How she would hate having to leave it. How she would hate having to leave the house, the Bay Area, everything.

Oh, come on, Lesley. Gardens can be planted any-where. There are lovely houses everywhere. Most places have their own special appeal. Loosen up, give a little.

Would the wife of the president of Hamilton House, Incorporated, have the time to plant a garden? she wondered. Would the poor woman even have time to look at a garden someone else had planted for her?

And why, when thinking about the fictitious wife of Hamilton House's president, did she always think of her as "the poor woman"?

At that moment Lesley heard a car pull into the driveway. A door slammed, the gate swung open, and Matt came up the flagstone walkway. She was always glad to see him but even more so when he wasn't expected.

"Isn't this a nice surprise!" she exclaimed.

He looped an arm around her and kissed her soundly. "What are you doing—talking to your plants?"

"Uh-huh. I'm telling them to straighten up and make me proud of them. I'm also thinking that I let that man from the nursery talk me into planting too many irises. The way those things multiply, two years from now I'll have to do some serious digging and dividing." She wrapped an arm around his waist and looked up at him adoringly. "So, what have you been doing today?"

"Settling disputes, mending fences, dispensing wisdom and making momentous decisions."

"All that? You have had a busy day. A man who works that hard deserves something cold to drink."

Matt shed his coat and tie as they went into the house. At the bar, Lesley mixed him a drink, then sat on a stool beside him. "So, tell me all the exciting things that happened today."

"Eric came to see me at the office," he began.

"You, too?"

"His chin was down to here." Matt indicated his breastbone. "He'd been to see Carol, and she had greeted him less than cordially."

Lesley gasped. "That's terrible."

"Not to worry. I got it all straightened out." He looked very pleased with himself. "Eric and Carol are going to open a clinic. At least, I assume they are. I left before things were actually resolved. But I'm betting they'll be working together."

Lesley was puzzled. "A clinic?"

"A skating clinic for handicapped children. Eric's really excited about it."

"How wonderful! Oh, that's just what Carol needs. Tell me more about it."

"I really don't know all that much, not the particulars. Eric visited one in Philadelphia, and that's what put the bee in his bonnet. I'm sure you'll hear everything in minute detail from Eric and Carol." Matt propped an elbow on the bar, cupped his chin in one palm and smiled at Lesley. "I see that gleam in your eye, sweetheart. Are you thinking the project is just what you need, too? All you'd have to do is say the word, and you'd be a partner. The kids would love it."

"Matt! No long-range plans, remember? Our fate is in Vanessa Hamilton's hands."

"Hmm. I guess we did more or less agree on that, didn't we? But if we're here when that clinic opens...?"

"That's different. If we're here, I'd love to be in on it, if they want me."

"They'll want you." Matt sipped his drink in thoughtful silence a minute. "Eric was in the mood to unburden his soul today," he finally said, changing the subject. "He confessed that he's crazy about Carol...in a man-woman sort of way."

Lesley's eyes widened, then she began to chortle. "Bingo! Patience has its rewards, right? I do so hope he tells her how he feels."

"He doesn't have to. I told her."

"You didn't!"

"Why not? It was better than a shot of penicillin for what ailed her. And Eric said that nothing he'd told me was confidential."

"Matchmaking, too, Mr. Logan? Busy, busy."

"Just doing what I can to make the world safe for young love."

"What about not-so-young love?"

"It doesn't seem to be in any danger. What would you say to having an overnight guest on a week-night?"

"I'd love it." He now had a permanent cache of supplies stored in her bathroom, and in one corner of her closet were several of his casual shirts and slacks.

Nothing for work, though. "Do you want to change? I'll have Clarice do up your shirt and steam your suit."

Matt looked at her in mock horror. "The vice president of Hamilton House, Western Division, doesn't wear the same suit to work two days in a row."

"Oh, excuse me, sir. I guess that would be a serious breach of etiquette."

"I'll go home in the morning to change before I go to the office. I can be late. I'm the boss. Or maybe I won't go in at all. Again, I'm the boss."

Lesley grinned. Sometimes she thought Matt said such things to prove to himself he really could miss a day at the office without armies marching. He'd once confessed that until her advent into his life, he only missed going into the office if he was out of town or needed immediate medical attention. She reached for his nape and wiggled her fingers through his hair.

"Does it need cutting?"

"No. Well...it might be a teensy bit longer than you normally wear it, but I like it."

"I suspect there's a bit of the bohemian in you, love."

"I suspect you might be right."

The minute Lesley said that, she regretted it, although Matt didn't appear to think the remark was anything more than idle chatter. The silliest things were magnified in her mind these days. Of course, she was much too conventional to be bohemian, but after all those years with Arturo and the writers and artists he'd liked to be around, she didn't find casual untidiness as offensive as, say, her mother or Olivia Bannister would. Or as the wife of a corporation president should. And her usual uniforms were leotards for the rink and jeans around the house. If they had to go to

Dallas, she would need to give serious attention to her wardrobe. And she probably was the only woman alive who regarded that as a major chore.

"Let me go tell Clarice you're staying for dinner," Lesley said, sliding off the stool. "I'll be right back."

She was gone five minutes, and when she returned to the game room, Matt was still seated at the bar, sipping his cocktail, staring straight ahead, deep in thought. Lesley studied him a minute. He seemed preoccupied, unusually so. He didn't even turn when she entered the room. She'd never seen Matt down, and he wasn't now, but he definitely had something on his mind.

"Anything wrong at work?" she asked.

"Huh? Oh, no, nothing at all."

"Can I fix you another drink? Dinner won't be ready for an hour. Matt, pay attention. I'm doing my devoted wife bit. How was work, dear? May I fix you a drink?"

Matt grinned. "I'll just nurse this one a little while longer. Aren't you having something?"

"Oh, a little wine, I guess." While she was behind the bar uncorking the bottle, she looked at him again, studying him thoughtfully. "Are you sure there's nothing wrong, darling? You look as though you're a million miles away."

Matt gave himself a shake, downed his drink and set the empty glass on the bar. "I've got a couple of things on my mind, but it's nothing for you to worry about. I think I will go up and change. It won't take but a minute."

While he was gone, Lesley sat at the bar, sipping her wine and frowning. Something was up; she'd bet on it. It wasn't unusual for Matt to try to see her at least once during the week, but never on Monday. Monday was the day when, in his words, "everyone in the organization has had all weekend to think about what's screwed up." He told her he often ate dinner at his desk on Monday evening and got home just in time to go to bed.

But this had been an unusual Monday—Carol and Eric and all. Still, Lesley couldn't shake the feeling that he was grappling with a problem. But she supposed if he wanted her to know what it was, he would tell her when he was ready. Then again, he hardly ever discussed business with her. What input could she give him?

The telephone behind the bar rang, but as usual, she waited for Clarice to answer it. The maid stuck her head in the door a minute later. "It's Carol for you," Clarice said.

"Wonderful!" Lesley exclaimed, reaching for the instrument.

"Carol?"

"Oh, Lesley!" Her voice sounded like a million champagne bubbles. "This has positively been the most wonderful day of my whole life! Eric was here."

"Your father told me. I'm so glad."

"I've got to come to see you tomorrow. Both of us will. We want to tell you about this great new project of Eric's. He thought you might want in on it."

"I'm dying to hear about it."

Carol's tone turned confidential. "He's taking me out to dinner tonight. And dancing afterward. He told me to get dressed up, that he was going to give me a night to remember. Isn't that something?"

A soft smile spread across Lesley's face. "It really is."

"Everything's changed between us. He was so sweet and caring. I have waited a long time for this...a long time. And, Lesley, I finally got kissed good. Really good."

Lesley started laughing. "Beats the heck out of doing triples, doesn't it?"

"You better believe it! Eric really knows how." There was a pause. "Which makes me think there have been a lot more girlfriends than he admits to. Oh, well, let's just hope I'm the last one. See you tomorrow."

Lesley was still laughing when Matt returned, dressed in slacks and a polo shirt. "What's so funny?" he asked, puzzled.

"Your daughter. Not funny, exactly. Happy. She's back in seventh heaven."

"It's going to be nice to have a happy Carol back with us. Ain't love grand?"

"I think so." Lesley's eyes raked him from head to foot. "You look much more comfortable. Want that drink now?"

"Please. I'll mix it."

"Let me." She took his glass and went behind the bar. "Carol and Eric are coming over tomorrow to tell me about the clinic. I'm sure they're going to ask me to go in on it with them. What do I tell them?"

"Tell them?" Matt shrugged. "Yes or no, I guess."

"Matt, I can't tell them anything yet, and they're going to think that's odd. Is it all right to tell them about the promotion, to tell them I can't make any plans while that's up in the air?"

Matt paused, then said, "Tell them whatever you want, sweetheart. I don't care. Play it by ear."

Lesley pushed his drink toward him, then came out from behind the bar. This time, instead of sitting down, she positioned herself between his legs, locked her hands behind his neck and kissed him thoroughly. When she pulled back, he was smiling at her speculatively.

"What was that for?"

"Do I need a reason? By the way, I don't think I'll be betraying a confidence if I tell you your daughter got kissed good today for the first time in her life."

"At nineteen? She's a late bloomer. How old were you when you got kissed good for the first time?"

"Forty... and that's a fact."

AFTER DINNER, Matt read the Sunday paper he'd had no time for yesterday, and Lesley watched an ancient movie on television. She'd seen it so many times she practically could recite the dialogue right along with the actors. When she heard Matt yawn lustily, she clicked it off. "Ready for bed? You look tired."

But he wasn't tired. Once they were upstairs with the door closed, Matt wanted to make love. When Lesley realized that, she began to undress, but he stopped her, saying he wanted to reserve that pleasure for himself. He coaxed her with kisses and tickles; she responded by pulling him down onto the bed and making love to him with reckless abandon. Sometimes their lovemaking was sweetly satisfying, very romantic. Other times it was hungry and desperate. Tonight, however, it was a delightful romp, the climax as satisfying as all the teasing foreplay.

"Oh, sweetheart," Matt groaned, releasing her slowly. "That was good. I don't know how you do it, but you always give me exactly what I want."

Lesley smiled against his arm, pleased with herself. "My goodness, you were frisky tonight."

If there was something on his mind—and she still thought there was—he hadn't let it interfere with his libido. She stretched like a lynx, then massaged him until he was absolutely limp. Then she slipped off the bed and went into the bathroom to wash and cream her face and put on a nightgown. She fully expected to find Matt sound asleep when she returned. Instead, he was under the sheets, propped up against a pillow, his hands behind his head. The blinds over the bed were still open; fingers of moonlight played over the linens.

"I thought you'd be dead to the world after all that exertion," she teased him.

"Don't be ridiculous. Our little romp was like getting a shot of vitamins. Come to bed, sweetheart. I want to talk to you."

Lesley lifted the sheet and slid in beside him. "Is it anything heavy? I feel much too good to handle anything heavy tonight."

"On the contrary. What I'm about to say might give you the best night's sleep you've had in a long time. I'm not going to Dallas."

"Matt!"

"I'm going to call Vanessa in the morning and tell her to take me out of the running."

"Oh, Matt!" It took a minute for the full impact of his words to hit her. She wondered why she wasn't squealing with joy. She had been hoping and praying they wouldn't have to go. Why didn't she feel happier?

"I mean it," he said decisively. "Admittedly, I arrived at this momentous decision by a circuitous route, but sometime between leaving Carol and driving over here, I made up my mind that was what I was going to do."

"Wh-what brought it on?"

"Don't ask me. A combination of things, I suppose. Carol and Eric, something Olivia said, even that damned iris bed...."

"Darling, you really aren't making much sense."

"I know. I'm not sure there's any sense to be made of it, but... I was feeling good about Carol and Eric and that clinic. I'd like to be around to see it become reality, and I know how much you would enjoy helping with it. And, too, I was thinking about something Olivia had said earlier. She admitted that, after spending years wanting Carol to quit skating, now that it had happened she found she didn't want it at all. How do I know I wouldn't feel that way about becoming company president? Then I got here, and you said the damned irises were going to have to be divided in two years. My immediate thought was, where will we be in two years, and what will we be doing? Running our tails off or enjoying life? It suddenly occurred to me that I'm having the time of my life right now, and I don't want anything to change. I don't want to be the kind of man who lets personal achievement take precedence over everything else. I was like that for too long."

Lesley searched his face in the moonlight, looking for some signs of misgivings and doubts. She found nothing but the face of a man who had made up his mind. She waited for good vibrations to hit her, but nothing came. "Is this because of me?" she asked finally.

"You affect everything I do, you know that."

"I mean, if I weren't in the picture, how would you feel about the promotion?"

"That's impossible to say. If you weren't in the picture, I wouldn't be having the time of my life, would I?"

Then he smiled, and Lesley felt a little better. Running her hand up and down his bare arm, she asked, "How is Vanessa going to take this?"

Matt pursed his lips. "Hard to say. She might be a little disappointed. And damned surprised. She'll certainly be that. Matt Logan, the quintessential company man, turning down a chance for the top spot? But she has others to choose from."

"I don't know, Matt," Lesley said worriedly. "I hope you've given this plenty of thought."

"I've thought about it so much my brain's worn out." He shot her a quizzical look. "I though you'd be sailing."

"Funny, so did I. I wanted this so badly. Now I've got it. Strange."

"Are you telling me you want to go to Dallas all of a sudden?" Matt asked incredulously.

"No, that's not what I'm saying at all. Naturally, I'd prefer to have things stay just as they are, but..."

"And have them you shall." He sighed the sigh of a man who'd just had the weight of the world taken off his shoulders. Sliding farther down between the sheets, he pulled the pillow under his head. "Good night, my love. When the time comes, we'll divide the irises together."

He was asleep in minutes, but Lesley lay wide awake, staring at the ceiling. She had everything she wanted. Matt, most of all. She was free of the fear of having to move. She could continue working with Carol and Eric, both of whom she adored. Everything. So where was the elation she should have been feeling?

Relax, Lesley, and enjoy it. What are you worried about?

She was worried that Matt had made a decision he would regret. That he was doing it more for her than for him.

Well, it was his decision, his choice, and he's a big boy. He's done all right so far. Relax.

She knew all that, but it still didn't feel right.

That was the crux of the matter. It didn't feel right to her. She chewed her lip, stewed and fretted. From off in the dark recesses of the house came the chiming of the grandfather clock: ten-thirty, ten forty-five, eleven o'clock. Lesley got up to get a drink of water, then returned to bed to stare at Matt's sleeping form. She thought she knew him so well, but she couldn't read his mind, couldn't know the thought processes that had brought him to his fateful decision.

As the hours ticked by, sleep became even more elusive. She prowled through the house, as she often did on restless nights, but all her getting in and out of bed, all her tossing and turning had no effect on Matt. He still slept soundly.

That should tell you something, Lesley, her maddening inner voice said. *Apparently his mind is at rest. Go to sleep.*

Sleep finally came just before dawn, and when she at last succumbed, she slept so soundly she never knew when Matt woke, dressed and left the house. It was almost nine o'clock when she first stirred and reached for him. Encountering only his pillow, she glanced at the bedside clock, then bolted upright. She had desperately wanted to talk to Matt before he went to the office. Maybe he was downstairs having coffee. Raising herself up on her knees, she looked out the window. From there she could see over the fence to the driveway. His car was gone.

Lesley sat back cross-legged on the bed, reached for the phone and dialed Matt's home number. Horace informed her that Mr. Logan had left for the office an hour ago. He must have gotten up shortly after she'd fallen asleep. She hung up, then dialed again. This time it was Helen's voice that came over the line.

"Oh, good morning, Lesley," the secretary said cheerfully. "May I have him call you back? He's on the phone with Vanessa, and interrupting that is a no-no. Unless it's an emergency, of course."

Lesley sighed. "No, Helen, no emergency. Thanks." Hanging up, Lesley stared into space for a few minutes before dragging herself off the bed and into the bathroom. So it was done, for better or worse. She followed her morning routine, then slipped on a pair of jeans and a T-shirt before going downstairs for coffee. She was halfway through her first cup when Matt returned her call.

"Good morning, Sleeping Beauty," he said. "Are you just now getting up?"

"Uh-huh. Downright decadent, isn't it?"

"You called?"

"Yes. You...talked to Vanessa." It wasn't a question.

"Uh-huh."

"Is everything all right?"

"I certainly hope so."

What did that mean? Lesley wondered. She waited a minute, hoping he would tell her exactly what Vanessa had said, but nothing was forthcoming. "Did she sound disappointed, angry?"

"No. I . . . Listen, sweetheart, there's another call waiting for me. I've got a bitch of a schedule today, but what say we meet at my house around six-thirty this evening? We'll have dinner. We . . . need to talk."

Lesley frowned. Something was wrong. He didn't sound right, not like Matt. "Of course."

"I'll see you then. Remember, I love you."

Remember? Why would she forget? "I love you, too, Matt. Goodbye."

IT WAS A LONG DAY. Again and again Lesley tried to imagine Vanessa's reaction to Matt's startling announcement. She couldn't forget how strange he had sounded on the phone. Maybe he was having second thoughts. If so, could he undo what he had done?

Midway through her ruminations, a frightening thought crossed her mind. Would Vanessa fire Matt? Would she do something that drastic? Even if she was disappointed, she wouldn't be outraged—would she? As Matt had said, she had others to choose from.

Then Lesley remembered that Vanessa Hamilton was getting ready to can her late husband's best friend because he had disappointed her.

But, she reminded herself, that man had done something covert and disloyal. In telling Vanessa he didn't want the promotion, Matt was being completely aboveboard and honest.

Oh, God, how awful he would feel if he had to leave the company. This was all her fault. The first time Matt had mentioned the promotion, she should have said, "How wonderful," and let it go at that.

A fine time to be deciding that, Lesley. We're all gifted with perfect hindsight.

So it went all morning. Lesley was relieved when Carol and Eric literally flew through the front door shortly before noon, bursting with excitement and plans and putting a temporary end to her private turmoil.

Carol, especially, was a delight. Her old vitality was back, now heightened by the dreamy-eyed look of a young woman who'd recently experienced being kissed "really good" for the first time in her life. Eric wore the bemused expression of a man who couldn't quite believe what was happening to him, but welcomed it, nevertheless.

Young love must be wonderful, Lesley thought. She wouldn't know since that was something she had missed out on entirely. But maybe middle-aged love was even better. Certainly it was better appreciated.

After listening to the two young people go on and on about the clinic, she readily agreed to help them in any way she could. Now that Matt had made his decision and relayed it to Vanessa, there was nothing to stop either of them from making all the plans they wanted.

Still, something didn't feel right. It had her on edge all day. By the time she began getting ready for dinner at Matt's house, a real uneasiness had built inside her.

As usual, Matt was waiting for her in his study when she arrived. Lesley was so finely attuned to him that the minute she stepped into the room she knew that her worries had not been unwarranted. He was troubled, dealing with something personal and difficult. The angles and planes of his face seemed chiseled in stone, and his eyes were etched with fatigue. He had shed his coat and tie but hadn't changed clothes, which was normally the first thing he did when he got home. Of course, maybe he'd just arrived. Then she noticed his glass, with perhaps a quarter inch of pale brown liquid in it. He'd been home long enough to finish a drink.

"Hello, sweetheart," he said, pulling her to him for a kiss.

"Hi," she said, forcing lightness into her voice. "Been home long?"

"Not long. Let me get you something. Would you like to go out or have dinner here?"

"I don't care," she said, settling herself on the sofa but never taking her eyes off him. "You're the host. You decide."

"Did you see Carol today?"

"Oh, yes. Eric, too. They're off in a world all their own." She made an upward spiral with her forefinger.

Matt returned, carrying a glass of wine for her and a fresh drink for him. He set both of them on the coffee table, hitched his trousers at the knee and sat down. "Was the traffic bad?" he asked inanely.

"No more so than usual."

"Did you get caught in any rain?"

"Oh, God, Matt, what's wrong? Traffic? Weather? Since when are we reduced to talking about those things? It's Vanessa, isn't it? She said something that has you upset. What did she do—fire you? I don't care. It isn't the end of the world. As a matter of fact, if you aren't working, we'll have more time to be together."

A smile played around the corners of Matt's mouth. "No, sweetheart, she didn't fire me." He glanced down at his hands, then back at her. The smile was gone. "She didn't say a thing, mainly because I didn't tell her. When push came to shove, I simply couldn't tell her I didn't want that promotion."

Lesley's eyes widened, and one hand flew to her mouth. Matt had had a miserable day, dreading this moment, while he was sure Lesley had spent a relaxing one, feeling more secure about their future than she ever had. Getting to his feet, he strode to the fireplace and propped one arm on the mantel. "She called me before I could call her. It was about the Canadian expansion. I'd swear the woman's a witch. She started hammering away about how comfortable she feels with me in charge of the expansion, about how she can always count on me, that I've never disappointed her. And then damned if she didn't mention every single wonderful thing I'd done for her during the past twenty years! She dredged up things I'd forgotten all about. She was on a real nostalgia binge."

He paused and glanced over his shoulder at Lesley, his face expressing his chagrin. "I had to sit and listen to this tribute to myself, and I thought, how can I accept all the things she's done for me through the years, all the promotions and privileges, and then when she wants something I don't particularly want, say no, thanks? The answer to that is, I can't."

Lesley hadn't moved. Her hand still covered her mouth. Her eyes were riveted on him, and Matt thought he detected a bit of misting over. Hurrying back to sit beside her, he touched the side of her face. "I'm sorry, love. I've dreaded telling you all day after that marvelous speech I made in bed last night. But...I just couldn't do it. I owe her too much. Even now, if I could come up with one legitimate reason... If you still were tied to Carol's skating, I wouldn't leave. If you refused to go with me, I wouldn't leave. If Carol needed me here... If, if, if. But none of that's true now, so the only reason I'd have for turning down the promotion is that I like things the way they are, which is damned flimsy.''

Matt paused to sigh. "Then I remembered all I said to Carol about adapting, going with the flow, changing with the circumstances. I don't know. Maybe I'll spend these next months hoping and praying that Vanessa will give the nod to someone else, but she'll have to be the one who takes me out of the running, not me.''

Suddenly Lesley's arms flew around him, and she hugged him ferociously. "Oh, Matt, I'm so glad! So relieved!''

He was stunned. "You are?''

She pulled back, and he could see there were tears in her eyes, all right, but they were tears of happiness. "I couldn't sleep last night for thinking about it. Nothing felt right, and I didn't know why. Then all of a sudden it occurred to me. It should be Vanessa's choice, not ours. If she wants you to be president of Hamilton House, she has her reasons, and you should accept gratefully. I called this morning to tell you not to call her. When Helen said you were on the phone with her, I was sure it was done. And I still didn't feel right about it. I was so afraid you were doing it for me, not for you.''

"No, I had plenty of doubts, too. Plenty of them.'' He looked at her, his eyes earnest. "Lesley, you'd better think about this long and hard. I can still say no, but once Vanessa points her finger at me, if she does, it's too late. We'll have to go.''

"I know, and that's what we'll do. You'll be a superb president, and I'll . . . well, I'll do my best. If the people in Dallas think I'm a bit odd, who will they complain to? I'll be the president's wife, for heaven's sake!''

"You? Odd? I doubt that.''

Lesley saw the relief wash over Matt. His shoulders slumped, and the fatigue in his eyes eased. She felt a great rush of tenderness for him. "You've had a bad day, haven't you, worrying about how I'd feel about all this?''

"It hasn't been an easy one,'' he admitted. "I was afraid you'd be disappointed, not only in me but in having the uncertainty still with us for a while longer.''

"What uncertainty? We're still getting married, aren't we?''

"Of course.''

"That's all that matters, isn't it?''

"It's all that matters to me,'' Matt assured her. "And there's a very good chance Vanessa will choose someone else.''

Lesley opened her mouth to say, "Hold that good thought,'' but quickly closed it. From this moment on, she was going to be the most flexible person alive. If fate deemed it that her future lay in being the wife of Hamilton House's president, so be it. She'd do the best she could. If she had to sell her house, she'd do it. It was, after all, just a place. Many times in her life she had bestowed far too much importance on unimportant things. It had taken a long time—possibly half her life—but now she knew where to place her priorities.

As if he could read her thoughts, Matt captured her nape and pulled her to him to extract a kiss. "I'll make a deal with you," he said.

"Deal? What is it, love?"

"No matter what happens, someday we'll wind up back here, back in your house, if you like. I don't see any need to sell it. If we have to leave it for a few years, perhaps we can lease it. It will be a nice place to wile away our dotage."

"Are you going to have a dotage? How disappointing. All right, it's a deal."

"There's more. If we do wind up in Dallas, promise me you'll live your life exactly as you want to. I don't ever want you thinking, oh, my God, I've got to do such and such. I'll be going there to run a company. Neither of us has a damned thing to prove, no one to impress, no points to score. We've already scored them. I just want you to enjoy, enjoy."

Lesley smiled, contented and very sure that the fragments of her life had at last been knitted together. "If I'm with you, I don't see how I could do anything else."

Harlequin
Superromance.

COMING NEXT MONTH

#414 BETWEEN TWO MOONS • Eve Gladstone
The scion of black princes and robber barons, Tony
Campbell had a reputation for ruthlessness. But
when he took over her store—the most fashionable
woman's specialty shop in Manhattan—Kelly
Aldrich sensed another side to him. Could she tame
the British lion? She had to. Or be consumed by him.

#415 STARLIGHT, STAR BRIGHT • Kelly Walsh
Federal postal inspector Chris Laval knew Ivy
Austin's family meant everything to her. So when he
began to suspect Ivy's brother was involved in a mail
fraud scam, Chris had a problem: how could he win
Ivy's love when he might have to send her beloved
brother to jail?

#416 PLAYING BY THE RULES • Connie Bennett
Police lieutenant Alex Devane swore he'd never again
carry a gun. He'd seen and done too much to ever
want to be reassociated with violence. Ivy Kincaid
helped make Alex see he would only be helping
people by working on the Brauxton Strangler case.
She also brought Alex's passionate spirit to life
again, but Alex was determined not to endanger the
life of another loved one....

#417 STORMY WEATHER • Irma Walker
Stormy Todd was a troublesome tenant. When Guy
Harris evicted her from her home, she and her kids
showed up at his beach house! Guy found Stormy
hard to resist, but was there any future for an
unemployed single mother and one of San Jose's
most prominent citizens?

HARLEQUIN
American Romance®

THE LOVES OF A CENTURY

Join American Romance in a nostalgic look back at the twentieth century—at the lives and loves of American men and women from the turn-of-the-century to the dawn of the year 2000.

Journey through the decades from the dance halls of the 1900s to the discos of the seventies . . . from Glenn Miller to the Beatles . . . from Valentino to Newman . . . from corset to miniskirt . . . from beau to significant other.

Relive the moments . . . recapture the memories.

Watch for all the CENTURY OF AMERICAN ROMANCE titles in Harlequin American Romance. In one of the four American Romance books appearing each month, for the next ten months, we'll take you back to a decade of the twentieth century, where you'll relive the years and rekindle the romance of days gone by.

Don't miss a day of A CENTURY OF AMERICAN ROMANCE.

A CENTURY OF
AMERICAN ROMANCE
1910s

The women . . . the men . . . the passions . . . the memories . . .

COMING SOON

In September, two worlds will collide in four very special romance titles. Somewhere between first meeting and happy ending, Dreamscape Romance will sweep you to the very edge of reality where everyday reason cannot conquer unlimited imagination—or the power of love. The timeless mysteries of reincarnation, telepathy, psychic visions and earthbound spirits intensify the modern lives and passion of ordinary men and women with an extraordinary alluring force.

Available in September!

EARTHBOUND—Rebecca Flanders
THIS TIME FOREVER—Margaret Chittenden
MOONSPELL—Regan Forest
PRINCE OF DREAMS—Carly Bishop

DRSC-RR